FAIRY TALE FINALE

THE BACKSTAGE MIRROR™
BOOK THREE

KELLI ROBYNS

MICHAEL ANDERLE

DON'T MISS OUR NEW RELEASES

Join the Florid Romance email list to be notified of new releases and special promotions (which happen often) by following this link:

https://floridromance.lmbpn.com/about/sign-up-for-our-newsletter/

Published by Florid Romance
an imprint of LMBPN Publishing
2375 E. Tropicana Avenue, Suite 8-305
Las Vegas, Nevada 89119 USA

Version 1.00, January 2026
eBook ISBN: 979-8-89790-068-8
Print ISBN: 979-8-89790-069-5

CONTENT ADVISORY

This novel contains depictions of mental health crises, including dissociation, depression, addiction-like behavior, and onstage crisis. It explores themes of psychological manipulation and gaslighting by supernatural entities. It includes multiple on-page consensual sex scenes, threats of assault, and instances of workplace danger.

DRAMATIS PERSONAE

- **Zoe Reeves:** A talented, optimistic actress cast as Cinderella.
- **Tyler Bacon:** A cynical journalist investigating the Meridian Theatre.
- **Cate Hart (Hecate):** The formidable director of the Meridian Theatre, with a secret past tied to its magic.
- **Malcolm:** The theater's quiet, steadfast technical director and Cate's partner.
- **Vivi Asbury:** A veteran actress and mentor to Zoe, survivor of the theater's magic.
- **Marc Middleton:** The theater's lighting designer and Vivi's partner.
- **Kevin Brooks:** A veteran actor and mentor, survivor of the theater's magic.
- **Sarah Kim:** A therapist and Kevin's partner.
- **Danny Kim:** The theater's pragmatic stage manager and Sarah's brother.

- **Carmen:** The theater's long-serving and observant costume mistress.
- **Prince Adrian:** The perfect, alluring entity from the *Cinderella* mirror world.

ONE

THE PERFORMANCE OF JOY

Months had washed away since the night the theater's magic nearly unraveled itself, leaving a quiet scar tissue of memory. The crisis had been contained, its story reduced to fractured whispers passed between members of the company, but for the small circle of guardians who stood at its heart, a brand they all shared. Autumn's lingering warmth had surrendered to the first real bite of winter, a crispness in the air that carried the promise of frost on the windowpanes. And with that change came the tradition that truly marked the start of the holidays at the Meridian, the annual auditions for the Christmas show. This year, it was *Cinderella*.

Zoe sat curled on the green room's worn velvet couch, a folder holding her headshot and sheet music resting on her lap. It felt less like a tool of her trade and more like a shield. The room was alive with the low, happy hum of her peers, a familiar symphony of anticipation. The air was thick with the scent of coffee gone stale in the pot and the sweet, almost cloying perfume of day-old donuts someone had brought in, a smell that clung to the upholstery like a ghost of celebrations past. This was supposed to be her natural habitat, this vibrant ecosystem of nerves and camaraderie. But today, the sounds felt distant and distorted, as if she were hearing them from the bottom of a deep well. Her attention was a tether, pulled taut toward the corner of the room where Vivi and Marc stood talking with Kevin and Sarah.

They were a picture of quiet, settled peace. The change in her mentors was something you could see, something you could almost touch. Vivi, who had once held herself with the rigid control of a drawn bowstring, now leaned into Marc's side with an effortless, unconscious grace. Her smile, once a rare currency she spent with caution, was now a soft, steady light that lived in her eyes whenever she looked at him. And Kevin. The transformation in Kevin was the one that truly shook Zoe to her foundations. The brooding, haunted artist she had known was gone, replaced by a man who seemed to finally fit inside his own skin, a man who wore his own peace like a well-loved coat. He held Sarah's hand, their fingers woven together, and the way he looked at her was with a calm, absolute devotion that felt more solid and real than the floorboards beneath Zoe's feet.

They had walked through a fire that should have consumed them, and they had come out the other side not merely whole but remade. Their happiness wasn't the bright, performative thing you put on for a crowd; it was deep and authentic, like the worn grain of old wood, beautiful because of the life it had weathered.

Suddenly, Carmen, the costume mistress, rushed in looking for Kevin.

"Kevin, I've been looking for you. Love, can you give me a minute? I need to try this adjustment I've made to your Phantom costume."

"Of course, anything for you, Carmen," he said while she draped a velvet black cape around his shoulders. "This fabric," she murmured, "it has the strangest smell. Like old roses and underground water." She looked directly at him. "I had a costume come back once that smelled like this. The actor who wore it... Well, he said he'd found the most amazing space to rehearse in. Somewhere private. Somewhere that felt more real than reality."

Kevin stiffened. "What happened to him?"

"Oh, he left the production suddenly. Family emergency, they said." Carmen's fingers were gentle but firm as she adjusted his collar. "I kept the costume, though. And the rose petals I found in the pocket. Pressed them into a memento book I've been keeping. They turned to silver powder eventually. Isn't that strange?"

A familiar ache bloomed in Kevin's chest, but he only looked down as Carmen smiled a knowing look.

"This is better now, thank you for indulging my perfectionism," she said, nodding at Kevin and Zoe, and then left the room.

When Danny Kim's voice cut through the chatter and called Zoe's name, she rose from the couch. Her smile was instantaneous, a bright and automatic reflex she had perfected over the course of her lifetime. It felt painted on, a familiar and comforting mask she knew how to wear. She walked out of the warm, cluttered intimacy of the green room, leaving the happy sounds to fade behind her. The backstage labyrinth swallowed her, the air growing cooler, the sounds shifting to the stark, professional quiet of the wings.

The stage was a vast, dark cavern, an empty universe waiting to be filled. The only light was a single, harsh spotlight that pooled on the floorboards at center stage like a fallen moon. It was like stepping into a vacuum, a place outside of time. Out in the consuming blackness of the house, she could make out the shadowy silhouettes at the directors' table. Cate Hart was a motionless, intense shape at its head, a queen surveying her empty kingdom. The air was cool and smelled of old velvet and the ghosts of a thousand shows, a scent like memory itself. Zoe found her mark, the light so bright that it almost seemed like a physical presence, isolating her in its stark, white glare. She handed her sheet music to the accompanist, a shadowy figure at the piano in the pit, his presence little more than a whisper of movement in the dark.

She took a moment. She closed her eyes and reached for the feeling she was chasing. Not the complex, messy, hard-won peace she saw in her friends. She wanted something cleaner. Simpler. A fairy tale. She summoned the pure, uncomplicated hope of a girl who believes with her whole heart that magic is real. She would perform it so perfectly, so convincingly, that it would have to be true.

The opening notes from the piano echoed in the vast,

empty theater, each one a clear, hopeful promise. Zoe opened her eyes, and she sang.

The song was "*A Dream Is a Wish Your Heart Makes*," a classic choice, almost dangerously simple in its sentiment. But the voice that bloomed and filled the theater was anything but a marvel of technical flawlessness. Every note was placed with crystalline precision; her pitch was unwavering, a stunning display of absolute control, as captivating and clear as a bell on a winter morning. She didn't just sing the song. She embodied its relentless, unyielding optimism. She moved with a dancer's practiced grace, her gestures open and hopeful, her face a radiant, beatific picture of innocent belief.

A brilliant performance, but also a desperate one.

To someone watching from the back row, she was the epitome of Cinderella, personified. But to anyone who knew what to look for, the strain was a visible tremor beneath the polished surface. The smile, vast and dazzling, was held with rigid control, speaking of a deep, underlying tension. The brightness in her eyes wasn't the soft glow of contentment but a feverish gleam, a frantic performance of joy that verged on hysteria. She was clinging to hope like a drowning woman to a piece of driftwood in a raging sea. She was pouring every last ounce of her insecurity, every whisper of her fear of inadequacy, into the creation of this perfect, unbreakable vessel of happiness.

When the final, hopeful note ascended and then faded into the cavernous silence of the theater, there was a beat of stunned quiet, a silence so profound it felt louder than the song itself. Then, a sharp, collective intake of breath from the darkness of the director's table.

"Thank you, Zoe," Cate's voice emerged from the void, perfectly level and devoid of inflection. "That was... compelling."

Zoe beamed, the blinding spotlight catching the wet shimmer of unshed tears in her eyes. She chose to hear the compliment, to accept the word as a victory, rather than feeling the strange, analytical weight behind it. She gave a curtsy, a gesture of storybook grace, and practically floated off the stage. Her heart hammered against her ribs with a feeling of dizzying, breathless triumph. She had done it. She had nailed it.

An hour later, the callback list was posted on the old corkboard in the backstage hallway. Zoe's hands trembled as she pushed her way through the small, anxious crowd of her fellow actors. And there, right at the top of the page, printed in stark black that seemed to sing just for her.

CINDERELLA..................ZOE REEVES

A genuine, involuntary gasp of pure joy escaped her lips. She had won. The validation was a warm, intoxicating rush, a flood of relief that finally silenced the quiet, gnawing voice of inadequacy for the first time in what felt like an eternity. She had proven it. She could do this. Her way worked. She turned, a real, unperformed smile finally gracing her lips, a smile that reached all the way to her eyes. She scanned the hallway, wanting to find Vivi or Kevin, wanting to share this moment with them.

But they weren't looking at the cast list.

They stood a few feet away, half-hidden in the dim, utilitarian light of the hallway. They had not been watching for her success. They had only been watching her. And the easy, authentic joy she had seen on their faces in the green room, the quiet, settled happiness she so deeply admired, was gone. It had been replaced by a shared, familiar dread, a grim understanding that passed between them in a silent, knowing glance that spoke volumes.

Vivi turned to Kevin, her voice too low for Zoe to hear, possibly. Still, the urgent, clinical precision in her tone was unmistakable, the voice of a doctor looking at a troubling X-ray, the voice of a lookout on the coast, spotting a familiar storm gathering on the far horizon.

"It's worse," Vivi's voice cut through the air between them. "The denial is deeper now. Our old way won't reach her."

CHAPTER

TWO

TYLER BACON

The assignment was offensively sentimental, a piece of journalistic fluff that landed on Tyler Bacon's desk like a sweet, sticky piece of candy he had no appetite for. *The Magic of the Meridian,* the pitch read. A feature for *Westgate Arts & Culture Magazine* on the inexplicable, enduring success of a local repertory theater. *Magic.* Tyler let out a humorless sound. Magic was a word people used when they were too lazy to find the structural wires holding everything up, the hidden mirrors creating the effect, or the clever financial maneuvering that really kept the lights on. He was a journalist. He dealt with the complex, verifiable architecture of facts, not the soft, hazy shape of fairy dust.

Armed with a fresh, cheap reporter's notebook, a digital voice recorder, and a cynicism so deep it became a load-bearing part of his own personality, he pushed through the heavy oak doors of the Meridian Theatre. The lobby was the first piece of evidence for the prosecution.

Grand, certainly, but a faded, trying-too-hard kind of grand that reminded him of an old Southern belle in a worn-out dress. The crimson velvet ropes were worn thin in places, their plushness worn away by time. The brass railings held a shine that spoke of dutiful, endless polishing, but it couldn't hide the constellation of dings and scratches from a century of patrons. High, arched windows let in the weak afternoon light, illuminating columns of motes that danced in the air like microscopic ballerinas in a forgotten show. It smelled of old wood, lemon polish, and the lingering ghost of popcorn, a scent of crowds and happy applause that only made the current emptiness feel more profound. This was a place clinging to its own history with both hands, and Tyler already had his opening line drafted in his head. *The Meridian doesn't just stage plays; it performs the role of a grand old theater, hoping no one notices the worn-out props.*

From behind a set of double doors, he heard the muffled thumps of set pieces being moved and the distant, tinny echo of music from a rehearsal in progress. He was early for his interview with the newly cast Cinderella, a detail that was both irritating and professionally useful. It gave him time to observe, to soak in the atmosphere he was supposed to be writing about. As he leaned against a pillar, jotting down notes on the decor with a precise, fine-point pen made for dissection, he saw a young stagehand, barely out of his teens, trip over his own feet near the main auditorium entrance. An older usher, a man whose face was a roadmap of theatrical seasons, helped him up with a quiet word and a knowing pat on the shoulder. As the kid recovered, flushed with embarrassment, he reached out and tapped the ornate brass doorplate twice with his knuckles before disappearing inside. A ritual. A superstition. Tyler noted it down, labeling it as local color, another quirky habit that fueled the theater's manufactured mystique. The brass on that spot was worn smooth, a soft, golden depression where countless hands had performed the same small act of faith. The kid didn't look quirky, though. He looked reverent, as if he were stepping onto holy ground.

"Can I help you?"

The voice was like a flute in a room full of low cellos, bright, clear, and so relentlessly cheerful it set his teeth on edge. Tyler turned. Standing before him was a young woman who could only be Zoe Reeves. She was a whirlwind of impossible color in his muted, grey-toned world, dressed in a bright yellow sweater and jeans, her blonde hair pulled back in a high, bouncing ponytail. She held a scuffed dance bag in one hand, a small, faded keychain of a cartoon sun hanging from its zipper. Her smile was a dazzling, high-wattage thing that seemed to defy the lobby's dim, historic gloom.

"Tyler Bacon, *Westgate Arts & Culture Magazine*," he said, extending his hand with a journalist's handshake, brief and all business. Hers was surprisingly firm, warm, and it held on to a fraction of a second too long, a small, unspoken offering of connection. "I have an appointment with Zoe Reeves."

"That's me!" she chirped, her smile somehow widening. "It's so exciting to have you here. This place is ... well, it's magic, isn't it?"

Tyler's internal cynic preened, settling back with a satisfied smile. Hook, line, and sinker. "That's what I'm here to find out," he said, the click of his pen sounding loud in the cavernous space. He gestured to a pair of velvet chairs in a quiet alcove. "Do you have a few minutes before you're called?"

"Absolutely." She sat on the very edge of her seat, practically vibrating with an energy that felt both genuine and exhausting to watch.

He started his digital recorder, placing it on the small table between them. "So, you've been cast as Cinderella—big role. You're following in the footsteps of Vivi Asbury and Kevin Brooks, who've had breakout success here. People talk about the Meridian having a special atmosphere. What does that mean to you, as a performer?" He kept his tone neutral, the practiced disinterest of an objective observer looking for a clean, usable quote.

"Oh, it's not atmosphere," she said, leaning forward. Her sincerity was a palpable force, thick and heavy in the air like summer humidity. "It's real. There's energy here—a history. You can feel it the moment you walk on that stage. It's like the building itself wants you to succeed, to find the truest part of your character."

The building wants you to succeed.

He wrote it down verbatim, a saccharine quote for the

puff piece he was already dreading, like trapping a butterfly under glass. Pretty, and completely lifeless. "So, it's a feeling of support?"

"More than that," she insisted, her earnestness unwavering. "It's a feeling of... possibility, like anything can happen. Like fairy tales can come true."

There it was. The thematic core of the article is wrapped in a gift and tied with a bow. He could almost see the headline now. *The Meridian's Modern-Day Cinderella Believes in Fairy Tales.* Perfect but also intensely, profoundly irritating. Nobody this earnest could be for real. It had to be a performance, just another role she was playing.

He decided to test the theory, gently poking at the façade to see what was underneath. "But Cinderella is a character who endures a lot of hardship before she gets her happy ending. Is it draining to maintain that level of sunshine-and-rainbows optimism all the time? Is that just part of the job?"

The question found its mark, and for a split second, the performance faltered. The high-wattage smile didn't go out, but it browned out, the light dimming for a crucial instant. In her bright, expressive eyes, he saw a shadow of something else, a glimpse into a well of genuine hurt, an exhaustion so deep it startled him. There and gone in a heartbeat, plastered over so quickly by her professional effervescence that he almost thought he'd imagined it.

But he hadn't. He was a journalist. His entire career was built on noticing the moment the mask slips.

He felt an immediate, unwelcome jolt of regret. He

hadn't meant to wound her, only to probe the professional armor. He quickly backtracked, his tone softening without his conscious permission, a reflex he didn't know he possessed. "I mean," he rephrased, the words feeling clumsy in his mouth, "it must be taxing always to project that level of positivity. How do you do it?"

Zoe laughed, a bright, clear sound that echoed slightly in the high-ceilinged lobby, but it didn't quite reach her eyes this time. "Lots of coffee!" she said, patting her dance bag with its little sun keychain. "And honestly, I believe in it. I think if you focus on the good, you make better happen. It's that simple."

This was anything but simple, and they both knew it. That one, tiny crack in her armor had changed everything. She wasn't a naive Pollyanna, believing in fairy tales because she'd never known anything else. She was a soldier. Her optimism wasn't a feeling, but a shield she held up against the world, and he could suddenly feel the immense weight of it. For some reason, that was infinitely more interesting than the trite narrative he'd come here to write. He found himself disarmed, his cynical categorizations failing him. This wasn't manufactured hype for a story. This wasn't very easy. This was real.

"I'd like to see that in action," he said, the words surprising him as much as they seemed to surprise her. "My editor wants a deeper dive. Would it be possible for me to sit in on a few rehearsals? To see the process firsthand?"

Her face lit up, the shadow of hurt completely gone now, replaced by a genuine, unshielded delight. "Really?

You want to watch us work? That would be amazing! Cate, our director, has to approve it, of course, but she's usually open to it if it's for a serious piece. I can ask her for you!"

"I'd appreciate that," he said, clicking his pen off. He had his quotes. He had his central figure. But his story had fundamentally changed. He was no longer here to dissect the "magic of theater." He was here to figure out Zoe Reeves.

Later that evening, sitting in the driver's seat of his beat-up sedan in the theater's empty parking lot, the rain fell, drumming a soft, pensive rhythm on the roof. The interior of the car was cluttered, with a faint smell of stale coffee and old newspapers, a messy, real-world fortress. He pulled out his notebook. He flipped to the first page, where he'd written his working title that morning, a perfect encapsulation of his initial, easy skepticism.

The Meridian's Magic: A Local Legend Built on Hype.

He stared at the words, at the cynical certainty of them. A lifetime ago. He thought of the reverence in the stagehand's gesture, a quiet prayer whispered to a brass plate. He thought of the palpable weight of history in the lobby, and the way Zoe's smile had faltered, revealing a glimpse of the machinery required to keep it so bright. The story wasn't the hype. The story was the reason for the hype.

With a decisive flick of his wrist, he scratched a thick, angry line through the title, the pen tearing slightly at the paper—a messy, yet satisfying, act of destruction that wiped the slate clean.

Underneath, in the shadowy gloom of the car, he wrote a new question, marking the beginning of a thorough investigation.

What is Zoe running from?

THREE

TYLER'S PERSISTENCE

Tyler Bacon figured he was something of a connoisseur of bad dates. He'd survived the ones that felt more like a job interview, where his five-year plan was cross-examined over appetizers. He'd endured the thinly veiled therapy sessions, listening to tales of cheating exes and childhood traumas between sips of lukewarm water. He'd sat through a multi-level marketing pitch for essential oils delivered with unnerving passion while he was trying to enjoy his calamari. But this was something else entirely. This wasn't a bad date, but an empty one, a beautiful room with no one home.

He had called in a favor to get the reservation at *The Gilded Vine*, a warm little Italian place tucked into a brick-lined alley in the Celadon Arts District, known for two things: soft lighting that made everyone look a little more honest and a decent Chianti that made them feel that way. He'd hoped the combination would coax some genuine warmth from the woman across from him. He had pitched the evening to Zoe as a continuation of his "research" for the article, a careful framing that gave them both the professional cover they needed to say yes—a comfortable lie, a piece of social architecture to protect them both from the weight of a fundamental question. But he was there because he was utterly fascinated by her, drawn to a defiant, sun-drenched optimism that was a foreign species in the gray, fact-based world he lived in.

She sat across the small table, a vision in a simple white dress that seemed to gather the candlelight around her. The soft glow caught the threads of gold in her hair, making them shine. She was smiling, with the same brilliant, practiced smile he'd seen her give for curtain calls, a masterful piece of stagecraft, flawless in its execution and completely hollow. It never reached her eyes. That was the most unsettling part. Her gaze kept drifting, a slow, lazy slide past his shoulder, as if she were watching a far more compelling story unfold on the painted brick wall behind him. A musician on the street corner outside played a mournful tune on a saxophone, the notes drifting through the open door on a humid breeze, but she gave no sign that she had heard it.

"So, Cinderella. That's a huge role. You must be thrilled,' he said.

"Oh, it's a dream come true," her voice was light and airy, floating somewhere above their table. The words were perfect, the enthusiasm technically present, yet it felt as if she were reading from a script she'd memorized years ago. "It's such a beautiful story. About hope. And finding your perfect match."

"Right. The prince," Tyler said, leaning forward enough to show he was engaged. Here was an opening. "What's your take on him? As a character, I mean."

For a breathtaking, deceptive second, Zoe's focus snapped sharp. A genuine light kindled in her eyes, a sudden and startling heat. "He's... wonderful," she breathed, and the word wasn't an actor's analysis but a woman's testimony. Filled with a strange, personal reverence that made the hair on his arms stand up. "He's everything you would ever imagine. Noble, and kind, and he sees you. He truly sees you, from the very first moment."

Her description wasn't that of an actress exploring a part, the breathless confession of someone describing a profoundly personal, lived experience. The sheer intensity of her conviction set him on edge. This wasn't the passion of an artist lost in her craft; the quiet fervor of a true believer, someone who had seen a miracle and couldn't speak of it in anything but hushed, sacred tones. He felt compelled to push gently.

"But is that realistic?" he asked, his voice softer than he'd intended. "Love at first sight? A perfect man who appears to complete you? Don't you think happy endings are a little more complicated in the real world?"

The conversational probe he'd been planning, a casual, cynical nudge meant to spark a bit of playful debate. He expected her to laugh, to argue back with that bright energy he found so captivating. Instead, her smile tightened, the warmth vanishing until it became a brittle, porcelain shield.

"Maybe your world is complicated," she said, and the

unexpected edge in her soft voice was like a shard of glass. "That doesn't mean everyone has to be. Some people are meant to find each other. Some love stories are simple. Perfect."

The words hung in the air, and the conversation died right there. A thick, heavy silence stretched between them, punctuated only by the distant clink of silverware and the low murmur of other people's happiness. The rich, comforting aroma of garlic bread and oregano that had filled the air now felt cloying, too heavy to breathe. He watched her take a delicate, deliberate sip of her wine, her posture perfect, her eyes once again unfocused, lost in her own private theater.

The romantic disappointment settled in his gut, a slow sinking. This wasn't going to work. Not tonight, maybe not ever. The easy, sparring chemistry they had in the theater lobby, the spark that had made him want to know the woman behind the actress, had vanished entirely. This strange, hollow performance replaced it. The woman he'd asked to dinner wasn't there. In her place was this polite, beautiful, and utterly absent stranger.

And that's when the second shift happened, a quiet click in the back of his mind, a familiar gear engaged. The journalist in him, the part that had been patiently waiting in the wings, observing from the shadows, stepped into the spotlight. The failed date was no longer a personal loss, a minor bruise to his ego, a professional lead, damn good one.

The emotional fog cleared, revealing the hard lines of a story. He started a mental catalogue, an analysis—the unfocused gaze, as if she were looking through him, not at him. The stilted, rehearsed-sounding answers were more like press release copy. And that fervent, almost defensive belief in a perfect, fairy-tale romance. This wasn't a woman distracted by the pressures of a new role. This was a woman actively, desperately hiding something. A secret so all-consuming it left no room for anything or anyone else.

He thought of the files he'd spent days reading through in the theater's archives. The brittle newspaper clippings and faded programs from the Meridian's long history. The sudden breakdowns. The actors who vanished without a trace from major productions. *Nervous exhaustion. Personal emergencies.* The official explanations were always neat. He looked at Zoe and saw the faint, purple shadows under her eyes that her bright smile and careful makeup couldn't quite hide. A certainty washed over him. He saw it happen. He was watching the "before" picture for one of those forgotten tragedies, a living, breathing prelude to another disappearance.

He subtly shifted his posture, the slight slump of a disappointed suitor straightening into the alert stillness of an investigator observing a subject. His focus changed. His questions were no longer personal, but diagnostic. He probed for symptoms.

"You seem a little tired. Rehearsals that intense?"

"Something like that," she murmured, her fingers picking at a loose thread on the heavy linen napkin in her lap. "It's a demanding role. You have to give all of yourself to it."

All of yourself. The phrase echoed in his mind, a direct quote from a 1958 review of an actor who'd played Hamlet and had a public collapse on stage. *He gave all of himself to the role,* the critic had written, weeks before the actor was institutionalized. Tyler made a careful mental note, filing the phrase away for future reference.

The rest of the dinner was a masterclass in deflection from her and subtle interrogation from him. He kept the conversation moving, asking about her process, the demands of musical theater, and the show's history. Her answers were a smokescreen of well-crafted platitudes about her craft and the magic of the stage. She was performing the role of a dedicated actress, and she was doing it flawlessly. But the person behind the performance was gone. He was interviewing a ghost, a beautiful echo of a woman who was already somewhere else.

When the check finally came, he paid with the credit card from the same worn leather wallet that held his press credentials. This encounter had officially become a matter of work.

Outside, the night air was cool, a welcome relief from the stuffy restaurant. It carried the distant, rhythmic sounds of city traffic and the lingering scent of rain on hot pavement. The silence that fell between them as they walked toward the corner where they would part ways was no longer awkward, but clinical. He was observing. She was hiding.

Under the hazy orange glow of a streetlight, she finally turned to him. Her smile was back in place, but this time it was fragile, and there was a genuine apology in her eyes.

"Tyler, I'm so sorry. I've been terrible company tonight. I think...I'm not feeling well."

He saw the lie, clear as day. But for the first time all evening, he also saw a brief, raw terror flash in her eyes behind it—a crack in the façade, a glimpse of the frantic person trapped inside. The *Save the Cat* part of his brain, that small, stubbornly empathetic piece he always tried to keep separate from his work, stirred with an unexpected ache. She looked lost. She looked frightened.

His journalistic instincts took a momentary backseat to a wave of genuine, human concern. He reached out, his movements slow, and placed a gentle hand on her arm. Her skin was cool to the touch, despite the humid night.

"Zoe," his voice softer than he'd intended it to be. "For what it's worth... if you ever need to talk about anything, I'm a pretty good listener. Off the record."

She stared at him, her eyes wide with a mixture of surprise and suspicion. For a heart-stopping second, he thought the dam might actually break. He saw the slight tremble in her lower lip, the raw vulnerability she fought so hard to conceal, rising to the surface. He saw the girl, not the actress. Then, as quickly as it had appeared, the mask was back. She composed her features, gave his arm a light, grateful squeeze that felt as rehearsed as her lines had been.

"Thank you, Tyler. That's sweet of you. I'll be fine."

She turned and walked away, her white dress a receding beacon in the Westgate night. She disappeared around the corner, leaving him standing there, feeling the phantom chill of her skin on his hand and the weight of her lie in the air. He watched the space where she had been, the romantic disappointment of the evening now entirely replaced by a sharp-edged sense of purpose. She wasn't fine. She was in serious trouble.

And she was the biggest story he had ever stumbled upon.

Later that night, the hum of the city outside his Spartan apartment was a distant murmur. The investigation became a physical thing. He uncapped a black pushpin and drove it into the large corkboard that hung above his cluttered desk. One by one, he pinned up the artifacts of his obsession. The timeline he'd constructed of disappearances and breakdowns from the Meridian archives: the photocopied newspaper clippings, their headlines about *nervous exhaustion* and *personal emergencies* highlighted in yellow. The list of psychologically intense productions seemed to correlate with the incidents. A constellation of forgotten tragedies, a seventy-year-old mystery with no motive, no suspect, and no solution.

For a long time, he stared at the board, at the scattered, disparate pieces of a puzzle he couldn't assemble. The paper trail was cold. History was mute. But his failed date with Zoe had given him the one thing he was missing: the key, the piece that made all the other silent, rusted tumblers in the lock finally begin to turn.

He pulled a fresh sheet of paper from his well-worn reporter's notebook, the one with the coffee ring stained onto its cover. He took a thick black marker from the cup on his desk. In large, clean, block letters, he wrote a single word.

ZOE.

He took another pushpin, this one a bright, blood-red one, and pressed it firmly into the very center of the corkboard, pinning her name over everything else. The old clippings and historical data suddenly receded, becoming a frame, a backdrop for the actual subject. The faces of the long-lost actors seemed to stare out from the yellowed paper, their tragedies no longer history, but a warning. The investigation was no longer about the past.

The past was just the prologue. The story was hers.

FOUR

THE DRESSING ROOM DISCOVERY

The trouble with the Meridian Theatre was that it was never truly quiet, not in the way that meant empty. An hour after Cate had sent the cast scattering into the humid evening air, the building still held its own kind of life. The low, constant hum you felt more in your bones than heard with your ears. A life made of the muffled thud of a stagehand working late, securing a flat in the cavernous darkness of the stage. A life in the slow, sleepy creak of the floorboards high up in the mezzanine, settling like an older woman in a familiar chair. The very breath of the ventilation, a system that seemed to inhale secrets in the wings and exhale them as whispers down the long, shadowed hallways. For Zoe, lately, she had the unnerving sensation of being perpetually seen.

Ever since rehearsals for *Cinderella* had tightened their grip on the company's schedule, Cate Hart's presence had become a permanent fixture in the corner of Zoe's eye, a haunting, a persistent ghost that wore a severe expression and silver-streaked hair. Zoe would be in the middle of a dance number, her body a blur of motion under the hot stage lights, and she'd catch a glimpse of the director's silhouette beyond the proscenium arch. She'd be in the music room, her voice climbing scales, and a shadow that could only be Cate's would stretch and retreat past the open doorway. It felt less like guidance and more like a quiet, constant judgment. It made the skin on her arms prickle, a steady, low-grade pressure to be perfect, to be *on*, when all she wanted was to fall apart a little. Cate's notes were another thing entirely, always delivered with an unnerving perception that made Zoe feel like the woman had been standing inside her own head, listening to the thoughts she tried so hard to hide.

She needed a place to be messy—a place to be genuinely, gloriously imperfect. The role of Cinderella, for all its fairy-tale sparkle, demanded it. That was the truth Vivi had tried to give her, wrapped in such solemn, heavy gravity. Finding the character's moments of quiet, gutting despair, that fragile moment of hopelessness right before the choice to believe again, wasn't something Zoe could excavate with Cate's piercing gaze boring into the back of her neck. Her own optimism, the primary tool in her personal and professional toolbox, was an external performance, a resilient shield she held up for the world to see. To find the character's internal truth, the raw and aching core of the girl in the cinders, she had to be completely and utterly alone.

That left only one place in the entire sprawling theater —her dressing room.

This was a small, functional space tucked away on the second floor, a known blind spot in Cate's ever-watchful network of security cameras. The room greeted her with the familiar backstage perfume of old wood, the faint metallic tang of greasepaint, and the lingering, sweet chemical cloud of hairspray. Cluttered with her life, an explosion of Zoe's own sunshine splashed against the room's drab, utilitarian beige. Her massive dance bag, a kaleidoscope of neon pink and electric blue, overflowed with brightly colored leg warmers. A half-eaten bag of sour watermelon candies, her secret rehearsal fuel, sat open on the vanity. Her script was a testament to her work ethic, a rainbow of highlighted passages and scribbled notes in every margin.

The room's single true feature, the one thing that held any sense of history, was the mirror. Huge, an antique left-over from the theater's very bones, its ornate gilt frame now tarnished and weary with age. The gold leaf was peeling in delicate flakes, revealing the dark, serious wood beneath like a secret being whispered. On the top curve of the frame, a small, carved cherub with a chipped wing seemed to be mid-flight, a silent, forgotten detail from a more romantic time. The mirror was her practice partner, a quiet, unblinking audience for her most private and vulnerable explorations of character.

Zoe closed the door, the latch clicking into place with a sound of satisfying finality. The muffled hums and thumps of the theater faded, wrapping her in a cocoon of relative silence. She took a deep, slow breath, the air tasting of settled history and old productions.

Here, she was unobserved. Here, she could let the cracks show.

She turned to face her reflection, her own image staring back from the great expanse of silver glass. Just a girl in simple black leggings and a faded tank top, the color of a washed-out sunset. Her blonde hair was pulled back in a severely practical ponytail, and a fine sheen of sweat coated her temples from the last run-through. She looked like a dancer. A worker. She didn't look like a princess.

This is the moment, she whispered, her voice a soft, private thing in the still room. She was working on the transformation scene, the one right before the Fairy Godmother's arrival, a moment of profound vulnerability, as a girl hit rock bottom, her only chance to attend the ball turned to ashes and rags.

"There's nothing left to believe in," she recited, trying to pour the weight of a lifetime of disappointment into the line. Her reflection mimicked the words, but the image felt as hollow as a drum. Her face, when she tried to pull it into a mask of sadness, still held a baseline of cheerfulness. The performance of happiness was so deeply ingrained in her muscles that it had become her default setting, the place she returned to without thought.

"No," she corrected herself aloud, giving her head a sharp shake. Feel it, Zoe. She closed her eyes, shutting out her own stubbornly optimistic face. She tried to conjure the feeling of raw, aching injustice—the sting of being left behind. The hard certainty that your dreams were nothing more than smoke, and your reality was a stone floor that would always need scrubbing. This was her artistic duty. She owed it to the role. She owed it to the audience who would be sitting in the dark, waiting to believe her. She had to find that truth.

She opened her eyes again, looking deep into her own mirrored gaze as if she could will the sadness into existence. She let her shoulders slump. She let her breath out in a ragged sigh. She delivered the line once more. "There's nothing left to believe in."

This time, something was different.

For a split second that stretched into an eternity, the reflection wavered. It happened at the edges first, the cluttered dressing room behind her seeming to dissolve like sugar in water. The image shimmered, losing its focus like a photograph left out in the rain. She saw not her own pale pink tank top, but a flash of something else—a swirl of nonexistent pale blue fabric that seemed to be spun from light itself, impossibly grand. The bare bulb hanging from the ceiling overhead was momentarily gone, replaced by the brilliant, crystalline glimmer of a thousand tiny lights hanging from a chandelier.

Zoe blinked, and her heart gave a startled little leap in her chest. The vision vanished. Just her, a little out of breath, alone in her dressing room. She let out a sharp, delighted gasp, a little intake of pure surprise. Her mind, conditioned by a lifetime of finding the silver lining, didn't register fear. It didn't register confusion or alarm. It registered pure, unadulterated wonder.

"Whoa," she breathed, a broad, genuine smile spreading across her face, one that felt different from the one she usually put on. It was real. Her imagination had never been that powerful before, never so vivid and complete. It had to be the magic of the theater, the energy of the story finally seeping into her—an *inspiration*.

A jolt of creative adrenaline surged through her, a current of pure, thrilling energy. She leaned closer to the mirror, her palms pressing flat against the cool, smooth surface of the vanity. The air around the mirror seemed to hum with a faint, invisible charge, and a clean, sharp scent, like the air after a summer thunderstorm, filled her nostrils. She could almost hear it, a faint, beautiful strain of music, the swelling strings of a waltz that seemed to be coming from a great distance, a melody from a half-remembered dream.

"Okay," she said to the mirror, to herself, her voice full of a new, giddy confidence. "Again."

She took another deep breath and plunged back into the scene, but this time it was different. She wasn't alone. She had a new, thrilling sense of partnership. The mirror was no longer a tool, but a muse.

"I can't go," she whispered, her voice thick with sorrow that now felt thrillingly accessible. "Not like this."

The shimmering came again, stronger this time, more confident. The worn, scarred floorboards at her feet were overlaid with the impossible image of a polished marble floor, so clear and bright she could see the reflection of phantom light dancing across its surface. The plain wooden door of her dressing room dissolved, replaced by a towering, gilded archway that seemed to reach the ceiling. And through it, she could see them. Couples, dozens of them, were waltzing in a vast, glittering ballroom. The men were impossibly handsome in their crisp, princely uniforms. The women were radiant in gowns of every color imaginable, spinning in a kaleidoscope of silk and satin. The light was golden and perfect, a permanent sunset that made everyone beautiful. The music was no longer a half-imagined thing, but a clear, soaring orchestral piece that vibrated through the floor, through the vanity, and up into her very bones.

Zoe stared, wholly and utterly enchanted. She felt no fear, no creeping sense of the impossible. It felt exactly like stepping into a dream, the kind of beautiful vision she had always believed her imagination was capable of creating. The world of the play came alive for her. She saw it all with the uncritical, wholehearted acceptance of a child watching a magic trick unfold. This wasn't a hallucination. This was a breakthrough.

This, she thought with a thrill of absolute, shimmering certainty, was what Vivi had been trying to tell her. Vivi's talk of darkness and despair had been a misdirection. The point wasn't to feel actual, gritty hopelessness. The point was to find an inspiration so powerful and beautiful that it made the fairy tale feel utterly and completely real. She had misunderstood the lesson entirely. This was how you played Cinderella. You didn't find the darkness. You found a light so bright and so brilliant that it blotted out all the shadows.

Her reaction was a universe away from the chilling, invasive fear Vivi had felt when the world of Illyria first bled through her own reflection. This was nothing like the dark, comforting allure Kevin had found in the Phantom's subterranean lair. For them, the magic had mirrored their inner conflicts, their secret wounds. For Zoe, it reflected her most profound, most cherished belief. That fairy tales were real. That optimism wasn't a weakness but a power. The magic wasn't a predator testing her defenses, but a confirmation of her entire worldview and validation in a swirling dress and a golden ballroom.

The vision receded, the beautiful ballroom dissolving like mist, leaving behind the familiar, comforting clutter of her own dressing room. The grand waltz faded out, leaving only the sound of her own ragged, happy breathing and the triumphant thumping of her heart against her ribs. She was left with a giddy, intoxicating sense of power. She had a secret. A secret, excellent tool that no one else in the cast had. This was her muse. Her own private wellspring of perfect, magical inspiration.

An insistent buzz from her dance bag made her jump. She glanced over, her focus slowly, reluctantly returning to the real world. Her phone was lit up, a text from one of the other dancers flashing on the screen.

> Drinks at The Gilded Bean? A few of us are heading over!

An hour ago, she would have gone without a second thought, her social energy a battery that never seemed to run down. She would have been the first one there, her laughter the loudest. But now, the thought of small talk and crowded coffee shops was a dull distraction, a waste of precious, magical time. The real party was here. In this room. In this mirror.

With a genuine, delighted smile that reached her eyes and made them shine for the first time that day, she pulled out her phone. Her thumbs moved quickly, almost gleefully, across the screen. A polite excuse flowed from her fingertips without a moment's hesitation.

> So sorry, have to pass! Totally swamped with character work. Rain check soon!

She hit send, and the decision didn't feel like a sacrifice, but a victory. She was protecting something extraordinary. She was carving out a new, secret appointment in her calendar for the next day. Another private rehearsal. More time with her muse. She looked back at the mirror, at her own ordinary reflection, and saw the promise of the extraordinary shimmering beneath the surface. The seduction had begun, and she was an utterly, blissfully willing participant.

FIVE

FIRST CONTACT

"Tell me," Tyler said with a confidential hum that cut right through the clamor of the backstage hallway. "Do you ever get the feeling this place is... watching you?"

For the space of a single, held breath, Zoe's practiced smile faltered. His question was a sliver of sharp steel, sliding neatly between the ribs of her carefully constructed cheerfulness. The feeling of being watched was the defining truth of her life these days, a constant, prickling pressure from Cate's unblinking gaze. But Tyler's eyes held a different kind of seeing. It wasn't the stare of a director judging a performance but the look of a man patiently searching for the hairline crack in a beautiful porcelain doll.

The well-oiled gears of her optimism, polished to a high shine over years of dedicated practice, ground into motion. A tiny, wild flutter of panic was caught, smoothed out, and repackaged into something that appeared to be amused curiosity. She tilted her head, letting a laugh bubble up from her chest. It sounded to her own ears like a string of hollow glass beads, pretty and bright and utterly false.

"Watching me?" she repeated, her tone airy and teasing. "Tyler, honey, this is a theater. A hundred people watch me every time I step on stage. It's pretty much the whole job." This piece of misdirection was a graceful side-step she had perfected long ago, answering the question she wished he had asked instead.

His expression never wavered. The small, knowing smile stayed right there, his eyes sharp with a knowing that unsettled her down to her bones. "That's not what I mean, and I think you know it."

He was too close, his perception a little too keen. He was a storm cloud on the horizon of the fragile, glittering world she was building for herself in the quiet corners of her own mind. She needed to pull back, to retreat to the one secret place he could never follow.

"I think," she smiled, shifting into something profes-sional and a little bit distant, "that you're a journalist hoping for a ghost story to spice up a slow news week." She gave his arm a light pat, a gesture meant as a friendly dismissal. The hallway air, thick with the smell of old velvet and leftover hairspray, seemed to press in on them. "If you'll excuse me, I'm plumb worn out. Big day tomorrow."

She didn't wait for him to answer. She turned and dissolved into the departing river of cast members, her heart hammering a frantic rhythm against her ribs. She didn't look back, but she could feel his gaze on her, a tangible warmth on her skin. He wasn't watching anymore. He was hunting.

The encounter left a film of unease on her spirit that clung all evening, like the damp chill of a coming rain. Her desire for her private sanctuary, for the comforting and inspiring presence of her mirror muse, sharpened into a craving so fierce and undeniable. But the theater was no longer a safe harbor. Cate was watching. Tyler was snooping. She needed a way to guarantee she would be completely, unequivocally alone.

The solution presented itself the next day, a flash of opportunistic brilliance born from a moment of technical failure. She was walking down the second-floor corridor when she noticed it. The small, dome-shaped security camera, mounted near the ceiling and pointed directly at the stretch of hallway outside her dressing room, was acting up. Its little red eye would glow steadily for a minute, then blink in a frantic, irregular pattern before going completely dark for several long seconds, as if it were struggling to stay awake. A small, unsteady gap in Cate's web of watchful eyes was a gift.

That afternoon, she put her plan in motion. She found Danny Kim near the stage manager's booth, his face a familiar mask of theatrical stress, a fine sheen of sweat on his brow. She put on her best performance of earnest concern.

"Danny, hey, I think one of the security cameras is on the fritz," she said, pointing up toward the ceiling. The floorboards groaned a little under her feet. "The one up there. Just thought you should know."

He glanced up, let out a long-suffering sigh, and made a note on the clipboard that seemed permanently attached to his hand. "Thanks, Zoe. I'll add it to the list. The whole system's older than dirt. Probably won't get a tech in to look at it for a couple of days."

A thrill, sharp and sweet as a sip of cold lemonade on a hot day, shot right through her. A couple of days. A perfect, private window.

That night, she waited. She went to dinner with a few of the other dancers, she laughed at their jokes, and she performed the role of the endlessly energetic and sociable Zoe Reeves with flawless precision. But her mind was somewhere else entirely, in a quiet room with a gilded mirror, counting down the minutes. By ten o'clock, the theater was settling into its nighttime quiet. By eleven, a tomb, populated only by the single, lonely ghost light glowing on the main stage and the low, circulatory hum of the building breathing around her.

She slipped back in through a side door she knew was often left unlocked, her rehearsal shoes making soft, scuffing sounds on the worn linoleum. The hallway with the broken camera was cast in a slow pulse of shadow and dim, unsteady emergency light. The long, dancing shadows made the corridor seem to breathe in and out—a sign. The universe was conspiring to give her this. The magic was making space for her.

She locked her dressing room door behind her. The simple click of the latch sounded as loud as a gunshot in the profound, waiting silence. The air in the room was calm and still, thick with the familiar, comforting smells of old wood, the ghosts of a thousand different perfumes, and the sharp, metallic tang of ambition. She was safe. She was alone. She turned to the mirror, her heart thumping with a giddy, illicit excitement. Her reflection looked back, a co-conspirator in the dim light, her eyes wide with anticipation.

"Okay," she whispered, her voice a fragile thread of sound. "Let's work."

She laid her script on the vanity and began the transformation scene again, the very pivot of the entire story. Cinderella, at her absolute lowest, stripped of every last scrap of hope. Zoe ran the lines, pushing herself deeper into the feeling, using the memory of Tyler's piercing questions to fuel the character's raw sense of being exposed and judged. She was at the part where the stepmother tears the beautiful dress to rags, a moment of ultimate humiliation she now felt in her own skin.

She moved through the motions of the scene, her body arcing in a silent pantomime of grief and despair. As she worked, she kept her eyes locked on her own reflection, waiting for the shift, for the shimmer of her muse. At first, nothing happened. It was just her, a girl in a tank top, pretending to be heartbroken in a quiet room. A knot of disappointment tightened in her chest. Had it all been a one-time thing? A stress-induced hallucination born of exhaustion and desire?

Just as the doubt crystallized into a hard little stone in her gut, her phone, resting on the corner of the vanity, buzzed against the wood. The screen lit up, casting a slight, modern glow in space. It was a text from Tyler.

Good night. Don't let the ghosts get you.

A genuine smile touched her lips, a small, warm bloom of affection in her chest that felt entirely her own. His cynicism was a kind of game between them, a familiar, comfortable rhythm. The thought of him, so grounded and honest and so relentlessly skeptical, was an anchor. For a split second, the frantic, buzzing need for the magic quieted. This was real. Dinner dates, teasing texts, and the easy comfort of a shared joke. This was good and enough.

Wasn't it?

The question hung in the still air, heavy and unanswered. The smile faded from her lips. She looked from the glowing screen of her phone back to her own reflection in the vast, tarnished mirror. In her own eyes, she saw the conflict, the two girls who lived inside her. One girl wanted the simple reality of a boy's teasing text. The other craved something more, something perfect. The real world was good, but the world in the mirror was flawless.

The choice wasn't a choice at all, but a surrender.

She put the phone face down on the vanity, a deliberate, almost ceremonial act. She was turning her back on daylight to embrace the twilight. She closed her eyes, took a deep, centering breath, and plunged back into the scene with a desperate, renewed focus. "There's nothing left," she whispered, pouring every single ounce of her manufactured despair into the words. "Nothing."

And the mirror answered.

It began as a soft glow, a warmth spreading from the glass that had nothing to do with the dim bulb overhead.

Then came the sound, not imagined this time, but a clear melody. A string waltz so exquisitely beautiful it made her heart ache, a song she felt she had known her whole life but had never heard before. The air grew heavy with an impossible scent, a wave of fragrance so potent that it was dizzying. The smell of a thousand wildflowers seemed to bloom all at once in a sun-drenched meadow, with sun-warmed earth and a hundred different blossoms opening simultaneously.

Zoe's eyes flew open. The dressing room was gone. The familiar peeling paint and vanity lights dissolved at the edges, melting away. She was looking not at her reflection, but through a window into another place. A world lit by a perpetual golden hour, where impossibly handsome princes and ladies in gowns the color of a summer sunset spun across a marble floor under the light of crystal chandeliers. Their smiles never wavered; their movements were impossibly gallant and graceful.

This was more vivid and real than it had been the last time. Her rational mind, the small, stubborn part of her that still clung to the laws of physics, screamed that this was impossible. But her heart, her artist's soul, which had been fed a steady diet of fairy tales and happy endings since childhood, sang with a single, triumphant word. Confirmation.

Driven by a curiosity so powerful it eclipsed all reason; she lifted a trembling hand. She had to know. She had to feel it. She reached out, her fingers extended, expecting to meet the unyielding shock of solid glass.

Her hand met nothing.

There was no impact. No resistance. Her fingers, then her palm, then her entire hand, slid through the surface of the mirror as if it were a shimmering curtain of warm, thick air. The sensation was a paradox, a physical impossibility that her brain struggled to process. One moment, her hand was in the cool, still air of the dressing room. The next, submerged in a world of impossible warmth and soft, golden light, a tingle ran all the way up her arm.

A sharp, involuntary gasp was torn from her lungs, and she jerked her arm back, her shoulder socket protesting the sudden, violent movement. She stumbled away from the vanity, her back hitting the opposite wall, her breath coming in short, shocked pants. Her hand was buzzing with residual energy, and it smelled... it smelled of summer and honeysuckle, and something else, something sweet and clean, like fresh rain and starlight.

The terror lasted for a single, thundering heartbeat, the primal, animal fear of the unnatural, the body's instinctive rejection of a world turned inside out, a shock of pure wrongness.

Then, it melted away. The shock wasn't horror, but of discovery. A wave of pure, unadulterated delight instantly overwrote the physical jolt. Her short, sharp gasps of fear dissolved into a breathless, wondering laugh that started deep in her belly and spilled out into the silent room.

This was real.

The visions, the music, the feeling of being on the cusp of something extraordinary. A real place. And she touched it.

The knowledge crashed over her, a euphoric, liberating wave. Vivi's fear, Kevin's desperation, Cate's grim warnings, they were all wrong. They didn't understand. They had found worlds of shadow and blood and pain because that is what they had been looking for. She had seen beauty, and she had found it. The magic wasn't a predator, but a reward and validation for every single optimistic belief she had ever held, proof that her relentless hope wasn't foolishness, but faith.

She lifted her hand, still tingling, and brought her fingers to her nose. The scent of wildflowers and something more, something impossible, was undeniable, a fragrant ghost clinging to her skin, the most beautiful thing she had ever smelled. Proof. Tangible, irrefutable proof.

A slow, determined smile spread across her face, a secret joy blooming in her heart for her. The world outside this room, with its cynical journalists, worried directors, and the endless, exhausting work of maintaining a sunny disposition, felt faded and drab in comparison. The real world was flawed and messy. This world, the one on the other side of the glass, was perfect.

She knew, with an addict's clarity, that she had to go back. It wasn't a question of if anymore, but only a matter of when. And for how long? And what parts of herself she was willing to leave behind to get there.

SIX

CATE'S RECOGNITION

The only sound was the low, electric prayer of the security monitors, a constant hum that had become the background radiation of Cate Hart's self-imposed vigil. Outside her second-story window, the humid Southern night hung heavy, thick with the scent of promised rain on hot asphalt and the ceaseless thrum of cicadas. But here, in the cloistered quiet of her office, the world was reduced to that single, synthetic note. The system had been installed for something as simple as catching teenagers trying to sneak in after hours. Now this was her watchtower, a grid of ghost-lit windows looking straight into the soul of her theater. A mug of forgotten coffee sat beside her, its contents as bitter as the feeling in her gut. The air tasted of aging electronics, the smell of a war room for a battle no one else knew was being fought.

Her finger traced the edge of a monitor, the glass a cool shock against her skin. A memory surfaced, unwelcome as a ghost at a wedding. Years ago, she and Malcolm would run backstage, their laughter echoing in the empty theater as they unboxed the cameras. *To catch stagehands napping in the wings,* he had joked. His smile had been so easy then, an honest and unguarded thing she saw less and less of these days. That memory was a chapter from a different book entirely, a story written by two people who thought they had already survived the worst. Now, the laughter was gone, a hollow echo in the chambers of her heart. The simple tool for catching trespassers had become her periscope, her only means of watching souls inching toward the abyss—a heavy, familiar weight, a crown she had never asked to wear.

The central screen dominated the main stage, bathed in a wash of grainy silver, with the ghost light standing lonely vigil at its center. Zoe Reeves moved across the scuffed floorboards, a bright, furious moth caught in the beam of a single light. Rehearsal had been over for an hour, but there she was, alone in the quiet dark. Cate leaned forward, and the old leather of her office chair groaned a protest that was lost in the hum of the machines. She watched Zoe spin, a flawless pirouette that ended in a perfect line. Then, for a fraction of a second, her shoulders slumped, a barely perceptible crack in the facade before she forced them straight and began the sequence all over again.

The pattern was there, sharp and clear as a shard of broken glass in her heart, terrifyingly familiar. She saw it in the obsessive, relentless intensity, in the refusal to stop, in the grinding need to drill a scene until there was nothing more than a shell of technical perfection, its spontaneous life bled completely away. This was the same hollowed-out, desperate drive for control she had watched consume Vivi from the inside out.

Cate's hand moved to the console, her fingers flicking a switch. The view jumped to a camera in the second-floor hallway. There was Zoe again, walking away from the stage, her energy still buzzing around her. She paused as she passed her own dressing room, her hand hovering over the doorknob as if it were hot to the touch. But she didn't go in. She continued down the hall, taking a few more steps, only to stop in front of the large, decorative mirror near the stairwell—an old, heavy thing, its gilt frame dulled by age, a silent witness to generations of actors' hopes and fears.

Cate's breath caught in her throat. Zoe wasn't looking at her reflection. She was looking *into* it. Her head was tilted with a kind of quiet, listening curiosity, her body utterly still. Her focus was absolute, pulled toward the reflective surface as if it were the only source of warmth in a cold world.

And there it was. The final piece she hadn't wanted to find. The two fatal symptoms of the theater's sickness. First, the obsessive practice that wore down the soul. Second, a fixation on its portals. Zoe was on the path.

Doubt came on her then, a sharp current pulling her under, like an old and unwelcome acquaintance. Her knuckles whitened where she gripped the edge of her desk, the past playing out in her mind like a reel of failed battle plans. With Vivi, she had been cryptic. She had spoken in riddles about pretty lies and hollow men. Vivi, lost in the fortress of her own intellect, had been unable to hear the warning until the walls were already crumbling around her. So, with Kevin, she had tried the opposite. She had been direct, brutal, tearing open the old wounds of her own trauma in *Macbeth* to show him the raw, bloody truth. And he, so convinced of his own unique artistic suffering, had looked right through her and dismissed her as unstable.

To call them mixed results was a kindness she no longer afforded herself. They were failures, each in their own way, each carved into her memory. A direct assault on Zoe's fortress of relentless optimism would only make the girl reinforce her walls, brick by painful brick. But to wait, to stand by until she suffered a public breakdown like Kevin's, a catastrophic betrayal, an abdication of a duty she had never wanted but could never set down.

Watching Zoe's small, still form on the screen, a wave of fierce, almost painful protectiveness washed over Cate. She didn't see a talented actress teetering on a precipice. She saw a kid, so full of a fragile, desperate light that it hurt to look at. This wasn't a problem to be managed or a situation to be contained, but a crisis. This was a person to be saved. Her hesitation wasn't cowardice but a deep, trauma-informed fear of making it worse—of choosing the wrong words or the wrong weapon and accidentally pushing Zoe closer to the very edge she was trying to pull her back from.

She would not repeat the same mistakes. She could not. She needed a new strategy. She needed a middle path.

The decision solidified in her chest, bringing with it a

clarity that cut through the fog of her fear. Phase one would be passive. She would begin making her presence known, not as a director looming with judgment, but as a silent, grounding force. She would happen to be working late in the rehearsal rooms. She would be organizing files in the wings when Zoe passed by. Her physical presence, a quiet tether to the real, messy, imperfect world, might be enough to disrupt the fantasy's seductive pull without setting off all of Zoe's defenses—a gentle, constant anchor of reality against the pull of a tide.

Phase two would be active, but it would be covert. This wasn't a fight she could wage alone, nor should she have to. She and Malcolm had forged their alliance in the crucible of a shared nightmare, a bond stronger than steel. They were no longer survivors. They were guardians. And it was time to activate their protocol.

Her hand, steady now, pushed back from the desk. The complaint about her chair was a loud, lonely sound in the silent office. She reached for her smartphone, its sleek, modern form a stark contrast to the bank of aging monitors. She swiped her favorites, her thumb pressing the first name on the list without hesitation.

It rang only once before he answered. His voice was a calm, familiar harbor in the sudden storm of her anxiety. She could almost feel the steady weight of his hand on her shoulder, a memory of support from a past crisis that lived not in her mind but in her bones.

"Malcolm," she said. Her voice was stripped of all pleasantries, honed down to its essential, urgent purpose. "It's starting again."

She heard the soft, sharp intake of his breath on the other end of the line, as the sound of a fellow veteran hearing the distant, familiar drum of a war they both thought they had left behind. There was no need for explanation or details. He knew.

"I need you to check the energy levels around the *Cinderella* set," she commanded, her tone low and firm. "Now."

CHAPTER

SEVEN

TYLER'S RESEARCH

The assignment was supposed to be a sweet-tea sort of story, easy to swallow and gone in an afternoon —a soft-focus, human-interest piece on the quirky, resilient world of community theater. Tyler Bacon had pitched it as a potential Sunday feature, something to fill the arts section with good local color. His editor, bless his deadline-addled heart, had signed off on it without a second thought. But from the moment Tyler first walked into the Meridian, the air thick with the scent of old velvet and something like sweet olive drifting in from the street, he'd felt the grit of a real story under his fingernails. This wasn't in the official history or the press releases but in the way the actors spoke about the place, with a strange cocktail of fierce love and whispered reverence. And in the almost-too-intense stare of the director, Cate Hart. And most of all, in the vibrant, blindingly bright star of their new show, Zoe Reeves, a woman who seemed to be powered by something more potent than ambition.

He found Cate Hart in her second-floor office, a cluttered command center that smelled of stale coffee and old paper. The director was staring at a bank of security monitors, the images on them swimming in a grainy, black-and-white dance. Her posture was ramrod straight, her expression a mask of grim concentration. She looked less like an artistic director and more like a general tracking enemy movement on a battlefield. When Tyler cleared his throat, she started, her eyes snapping to him with an unnerving focus before a veil of distraction dropped over them. She looked exhausted, her formidable energy frayed and thin, a rope worn down to its last few threads.

"Mr. Bacon," her voice was a dry rasp. "Right. The article."

"Just Tyler. And yes. I was hoping I might get a look at the theater's archives. Old programs, reviews, that sort of thing. For historical context." He had his reporter's notebook in his hand, the professional armor he had worn for a decade.

Cate waved a dismissive hand toward the hallway. "Basement. End of the hall. Door's unlocked. Knock yourself out."

The permission was granted so swiftly and carelessly that it caught him off guard. He had expected to have to cajole, to flatter, to promise glowing coverage. But Cate was already turning back to her screens, her attention consumed by the silent, grainy figures moving across them. He saw the genuine distress in the lines around her eyes, the unfocused anxiety that had replaced her usual sharp authority—a pang of something that felt danger-ously like empathy pricked at him.

"A rough day," his voice softened. "If now's not a good time, I can come back."

She glanced at him again, and for a second, he thought she actually saw him, the man and not just the reporter. "The day's not the problem," she muttered, more to herself than to him. Then she shook her head, a quick, sharp motion of dismissal. "No. Go. It's fine."

He took the unspoken command and retreated, navi-gating the utilitarian backstage hallways down a flight of creaking wooden stairs into the basement. The air grew cooler here, thick with the dry, slightly sweet scent of aging paper and bookbinding glue, a smell that reminded him of forgotten attics and summer afternoons spent in county libraries. He found the archive room at the end of a dimly lit corridor. Exactly as he had imagined. Tall, gray metal shelves stretched to the ceiling, groaning under the weight of overstuffed binders and stacked boxes whose cardboard had softened in the damp southern air. The quiet was a physical thing, a dense, heavy hush broken only by the low hum of the building's circulatory system.

This was his element. The hunt. The slow, methodical process of sifting through the dross for the glint of a story. He started with the basics, pulling down logbooks and photo albums from the theater's early years in the 1920s. He moved on to stacks of yellowed newspapers, the pages as brittle as autumn leaves, some bearing the faint, silvery trails of long-dead insects. He set himself up at a small desk with a microfilm reader, the machine whirring to life with a rhythmic click. The squeal of the reel turning was a familiar sound, a prelude to discovery that cast a greenish, ghostly glow on his face as he scrolled through decades of local arts coverage.

For hours, this was precisely what he expected. Rave reviews, occasional flops, casting announcements, fundraising drives, the mundane, cyclical life of a regional theater, a story he'd written a dozen times before. He made notes on his legal pad, the scratch of his ballpoint pen a sharp counterpoint to the soft rustle of old paper. He was looking for the angle—the one unique detail that would elevate his piece from fluff to a feature.

He found it around nine o'clock that night.

There were no explosive revelations, but a pattern, faint at first, then troublingly consistent—a slow drip of poison in the theater's veins.

It started with a small clipping from a 1958 edition of the *Westgate Chronicle* about a production of *A Streetcar Named Desire*. The lead actress, Eleanor Vance, had withdrawn from the production due to a sudden illness a week before opening. The paper cited nervous exhaustion. Tyler jotted it down—standard industry pressure.

Then came a 1972 microfilm article about *Macbeth*. The headline read, *Meridian's 'Macbeth' in Turmoil as Leading Man Exits*. The actor, a promising talent named Richard Doyle, had apparently suffered a complete breakdown and been institutionalized. The production was canceled. A tragic story, but not unheard of in such an intense role.

A note in a 1994 production log for *The Glass Menagerie*

caught his eye next, a hasty scrawl from the stage manager.

Laura is an understudy. Amelia gone. Cate says she's not coming back. No details.

He thought for a moment. Who was Cate? He flipped back through a stack of old programs until he found the one she had. Hecate Hart was listed as an actress in a few shows before she took over as director. *Hecate was her old stage name,* he recalled someone mentioning. *She shortened it to Cate when she started directing.* Interesting.

He kept digging, and the list grew longer—a dancer who vanished mid-run in the eighties. A tenor in a musical in the early 2000s quit overnight, forfeiting his contract and disappearing from the local scene entirely. The reasons were always vague, always attributed to burnout, exhaustion, or personal emergencies. Rational. Plausible. But when he laid them all out chronologically, the plausibility frayed at the edges. The incidents clustered around productions known for their psychological intensity. They occurred deep into the rehearsal process, when the pressure was at its highest. And there were too many of them. This secret, a small town would keep, buried deep under layers of politeness and Sunday sermons until it became part of the landscape.

His journalistic skepticism, the most vital tool in his professional arsenal, kicked into high gear. He was a man who dealt in facts, in verifiable sources, and on-the-record quotes. The idea of anything supernatural was absurd, the stuff of late-night cable shows and conspiracy forums. There had to be a logical explanation. A gas leak causing hallucinations? Unlikely to be so specific over seventy years. A tradition of brutal, psychologically damaging directorial methods? That felt more possible. Cate Hart certainly had the intensity for it. Perhaps the theater had a history of being a toxic workplace, consuming and discarding its most vulnerable artists.

That was a story. A real story. He could already see the headline, a piece of tragic bait his editor would gobble up. *The Dark Side of the Footlights: The Hidden Toll of the* Meridian's *Magic.*

He remembered reading an old article about the theater where Vivi Asbury, the previous season's leading lady, mentioned her own deep dive into the archives. She was researching her role as Viola, she'd said. He wondered what she had found, what she had been looking for. She did not seem like someone doing character work. She'd had the haunted look of a woman searching for an answer to a question she was terrified to ask. Tyler, on the other hand, had no fear, only professional curiosity. He was an objective observer, and he would find the objective truth.

However, the clippings were vague, and the notes were circumstantial. He could not build an investigative piece on whispers and coincidences. To get the real story, he needed a primary source. He needed to talk to the people living in the middle of it right now. He needed to see if the historical pattern had a modern-day echo.

And just like that, his professional and personal interests merged, flowing together into a single, sharp point of focus. Zoe Reeves. She was the heart of the current production, embodying the theater's vibrant energy. But he had seen the flash of panic in her eyes when he had pressed her, the brittle perfection of her smile. She was holding something back. If the theater was a high-pressure cooker, she was standing right at the center of the heat. She was the key.

He packed up his notebook; the pages now filled with a timeline of forgotten tragedies. He had his thesis. He took his next step. He left the quiet, heavy tomb of the archives and headed back upstairs. The muffled, distant sound of a single, clear soprano voice practicing a scale grew louder as he ascended, pulling him back into the world of the living.

He emerged into the backstage hallway as rehearsals were letting out. The air was suddenly filled with the loud, overlapping chatter of the cast, their energy spilling out of the studio. He spotted her immediately, a beacon in the crowd. Zoe was talking to one of the other dancers, laughing at something she said. The laugh was bright and practiced. It didn't quite reach her eyes.

He waited for her to break away, then intercepted her with a casual smile he hoped looked more genuine than hers, his own reporter's mask, honed to perfection over years of practice.

"Zoe, hey."

She turned, and her professional smile clicked into place. "Tyler! Still haunting the halls?"

"Just doing my due diligence. Got a second? I'm writing a piece on the theater's history and its personality.

The ghosts, so to speak." He oversaw her, letting the word hang in the air between them. Her smile didn't waver.

He held her gaze, watching the calculation bloom behind her eyes, the immediate, reflexive denial, and finally, the quick construction of a smile bright enough to blind, a fascinating and terrifying thing to behold.

EIGHT

THE VETERAN'S WISDOM

The green room held the low, thrumming anticipation that always came before a first blocking rehearsal, a place built for comfort, a history of nerves and relief soaked into its chaotic collection of furniture. A faded velvet sofa was shedding its pile, and a pair of armchairs held the permanent impressions of actors who had found their home there long ago. Most of the makeup mirrors lining one wall were dark, their bright ring lights waiting for the focused intensity of tech week. On a coffee table buried under discarded scripts and half-empty mugs, Zoe's own script for *Cinderella* stood out, its pages a rebellion of brightly highlighted lines.

Vivi watched her from across the room, a mug of black coffee warming her hands. Zoe was a splash of wildflower color in the room's muted, comfortable tones. Her posture was a study in bright, unyielding energy as she laughed at something an ensemble member said. The sound was clear and cheerful, but a little too loud, a performance of ease that didn't quite match the tight, white-knuckled grip she had on her water bottle.

A familiar, protective ache settled deep in Vivi's chest, the same feeling that surfaced whenever she saw a delicate prop left too close to the edge of a stage, a feeling she had come to recognize as a quiet alarm. She had walked this path before. She knew the deceptive promise of a perfect, polished role, the way a character's curated emotions could feel so much safer than your own messy, unpredictable ones. She and Kevin had survived their own seasons of madness, emerging into a settled, easy happiness that now felt as natural as breathing. But that hard-won peace had come with a new and solemn responsibility. It came with the duty to recognize the low, dark clouds of a storm gathering on someone else's horizon.

Zoe wasn't an optimistic understudy anymore. She was the lead. She was standing at the very center of the stage, directly in the path of the theater's sweet, hungry magic. And Vivi, a survivor of that particular fever, could not stand by and watch it take another.

She picked her moment, waiting until Zoe was momentarily alone, her head bowed over her script. The old building seemed to hold its breath as Vivi crossed the room, her footsteps silent on the worn rug. The space around Zoe smelled of old paper and the sharp, clean scent of opportunity.

"Hey," Vivi's voice was soft, a quiet note in the room's scattered sounds of muffled thuds from the stage crew and the low hum of the building's ventilation.

Zoe looked up, her face immediately breaking into that

radiant, high-wattage smile. "Vivi. Hey. Are you excited about today? I've been going over the ballroom scene, and I think I have a fun idea for the waltz."

She was already filling the air with professional enthusiasm, a beautiful and sturdy wall of it. Vivi offered a gentle, genuine smile in return, not the tight, practiced one she used to wear. "I am. But I was actually thinking about you. About Cinderella."

Zoe's expression turned earnest, her focus sharpening. "Oh? Any tips? You're the master of these classical roles."

This was the opening she had been waiting for. Vivi sat on the arm of the worn sofa, lowering her voice to create a small pocket of quiet between them. "It's just that she's a difficult character. More than people think. It's easy to play on the surface, the relentless optimism. But the real magic of her, the part that makes an audience feel her story in their bones, is what's underneath."

She paused, choosing her words with the care of someone disarming a bomb. This had to be a warning, but a warning wrapped so carefully in craft that Zoe's defenses would not immediately reject it. "The audience sees her suffering. They see the cruelty she endures. If her hope doesn't have weight, if it doesn't feel like a choice she has to make every single day against a tide of despair actively, then it's just smiling. It's not a character. It becomes a cartoon."

Vivi leaned in a fraction, trying to pour the gravity of her words into the small space between them. "You have to find the moments where her smile is a shield, not a feeling. The moments she's scrubbing the floors and her hands are raw, and for a second, she almost gives up. You have to feel that quiet moment where the belief almost gutters out before she chooses to believe in something better. That choice, that's the heart of the role. Without the darkness, the light doesn't mean a thing."

She had laid it bare, the core of her own hard-won truth, the lesson she had learned in the gilded cage of Illyria. Authentic joy wasn't the absence of pain, but the courage to feel it and keep going anyway, the most crucial piece of wisdom she had to offer, a fragile seed of knowledge she hoped would take root.

Zoe listened with rapt attention, nodding thoughtfully, her brow furrowed in concentration. For a moment, a fragile hope bloomed in Vivi's chest. Maybe this was working. Perhaps the words were finding their way through.

Then Zoe's face cleared, brightening with the sudden, triumphant flash of someone who had solved a complex technical problem.

"Oh, I get it," she exclaimed, her voice returning to its chipper, stage-ready volume. She grabbed a highlighter from her dance bag and uncapped it with a decisive click. "So, for the scenes with the stepmother, I should use a slightly lower vocal register to show the pressure she's under. Then, when I sing *'A Dream Is a Wish,' I can transition* to a brighter, more open head voice for contrast. The emotional journey is in the vocal dynamics. Got it. That's a great note, thank you."

She beamed at Vivi, her eyes shining with gratitude for

the brilliant piece of technical advice. And in that moment, Vivi's hope turned to dust in her hands.

Zoe had not heard a single word. Not the real ones. She had taken a profound, cautionary lesson about emotional vulnerability and, with the reflexive speed of a master craftsman, had translated it into the sterile, manageable language of acting jargon. Vocal register. Dynamics. Contrast. She had taken the soul of the advice and discarded it, keeping only the empty, technical shell.

This act of self-defense was so complete, so unconsciously perfect, so utterly terrifying. A draft that had nothing to do with the old windows snaked around Vivi's heart. This was an active, unbreachable shield. Zoe rephrased emotional depth as a technical problem to be solved, rendering her unreachable to any perceived emotional threat.

As Vivi stared, momentarily speechless, her gaze drifted past Zoe's shoulder to the gallery of framed photos on the wall. They were black-and-white portraits of past Meridian leads, a silent chorus of the theater's history. Her eyes landed on one, a young woman from the 1950s, her hair in a boyish crop, in costume for *A Streetcar Named Desire*. Her smile was elfin and full of a wild, mischievous hope. Vivi remembered Cate mentioning her once, her voice tight and distant. "Eleanor Vance," she had said. "A brilliant Blanche. Then one day, during the run, she flew away and never came back."

A euphemism. A ghost story. A warning.

Vivi looked from the smiling, forever-young face of Eleanor Vance, lost in a fantasy of eternal childhood, back to Zoe, so bright and hopeful, full of a desperate, manufactured belief in fairy tales. History was preparing to repeat itself, verse for verse. A profound sense of duty settled over Vivi. She could not let it happen again.

She had to save this girl. But the way she had saved herself, by confronting the lie head-on, would never work. Zoe's entire identity was built on the lie being true. A direct assault would only make her build her walls higher, stronger, more perfect.

"That's one way to think about it," Vivi managed, her voice quiet.

Zoe, completely oblivious, was already gathering her things, her energy focused on the rehearsal ahead of her. "Thanks again, Vivi. You're the best."

As Zoe started for the door, Vivi reached out, her hand landing gently on Zoe's arm. The sudden, simple contact made Zoe pause. Vivi forced a soft smile, one that cost her more effort than anything she had ever had to produce on stage. "Break a leg, Zoe. And take care of yourself in there, okay?"

Zoe's smile was genuine this time, warmed by the simple, human gesture. "Always. You too."

And then she was gone, practically skipping out of the room, leaving a trail of bubbly energy and the faint scent of floral perfume in her wake.

The sudden quiet she left behind was heavy and absolute. Vivi sank onto the old velvet sofa, the stuffing groaning in protest. The weight of her failure settled onto her shoulders. This wasn't about giving bad advice. She had looked into the eyes of the theater's next potential victim and had seen the intricate lock on the cage, but she had discovered she didn't have the key.

She realized with a sinking dread that she wasn't simply mentoring a young actress; she was mentoring a young actress who was also her daughter. She was guarding a soul who had painstakingly built her entire world out of spun glass and was about to step onto a stage where hurricanes were born. And she had no idea how to warn her that the first gust of wind was already on its way.

NINE

TYLER'S INVESTIGATION

The lie was a piece of grit lodged under his eyelid, a sharp, persistent irritation he could not blink away. For more than an hour, Tyler had been sitting in the gathering dark of his apartment, the only light coming from the cool blue-white glow of his laptop screen. It cast a sterile wash over a constellation of open browser tabs, interview transcripts, and scanned newspaper clippings that felt more like ghost stories than history. He was a journalist. His world was built on a foundation of facts, timelines, and truths that could be scrutinized and verified. And Zoe's story, a pretty, fragile thing, didn't track.

The first reports had come from a grim Vivi and a Kevin who looked as if he'd been pulled inside out. They had cornered him after rehearsal, their usual easy banter stripped away, leaving only a raw and shared urgency. Both had tried to talk to Zoe. Both had come away with nothing but the chilling sense that they had been speaking to a stranger. Their stories, filtered through the strange trauma that seemed to cling to them, sounded half-mad, tinged with something he couldn't name. But the heart of it was a language Tyler understood perfectly. Zoe was lying. She was pulling away, building a wall around herself brick by quiet brick. She was in trouble.

Her excuse for missing their dinner, the one he'd heard her give over the phone with a cheerfulness that felt painted on, was flimsy as a stage prop—a late rehearsal. Cate is on a tear. He had checked it, a knot of guilt tightening in his stomach as he'd called Danny Kim, the stage manager, under the pretense of a follow-up for his article. The rehearsal, Danny confirmed, had wrapped on time. The lie was a clumsy one, an unnecessary one, and it set every one of his professional instincts humming. You didn't tell a weak lie unless the truth you were hiding was too heavy and complicated to move.

His laptop screen illuminated his research folder on the Meridian Theatre, a project that had begun as a light arts and culture piece—a puff of sweet smoke—but was slowly twisting into something much darker. He scrolled past a brittle article from 1972 detailing a fire that had gutted the original costume shop, and another from 1988 about a last-minute donation that saved the theater from bankruptcy. He stopped, his cursor hovering over a file labeled simply **ANOMALIES.**

Inside were his notes on the unnerving pattern he'd stumbled upon weeks ago. Actors who had left. A promising leading man in the sixties who quit mid-run to "travel the world," mailing a single, cryptic postcard from Lisbon before vanishing from the face of the earth.

A gifted ingenue in the eighties who suffered a supposed breakdown and was quietly sent home to a family that later swore she never arrived. A character actor in the late nineties who walked out between acts one night and was never seen again, his street clothes still hanging in his locker. The stories were all different, but the timing was always the same, clustering around intense, emotionally demanding productions like moths to a flame.

He raked a hand through his hair, the conflict a bitter acid in his gut. This felt bigger than a flaky girlfriend, bigger than a simple lie. However, chasing this was a betrayal, since he cared about Zoe. He was beginning to think he might be falling for her, a truly terrifying thought for a man who had built a career on the solid bedrock of cynical detachment. He wanted to trust her, to believe in the bright, easy smile she offered the world. But the facts were a stubborn jury, and they weren't on her side.

Just as he was about to close the laptop, to try and force the thick unease from his mind and pretend this was a regular Tuesday night, his phone buzzed. The sound was sharp against the wooden table—a text from Zoe.

> So sorry again about the other night!
> Rehearsals are eating my brain.
> Raincheck soon? I promise to make it up
> to you! XO, Z.

The cheerfulness was a physical force, a wall of bright, happy emojis and breathless exclamation points, so perfect, so performatively Zoe that it felt completely alien. This text was written by a stranger, in her name.

That was it. The grit in his eye was now a stone in his throat. He could not swallow it down. He could no longer ignore it.

He stood and pulled on his jacket. He was crossing a line; he knew it. This line was drawn in sand between the man he was supposed to be and the man he was becoming. The journalist in him was at war with the man who was falling for the subject of his investigation. For a long moment, he hesitated, his hand resting on the cool brass of the doorknob. He pictured her face, that genuine, unfiltered smile from their first real conversation, before the missed dates and the flimsy excuses had started to build a wall between them. He remembered the vacant, distracted look in her eyes the last time they'd spoken, as if she were listening to a song only she could hear, a melody playing from a million miles away. A wave of protective fear washed over him, turning his hesitation to steel. This wasn't for a story anymore. This was for her.

The Meridian Theatre was eerily quiet when he slipped in through a side entrance, the heavy door propped open by a canvas sandbag leaking a fine trail of grit onto the floor. The main stage was a cavern of darkness, but a few ghost lights cast long, distorted shadows across the rows of empty velvet seats, making them into a silent, waiting congregation. The distant, rhythmic clang of a pipe in the boiler room was the only sound, a slow, metallic heartbeat in the building's deep chest. He made his way into the backstage hallways, his own footsteps sounding unnaturally loud on the worn floorboards.

He found her dressing room at the end of the hall. The little star-shaped nameplate seemed to gather the dim light to itself. And from behind the door, he heard it—a voice.

Zoe's voice, but not the sound of someone running lines. Rather, a low, continuous murmur. Intimate. Adoring. He crept closer, his heart beginning to pound a slow, heavy rhythm against his ribs. He held his breath, straining to catch the words through the thick wood.

"...yes, that's exactly it," she was saying, her voice soft and full of a breathtaking tenderness he'd never heard from her before. "You always know what I need to hear. It's like you see right into my heart."

Tyler frowned, the sound setting his teeth on edge. Who in God's name was she talking to? He pressed his ear closer to the door, the old, warped wood cool and solid against his skin.

"No one else gets it," she continued, followed by a soft, happy sigh that twisted something inside him. "They think it's an escape. But this... being with you... It's the most real thing in my life."

A long pause followed. Tyler found himself holding his own breath, waiting for the other side of the conversation. There was only the deep, humming silence of the old building. Then Zoe's voice came again, a little brighter this time.

"You're right. I shouldn't listen to them. They don't understand happiness."

A chill seeped into his blood. He was a journalist. He interviewed grieving widows, corrupt politicians, and pathological liars. He was accustomed to the cadence of one-sided conversations. She wasn't on the phone. She was talking to someone in that room. Or she was talking to herself.

Driven by a reporter's instinct he could not name, he crouched down. The old door was warped at the bottom, leaving a thin, dark gap between it and the floor. A sliver of warm, golden light spilled out into the hall. He angled his head, pressing his cheek against the gritty floorboards that smelled faintly of lemon polish and time. He could see a narrow slice of the room. Her feet, clad in fuzzy pink slippers. The scrolled leg of the vanity. And the heavy, ornate base of the large, antique mirror.

He watched, his own breathing shallow in his ears, as she paced back and forth in his limited field of view. Her slippers made a soft, whispering sound against the floor. She was always facing the mirror.

He had to know. He had to see. He rose slowly, his knees groaning in protest. He reached out and knocked on the door, the sound exploding.

The murmuring stopped instantly. The silence that poured from the room now was absolute, a heavy, listening thing. A few seconds later, he heard a faint scuffling noise, and then the sharp, loud click of the door latch turning.

The door swung open, and Zoe stood there, blinking in the dim hallway light. Her face was a mask of startled innocence, her eyes wide, a classic deer-caught-in-the-headlights expression that was a little too perfect, a little too practiced.

"Tyler! What are you doing here?" Her voice was high, a nervous, tinkling sound that grated on his nerves.

"I could ask you the same thing," his own voice coming out low and steady, cutting right through her performed surprise. He stepped forward, a single deliberate step that forced her to back into the room. "Who were you talking to, Zoe?"

She laughed, a short, sharp burst of air that held no humor at all. "Talking to? I wasn't talking to anyone. I was in here, going over my lines."

"It didn't sound like lines," he said. His gaze swept the small, cluttered room that was empty. There was nowhere for anyone to hide. His eyes landed on the mirror. Its silver surface shimmered under the harsh glare of the vanity bulbs. It dominated the room, a silent, liquid presence. "Conversation. A very intimate one."

Her face flushed, a tide of angry red creeping up her neck. She crossed her arms over her chest, her whole body screaming a defiance that looked as brittle as spun sugar. "I don't know what you think you heard, but I was alone."

"I heard you say, 'being with you is the most real thing in my life'," he quoted, his voice flat and unforgiving. He felt cruel satisfaction in using her own words against her. "Who, Zoe?"

She panicked. He could see it plain as day in her eyes, a frantic search for a story that would hold. She looked around the room, her gaze darting from the rack of shimmering costumes to the makeup-strewn table, anywhere but at him. Anywhere but at the mirror.

"I was... I was method acting," she finally stammered, the words tumbling out in a rush. "It's a technique for the character. You talk to yourself, as the character, to... to find her emotional truth. To stay in the moment."

The lie was so thin, sharp, and pathetic. And in its utter weakness, the most critical clue he had ever gotten.

The trigger. A filing cabinet in the back of his mind flew open, and an old, yellowed newspaper clipping flashed behind his eyes from his research: the *Westgate Chronicle, November 1958.* The article was about a promising young actress named Eleanor Vance, the star of Meridian's production of *A Streetcar Named Desire.* A quote from a fellow cast member, interviewed after Vance's sudden and bizarre disappearance, blazed in his memory, the newsprint suddenly as clear as if it were in his hands. *"She was brilliant, but intense. Towards the end, she'd spend hours in her dressing room, talking to her reflection. She said it was her method. To stay in character."*

Eleanor Vance had vanished without a trace three days before closing night, leaving behind nothing but a half-empty cup of cold coffee and a dressing room that smelled of lilacs.

This wasn't a delusion. This wasn't a personal crisis but a pattern. A historical, repeating, and terrifying pattern. The theater, the emotionally demanding role, the strange behavior, and talking to the mirror. And then, the disappearance.

Zoe wasn't in trouble. She was next in line.

His expression must have changed; the shock and concern on his face hardened into something else—a kind of analytical dread—because her defensive posture finally faltered.

"What?" she asked, her voice suddenly small, the anger gone. "What is it?"

He didn't answer her. He just stared, his gaze moving from her frightened face to the vast, silent mirror, the pieces of the puzzle clicking into place with a horrifying, inexorable speed. The disappearances. The strange, reverent way the theater veterans spoke about the building, as if it were a living thing. Vivi and Kevin's wild, impossible stories that he had tried so hard to dismiss. This was all connected. And the mirror was at the very center of it all.

"You're lying." This wasn't an argument, but a statement of fact—a variable he was analyzing.

Zoe flinched as if he had slapped her. A new kind of fear bled into her eyes, the fear of being caught in a lie and the primal fear of being seen. The fear of something hidden being watched. In a blink, her face shuttered, her expression twisting into something paranoid and hostile.

"Get out," she whispered, her voice trembling with a potent mixture of anger and panic.

"Zoe, listen to me."

"I said, get out!" she shrieked, her voice cracking as she pointed a shaking finger toward the door.

He held up his hands in a gesture of surrender, his mind racing faster than it ever had on a deadline. Pushing her now would be pointless. He had his lead. A terrifying, impossible lead, but a lead, nonetheless. He backed out of the room slowly, his eyes never leaving the shimmering surface of the mirror until the very last second.

Zoe slammed the door shut. He heard the distinct, final click of the lock turning.

The distant rumble of city traffic outside the theater's thick, insulated walls seemed to come from another world, another lifetime. He wasn't dealing with relationship problems anymore, not a cheating girlfriend or a simple misunderstanding. He was dealing with a sixty-year-old mystery, and the woman he was starting to care so much about was poised to become its next victim.

He pulled his phone from his pocket, his thumb swiping across the smooth glass with a desperate purpose. He scrolled past his contacts, past the half-written draft of his fluffy article about the theater's charming history. He opened a new, clean browser window.

His face was a grim mask in the dim, blue-white light as his fingers flew across the keyboard. His practiced journalistic realism had been burned away, replaced by an urgent, chilling focus. He typed the only words that mattered now.

CHAPTER

TEN

THE NEW GIRL

The scent of wildflowers had taken root in Zoe, but instead of the romantic perfume she expected, it carried an undertone of lye soap and coal dust. She had showered twice, scrubbed until her skin was pink, but the strange mixture clung to her, half fairy tale, half scullery maid.

The pull was irresistible. By mid-morning, she was back at her dressing room mirror, heart racing with anticipation. She pressed her palms against the cool glass, closed her eyes, and poured every ounce of her Cinderella dreams into that surface.

The mirror warmed. The air grew thick. The melody was not quite the waltz she remembered, but something repetitive like a work song.

Her eyes snapped open. The mirror was an archway, but instead of a ballroom, she saw a massive kitchen. Steam rose from copper pots the size of bathtubs. The floor was stone, scrubbed raw, and the air reeked of onions and old grease.

She stepped through and immediately slipped on a wet patch of floor, landing hard on her tailbone in a puddle of wash water.

"Finally!" A red-faced cook grabbed her arm, hauling her up. "The new girl! You're late! The breakfast dishes have been sitting for hours!"

"I... what? No, I'm not—"

"No excuses!" The cook shoved a rough brown dress at her. "Change quickly. If the Mistress catches you in those strange clothes, she'll have you whipped for witchcraft."

Before Zoe could protest, she was pushed behind a flour-sack curtain. The beautiful kingdom she'd imagined was apparently on the other side of about ten thousand dirty dishes.

She changed, the rough fabric scratching her skin. When she emerged, the cook pointed to a mountain of encrusted pots. "Start there. When you're done, the fireplaces need cleaning. Then the silver needs polishing for tonight's ball."

"Ball?" Zoe's heart leaped. "There's a ball tonight?"

"Not for the likes of us," the cook snorted. "Prince Adrian's choosing a bride. Every eligible lady in the kingdom will be there. Well, every lady who doesn't have dishpan hands."

Zoe looked down at her hands, already reddening from the lye. This wasn't how it was supposed to go.

She spent the next three hours scrubbing, her Broadway-trained body screaming in protest. Every time she tried to sneak toward the door, another servant appeared with more work. The irony wasn't lost on her; she was literally playing Cinderella but stuck in Act One with no fairy godmother in sight.

"You there! Serving girl!"

Zoe turned. A woman in elaborate purple silk stood in the doorway, her face a masterpiece of surgical enhancement, or perhaps corseting pulled to medieval extremes. Two younger women flanked her; their faces painted in identical expressions of disdain.

The Stepmother and Stepsisters. Of course.

"You'll prepare our baths," the Stepmother commanded. "The water must be exactly blood temperature, not body temperature, blood temperature. There's a difference."

"And add rose petals," the first stepsister added. "But only the ones that fall naturally. If you pluck them, they lose their essence."

"And they must be from roses that have been sung to," the second added. "In B-flat. Minor."

Zoe stared. "How am I supposed to know what key roses have been sung to?"

The Stepmother's hand cracked across her face. "Did I ask for your opinion?"

Zoe touched her stinging cheek, fury building. In the real world, she would likely face HR, a union representative, and a lawsuit. Here, she had a bucket and was gradually developing blisters.

As she hauled water up three flights of stairs *(because of course the magic kingdom hadn't discovered plumbing)*, she heard male laughter from below. Peering over the banister, she finally saw him.

Prince Adrian. Impossibly more handsome than she'd imagined, standing in the main hall in a shaft of golden light that seemed to follow him around. Her heart performed the full gymnastics routine from her high school production of *West Side Story*.

She started down the stairs, but the moment his eyes passed over her, they went... blank.

"Excuse me," she said.

He walked right through to where she was standing. Not around. Through. She was a ghost.

She stumbled back, shocked. "Hey! I'm right here!"

A footman leaned over. "Servants are invisible to royalty until the Plot demands otherwise. Don't you know anything?"

"The... Plot?"

"The Story. The Way Things Are." He shrugged. "Prince can't see servants until the ball. That's when the magic happens. It's in the rules."

"What rules?"

He pointed to a tapestry on the wall. In elaborate calligraphy, it read:

The Laws of Narrative Structure. Chapter 12: Class Invisibility Protocols.

This was unbelievable. She was trapped in a story that operated on completely arbitrary rules that changed based on... what? Which version of Cinderella was playing out?

That evening, as she helped squeeze the stepsisters into their ball gowns (a two-person job requiring a pulley system), the first one grabbed her chin, examining her face.

"You know, you're almost pretty. In a common, peasant sort of way."

"Thank you?" Zoe ventured.

"It's a shame you're a servant. My sister and I need someone to practice with."

"Practice?"

The second sister smiled wickedly. "Kissing. We can't go to the prince inexperienced. You'll do nicely. You there!" She called someone in the hall. "Bring the other servant. The new one. The boy."

Zoe's blood went cold. "The boy?"

The door opened, and Tyler Bacon stumbled in, wearing britches and a rough tunic, his hair messed up and his face bearing the same expression of utter bewilderment she'd worn hours ago.

CHAPTER

ELEVEN

TYLER'S TERRIBLE JOURNEY

Tyler Bacon stood outside Zoe's dressing room door, his reporter's instincts screaming that something was catastrophically wrong. He'd seen her slip away after the disaster of their dinner plans, had watched the light in her eyes dim to nothing. The hallway was empty, the theater settling into its nighttime quiet, but from behind her door came the soft murmur of her voice—not practicing lines but engaged in what sounded like an intimate conversation.

With someone who wasn't there.

He knocked. "Zoe? Are you okay in there?"

The murmuring stopped instantly. Tyler pushed past the door.

The mirror dominated the wall, ornate and ancient. As he approached it, he could have sworn he saw movement in its depths—not his reflection, but something else. A golden ballroom. Swirling figures in impossible finery.

He reached out to touch the glass, and his hand went through.

One moment, he was in Zoe's dressing room; the next, he was stumbling into a castle corridor, the stones beneath his feet worn smoothly by centuries of passage. His jeans and button-down had transformed into rough servants' clothing—britches, a coarse tunic, leather boots that pinched.

"You there! Boy!"

Tyler spun to find two women bearing down on him. They moved wrong—too smooth, like they were gliding rather than walking. Their faces were beautiful in the way mannequins were beautiful: perfect features, empty eyes.

"You're the new footman," the first one announced. "Perfect timing. We need someone to help us prepare for the prince's ball."

"I'm not—"

"Silence!" They said it in perfect unison, their voices harmonizing in a way that made his skin crawl. "You exist only for our preparation!"

What followed was the most surreal two hours of Tyler's life. The stepsisters—for that's what they had to be, he realized with dawning horror—subjected him to a bizarre routine of "preparation." He was forced to listen to them practice the exact angle of a curtsey ("seventeen degrees, no more, no less!"), judge which shade of pink best complemented their complexions (they all looked identical), and worst of all, serve as a practice partner for "swooning."

"You must catch us at precisely the right moment," the

second stepsister explained, demonstrating by falling backward. Tyler barely managed to catch her, her body strangely weightless, as if she were made of hollow porcelain. "Too early and it's not dramatic. Too late, and we hit the floor."

Through a window, he could see Zoe in the courtyard below, dressed in rags, hauling water from a well. Their eyes met across the impossible distance, and he saw his own horror reflected in her face. They were both trapped in this story.

But Tyler's journalistic mind was working through the surreal terror. The stepsisters couldn't deviate from their script. When he asked them about their lives before preparing for the ball, they stared at him blankly before resuming their practiced speeches about the prince's beauty. When he tried to leave the room, he found he physically couldn't until they dismissed him. The story had rules, rigid and unbreakable.

"Now," the first stepsister announced after what felt like an eternity, "you must help us practice being interesting."

"How?"

"Tell us things to say to the prince. Compliments. Witty observations."

Tyler stared at them. "About what?"

"About... about..." The first stepsister's face went slack, her expression vacant as she searched for something that wasn't in her programming. "About his... his beauty?"

"You already said that."

"His... wealth?"

"That too."

The stepsisters looked at each other, and for a moment, Tyler saw something flickering in their eyes, not exactly, but a kind of systemic panic, a computer program encountering an error it couldn't resolve.

"We must be beautiful," they said in unison, their voices taking on a desperate edge. "We must be chosen. We must be perfect for the prince."

That's when Tyler understood. This wasn't a fantasy world, but a trap—a beautiful loop that would play out the same way forever. And somehow, Zoe had been coming here voluntarily.

The thought of her choosing this terrified him more than being trapped here himself.

But his journalist's mind was working. The story had rules. Stupid, arbitrary rules, but rules, nonetheless. And if there were rules, there had to be loopholes.

Tyler burst through the glass, landing in a heap on her dressing room floor, his medieval costume smoking slightly at the edges.

"NEVER. AGAIN." He gasped, pulling himself up. "Those stepsisters made me rate their eyebrow arches for two hours. TWO HOURS, Zoe. Apparently, there's a 'correct' angle for enchanting princes."

Despite everything, Zoe found herself laughing. "They made me sort lentils from ashes."

"Why?"

"I don't know! Something about proving worthiness through pointless tasks!"

Tyler looked at her, his cynical armor completely gone,

replaced by a man who'd survived his own fairy-tale nightmare. "The prince—did he?"

"He can't see servants until the ball. Literally. I'm furniture to him until the plot demands otherwise."

"The stepsisters can see me. Unfortunately." He shuddered. "They wanted me to practice 'swooning catches.' Apparently, there's a technique."

They stared at each other, then burst into exhausted, hysterical laughter. Here they were, two modern people who'd literally been through the looking glass and discovered that fairy tales were bureaucratic nightmares with terrible labor laws.

"We're never going back there," Tyler said firmly.

"Never," Zoe agreed.

But as she said it, she could feel the pull of the mirror, weaker now but still there because the story wasn't finished. Cinderella hadn't gone to the ball. The shoe didn't fit. The happy ending hadn't been achieved.

Tyler's notebook contained two sets of notes now:

Regular world: "Zoe showing signs of dissociation, escapist tendencies."

Fairy tale world: "Thursday—Rated eyebrows for 2 hrs. Friday—Taught proper 'swooning posture.' Saturday—Judged competitive poetry about their eyes. (The rhymes were crimes against literature.)"

The fairy-tale world didn't like unfinished stories.
And patient.

TWELVE

THE PULL OF THE STORY

Tyler discovered he could only stay in the fairy-tale world for exactly as long as his real-world absence went unnoticed. The moment Danny Kim came looking for him to discuss a scheduling conflict, Tyler felt himself yanked backward through reality, tumbling through the mirror to land hard on Zoe's dressing room floor.

Danny found him there, disoriented and mumbling about stepsisters.

"You okay, man? You look like you've seen a ghost."

Tyler managed to pull himself together, made excuses about feeling faint, and stumbled out. But he couldn't stop thinking about what he'd witnessed. Zoe was going there regularly. He could see it now in her behavior—the way she'd disappear for precise amounts of time, the strange smell of lye and roses that clung to her, the exhaustion she tried to hide behind her smile.

He started documenting everything in his reporter's notebook:

Note 1: The fairy-tale world operates on strict narrative rules. Characters can't deviate from their prescribed roles. Time moves inconsistently—an hour there might be five minutes here, or vice versa.

Note 2: Zoe's being pulled in at specific times that correspond to story beats. 3 PM is always "prepare the stepsisters' tea." 7 PM is "polish the silver." She's not visiting—she's being conscripted into service.

Note 3: The stepsisters recognized me immediately as "the new footman." The story was waiting for me. It had a role prepared. That means it's adaptive and responsive. It's hunting for players.

Over the next few days, Tyler found himself pulled back three more times. Each time, he learned more about the world's horrifying perfection. The food all tasted like cardboard. The music was a three-minute loop that no one else seemed to notice. The prince was never actually present—he was always about to arrive, perpetually five minutes away from making his entrance.

During one particularly awful session where the step-sisters made him judge their "competitive poetry" about their own beauty (every poem rhymed "eyes" with "prize"), Tyler caught another glimpse of Zoe. She was in the garden, dancing alone, her face radiant with happiness that chilled him to the bone. She was falling in love with this empty world.

The worst part was that he couldn't talk to her about it directly. Whenever they were both pulled in, they were kept in separate areas by the story's iron logic. Servants didn't mingle during work hours. The few times their paths crossed, they could only exchange desperate looks before being dragged back to their assigned tasks.

Note 4: The world is hollow but seductive. It offers Zoe perfect love without risk, beauty without decay, happiness without the possibility of sorrow. I understand why she keeps going back. I also know why it's killing her.

The last time Tyler was pulled through, something different happened. The stepsisters were preparing for the ball itself, and their desperate energy had reached a fever pitch.

"The prince will choose tonight," they told him, their movements increasingly frantic. "One of us will be chosen. Or her. The servant girl. Someone must be chosen."

"What happens if no one is chosen?"

They both turned to stare at him, and their faces weren't beautiful anymore. They were terrified in their blankness.

"Someone is always chosen," they said. "The story demands it. The story must end happily ever after."

"And if it doesn't?"

"Then it begins again. And again. And again. Until someone stays."

Tyler felt ice in his veins. "Stays?"

"Forever after," they said in unison. "That's how the story ends. Forever and ever and ever after."

That's when Tyler understood the real danger. The story wasn't just seductive but patient. It would wait, pulling Zoe back over and over, until she finally chose to stay. And once she did, she'd become like the stepsisters—a beautiful, hollow thing, forever playing a role in a story that never changed.

Through trial and error, Tyler began to piece together the rules of how the mirror actually operated. After reviewing these notes, he created a SOP (Standard Operating Procedure) for The Backstage Mirror.

Rule 1: The mirror was hungry for players.

Rule 2: It became active only during productions in process. It would pull an actor in when the story needed a role filled.

Rule 3: You could resist the pull, but only if someone in the real world actively needed you. A direct question, a physical touch, an urgent call of your name, these were anchors that could keep you grounded. But the moment you were alone and unobserved, the mirror would try again.

Rule 4: Time adjusted according to narrative needs.

A musical number might take hours in the fairy tale but pass in seconds in reality. Conversely, scrubbing a floor for five minutes there might cost you three hours here.

Rule 5: The mirror world adapted but couldn't create. It could cast you in a role, but it couldn't make new ones. It could give you Prince Adrian's love, but he could only speak lines that existed in some version of the Cinderella story, somewhere.

Rule 6: Objects crossed over but transformed to fit the narrative. Tyler's notebook became a footman's ledger. Zoe's phone became a "magic speaking glass" that only reflected her own face, always smiling.

Rule 7: The physical form you took there depended on your emotional state when entering. The more you wanted to escape yourself, the more the story would transform you into your role. The more grounded you were, the more you retained of your authentic self.

Rule 8: And most terrifying of all—the story was patient. Each time you return, it feels more real than reality. Each time you left, the real world felt a little grayer, becoming a slow seduction—a gradual erosion of the boundary between fantasy and reality.

Tyler documented all of this first in his notebook,

which in the fairy-tale world contained only an endless list of the stepsisters' beautiful qualities ("Eyes like... eyes! Hair like... hair! Feet of an appropriate size!"). But he memorized everything, building a map to ensure they were never permanently trapped.

THIRTEEN

KEVIN'S OBSERVATION

From the shadows of the wings, a space thick with the smell of old velvet and rosin, Kevin watched the rehearsal bleed out onto the stage. The floor was a vast, dark sea of scuffed Marley floor, reflecting the stern, clinical glare of the work lights. This was the theater, its bones showing, a place where the magic was stripped away to reveal the sweat and mechanics, the raw architecture of a lie told beautifully.

At the center of it all was Zoe Reeves, a star burning so bright it hurt to look directly at her. As Cinderella, she was nothing short of incandescent. Her every move was a sharp, clean note of joy, her voice a sun-drenched cascade of hope that wrapped around the cavernous emptiness of the house and made it feel full. By every technical measure, she was perfect.

And the sight of it made a ghost of an old exhaustion ache deep in Kevin's bones, a painful thrum in the marrow.

He knew this performance. Not the lines she spoke or the songs she sang, but the desperate, furious burn of energy it took to keep that much light held in one place. He recognized it the way a veteran recognizes the specific report of the rifle he once carried into battle. For years, he had held a similar weapon, had aimed it at the world, had aimed it at himself. He had been forged from shadow and silence, a bespoke armor of brooding intensity and pain he'd worn as a second skin. It had been his shelter. It had been his cage.

Zoe's was the very same design, built from the opposite material. Hers was a fortress of impossible light, an impenetrable bulwark of weaponized optimism.

He watched her as Cate Hart called a brief hold to adjust a cue. One of the younger ensemble dancers, fresh out of college and swimming in her first professional gig, missed her mark. A low wave of frustration, humid and heavy, rolled through the cast. But not from Zoe. She smiled, her teeth a white line in the harsh light, and offered a soft word of encouragement that was as bright and uncomplicated as she was. Her very presence was a kind of soothing performance, a balm of effortless positivity. She showed no sign of her own fatigue, no hint of annoyance, no need for anything from anyone. She was the sun, a constant source of warmth, and everyone else was expected to orbit.

This was the spectacle of strength he had spent a lifetime perfecting. A memory washed over him, not as a sharp sting but as a slow, familiar tide. The sheer, draining weight of it. The effort it took to project an aura of indifference was not something he felt he had to maintain constantly. He remembered the endless days of forcing his face into a scowl when all he felt was a hollow ache, of crafting a cynical barb when all he wanted was the grace of silence. He felt the echo of that self-inflicted solitude, the profound loneliness that comes from being the sole architect of your own unbreachable walls.

He saw it all in her now. In the paper-thin tightness around her dazzling smile, a smile that never quite found its way to her eyes. In the way her laughter, though frequent and clear as a bell, seemed to hang in the air for a moment too long before dissolving, never truly settling into her. She was working so damn hard. And it seemed no one else in the entire building could see it.

When Cate Hart's voice finally cut through the tension, the fragile focus of the rehearsal broke apart. The overlapping murmur of the cast rose to fill the space as they scattered, a sudden rush for water bottles and phones. The low, constant hum of the building's massive HVAC unit, a sound he hadn't noticed before, suddenly became a droning, foundational presence, the theater's own mechanical breath. Zoe, still radiating that high-wattage energy, was instantly a magnet, surrounded by a small cluster of younger actors as she launched into a story, her hands gesturing with practiced animation.

Kevin remained in the shadows, his stillness a quiet rebellion against the frantic energy she projected. He was a patch of night bordering her relentless day. Vivi's words from the day after the audition came back to him, her voice wound tight with a dread he knew all too well. *The denial is deeper now. Our old way won't reach her.* Vivi had tried the subtle approach, the veteran's gambit, a coded warning about finding the character's darkness disguised as a technical note. It had glanced right off Zoe's optimism shield, leaving not so much as a scratch. A direct attempt from Vivi, the woman Zoe saw as a flawless mentor, had failed.

But maybe, he thought, an approach from a different direction could work, not from a mentor to be admired, but from a cautionary tale. He was the recovered wreck, the man who had walked her same path in a different set of shoes. He wasn't a standard to live up to. He was a warning. The 'Phantom Protocol' they had all quietly built after his own crisis began with this exact step: a gentle, one-on-one offer of shared experience, the least invasive, the kindest way in, and the key that Sarah had used to begin picking the lock on his own cage, finally.

He waited, a statue in the wings, letting the small group around her thin out until she was alone. He caught her eye as she bent to retie the pale pink ribbon on her ballet flat. He gave a slight, quiet nod. An invitation. She straightened, and the automatic smile clicked into place, a well-oiled machine. She walked toward him, her move-ment effortless and poised. The air around her seemed to shimmer with a manufactured brightness.

"Hey, Kevin! You were so great in that last run. The way you found that moment of quiet despair for the prince when he thinks he's lost her. Chills." Her praise was genuine enough, but a tool he recognized as such. A finely honed deflection, a way of keeping the conversation safely on the work, on the craft, on anything but the person standing in front of him.

"Thanks, Zoe," he said as a low counterpoint to her bright soprano. He didn't return the compliment, a deliberate choice he hoped would break the familiar rhythm of their actor-to-actor pleasantries, a minor disruption in the script. He gestured vaguely with his chin back toward the empty stage. "That was a long scene. You have to be exhausted."

This was a simple observation—a human one. But for Zoe, he knew this was a test. Her smile tightened, a fraction of an inch at the corners, the only sign of the effort it took to hold it up. "Oh, I'm fine. I'm running on pure excitement. And coffee. Lots and lots of coffee." She laughed, a sound that was bright and a little too loud, forced up from her diaphragm.

He didn't laugh with her. He held her gaze, his own expression one of quiet, unwavering calm. This was the moment. He had to offer her the key.

"You know, it's okay not to be fine. It's okay to have a bad day. It's okay to be frustrated when a scene isn't landing or when someone keeps stepping on your line." He let the words hang in the air between them, a simple offering of permission. An amnesty. He saw the little red eye of a security camera glowing from the wall high above them and wondered if Cate was watching, holding her breath as he was. "You're allowed to be human, Zoe. No one here expects you actually to be Cinderella all the time."

The effect was instantaneous and absolute. The light

in her face didn't fade; it went out completely. For a terrifying half-second, he saw everything she was holding back. The raw, animal panic. The profound, bone-deep exhaustion. Her eyes widened, her posture grew rigid. She looked cornered, a small, beautiful thing caught in a spotlight she couldn't escape.

Then, as quickly, the mask was back. This time, it was brittle, the cracks hastily sealed with a frantic coat of good cheer.

"Oh my gosh, you're so sweet to worry." Her voice was a full octave higher than before, thin and sharp. She let out another flustered little laugh and gave his arm a playful punch, a gesture so jarringly out of place, so miscalibrated. "But I am great. Seriously. This whole thing is a dream come true. Who could have a bad day when they're literally living a fairy tale? That would be crazy, right?"

She didn't wait for an answer. She glanced down at her wrist, a pantomime of checking a watch she wasn't wearing, a gesture of someone who had someplace vital to be. "Wow, look at the time. Break's almost over. I gotta run. See you out there."

And with one last dazzling, empty smile, she turned and fled. She practically sprinted, her bright ponytail bouncing behind her as she hurried back toward the perceived safety of the ensemble, a place where she could become one of many instead of one alone.

Kevin stood motionless in the shadows. The only thing she'd left behind was the faint disturbance in the air from her hurried departure and an awkward, ringing silence. He hadn't failed. He had confirmed the diagnosis. Vivi was right. The denial was deeper. The shield was absolute. Step One of the protocol had been a catastrophic failure.

Simple warnings, gentle probes, quiet offers of empathy. They were all useless against this. Her optimism wasn't a performance anymore, but a reflex—an autoimmune response to authenticity.

A profound, chilling clarity settled over him. Her performative happiness was functionally identical to his old performative darkness. They were both strategies to keep the world at arm's length, to keep anyone from getting close enough to see the frightened, inadequate person hiding behind the curtain. He knew, with a certainty that made his stomach clench into a knot, that the theater's hungry magic didn't give a damn about the flavor of the lie. It only cared about the desperation of the soul telling it.

And in that moment, he understood that Zoe was in more danger than he had ever been. She was more vulnerable because she honestly believed her poison was the cure. She was drinking it down with a smile.

A direct, one-on-one approach was not only futile but also counterproductive. It only made her reinforce the walls, slapping more mortar into the cracks. Pushing harder would drive her further into her glittering isolation, deeper into the waiting arms of the perfect, smiling, and utterly vacant fantasy he knew was stirring in the mirrors of this building, waiting for its star to arrive.

He couldn't do this by himself. An older version of him, the man he used to be, would have retreated right then and there. He would have stalked back to his own solitude, frustrated and angry, and let the failure curdle into proof that no one could be reached, that everyone was alone.

But that man was gone. That man had been a ghost for a long time now. That man didn't have a support system. That man didn't know how to ask for help.

He pulled his phone from his pocket. The screen cast a stark, blue-white light on his face in the dimness of the wings. His thumb moved with practiced, deliberate ease across the glass. As he held the device, he could almost smell the faint, clean scent of Sarah's shampoo, a scent that seemed to have permanently infused the cool plastic case. This was a constant, grounding reminder of the reality he had fought so hard to reclaim. His anchor. His partner.

He typed out a short, urgent message. The quiet tap of the virtual keys was the only sound in his small patch of darkness. He hit send, the single word hanging on the screen for a moment before a small checkmark bloomed beside it.

Sent.

The screen of Kevin's phone showed the message, stark and clear.

Need to talk tonight about Zoe.

CHAPTER

FOURTEEN

MALCOLM'S CONCERN

The sound was back.

Really, less a sound and more pressure building behind his eyes, a high, thin hum that sang at the edge of hearing, like a tuning fork struck in a room down a long hall, a vibration that belonged to another world. Malcolm stilled his feet in the dim backstage corridor. The two cardboard coffee cups in his hands felt suddenly foolish, a flimsy offering of the real world against the thing he knew was waking up in the walls. He closed his eyes. He willed away the bright, tinkling piano and the rise and fall of cheerful voices bleeding from the main stage, where Cinderella was taking shape. He needed to find the hum.

The hum was stronger today. Sharper, too. It sang to him with a melody of honey and rot, the sickeningly sweet perfume of a story beginning to bloom.

This was the reason he walked through these halls. He was a man haunted by a past that breathed on his neck, more real sometimes than the present moment. He had become a sentinel for the Meridian, a quiet ghost watching over the living. Cate's call the night before had only put a voice to the dread already coiling in his gut. He knew this feeling. The theater was stirring, its peculiar magic awakening, and it had found its next meal.

He pushed open the heavy door to the house, letting the scent of stale air and sawdust settle him, the smell of work, of reality, an anchor in the storm he felt brewing. Across the dark expanse, he saw Cate at the tech table. She was washed in the cool glow of a monitor, her face a familiar map of weary focus. Her watchfulness was a reflection of his own, and a burden they shared, one forged in a world of blood and prophecy that they had been lucky enough to escape alive. The coffee was an excuse, a simple, human thing to do, the kind of ritual that gave him cover to walk these halls, to listen for the vibrations of a world coming undone at the seams.

He moved through the cavernous darkness of the house, his path taking him past rows of vacant velvet seats, their surfaces holding the quiet of generations. With every step, the hum grew louder, more insistent. It had become a physical thing now, a sharp pressure inside his skull. A phantom current tugged him forward, pulling him toward the second-floor dressing rooms. He took the stairs two at a time, his boots making quiet thuds on the worn treads, a lonely heartbeat in the theater's silence.

The upstairs corridor was quieter, the sounds of rehearsal muffled to a whisper. Here, the hum was a clear, piercing note. It felt clean, pure, and terrifying. It led him on a short pilgrimage past Vivi's old room, then Kevin's. Their doors were closed, the nameplates blank now, hollowed-out memories of battles won. The magic inside them slept. But the vibration grew stronger at the end of the hall. It radiated from a single door, a solid, pulsing wave of impossible energy. A bright, cheerful star was taped to the wood. On it, in bubbly letters, was the name: **ZOE REEVES.**

A dread settled in his gut, sharp and familiar as a winter frost. His investigation was over. He had found the next victim in the story.

Before the knowledge could fully take root, his gaze snagged on a dark corner of the landing. The space was a graveyard of forgotten productions, a pile of theatrical bones. A stack of prop crates sat in the shadows, veiled in the soft gray of neglect. The stenciled lettering on the top one was faded, but the name was as clear as a scream in a quiet room. *MACBETH.*

The name struck him. Without thinking, he reached up, his fingers finding the faint, silvery line of a scar above his eyebrow, a permanent souvenir from a dirk that had been all too real. For a single, splintering second, the warm scent of coffee vanished, replaced by the coppery tang of hot, spilled blood. The hum in his ears deepened, twisting into the memory of witches' laughter, a cackle that promised ruin. He had fought a mad king for his life on a stage. He had watched a good man become a monster, swallowed whole by the perfect, murderous logic of a story that refused to end. He knew what this building was capable of. He knew what it would try to do to Zoe.

His hand tightened around the warm coffee cups. The fragile cardboard, a thin connection to this world, was this beautiful, imperfect reality. *No,* he thought, the word was a solid thing in his mind. *Not again.* He would not let it happen again.

He forced himself to look away from the crate, his gaze finding a brightly colored poster for *Cinderella* tacked to a nearby bulletin board. A princess in a glittering gown, a handsome prince, a promise of a midnight kiss that changed everything. This world was made of hope and glass slippers. He and Cate had come from a world of blood and iron. A cruel trick, he thought, that the same magic powered them both, that the path to a fairy tale could be built right next to the one that led to a slaughter.

An hour later, during a break in rehearsal, he found his moment. He had delivered Cate's coffee first, their eyes meeting over the rising steam in a silent, grim understanding. Words were unnecessary between them. They were two people who had survived the same shipwreck, and they both knew the look of a storm gathering on the horizon.

Zoe was in the green room, stretching out the pleasant ache of rehearsal. Her face was flushed, glowing with a sheen of happiness from her work. But the smile she wore, that brilliant, sun-drenched thing that was her signature, seemed to be miles away. Her eyes were bright, yes, but unfocused, as if she were looking right through the faded floral wallpaper at a landscape only she could see. This was a look Malcolm knew all too well.

And Zoe kept disappearing for "bathroom breaks" that lasted exactly seven minutes—long enough to scrub one pot in fairy-tale land before someone noticed she was gone. She's developed a system: set the phone timer, dash through the mirror, complete whatever degrading task the Stepmother has assigned, and sprint back before anyone comes looking.

"Zoe," he whispered.

She turned, and her distant smile clicked into a bright, present one, a light switched on for a visitor. "Malcolm. Hey. Did you bring Cate more of that fancy tea she likes?"

"Coffee today," he said, leaning a shoulder against the doorframe. He made sure his posture was loose, his voice gentle as a summer evening. He'd learned a hard lesson with Kevin. A direct charge made the wounded thing run for cover. "I was watching you all rehearse. It's a beautiful world you're building out there."

Her whole face lit up with pleasure so pure it almost hurt to look at. "Thank you. It is. Just so full of hope."

"It is," he agreed, his own voice sounding rough against the silver of hers. He paused, choosing his following words with the care of a man trying to talk a bird down from a high wire. "But you have to be careful with beautiful worlds, Zoe. Especially the perfect ones."

"Careful?" she asked. She tilted her head, her expression a watercolor painting of polite confusion: a lovely painting, but a painting all the same.

He gestured vaguely at a vase of silk flowers on a

side table, their petals perfect and changeless. A faint layer of grime coated their perfection, a detail a person lost in a dream would not notice. "The danger of perfect worlds," he said, meeting her bright, unblinking gaze. He tried to pour every ounce of his own complicated history into the words, to make them heavy enough to land. "Is that they don't leave any room for you. The real you. The messy, complicated, gloriously imperfect you. A perfect world asks you to be perfect, too. And if you stay in a place too long, you can forget how to be anything else."

He held his breath, praying that some part of his desperate plea would find purchase in her. He was handing her the single most important truth he had ever clawed his way toward, the lesson that had been the lifeboat for him and Cate. *The imperfect gifts of this world are the only ones that are real.*

Zoe listened; her head cocked with the sweet, studious attention of a prize pupil. When he was done, she beamed, her smile warmer and more genuine than it had been all afternoon. "Malcolm, that's beautiful," her voice brimming with a bright, uncomplicated admiration that felt like a slammed door. "It's so poetic. Is that from a play?"

The air went out of his lungs in a silent rush. His words, a life-or-death warning forged in the fires of his own past, had been taken as a charming bit of philosophy. She had not heard an alarm bell. She had heard a wind chime tinkling pleasantly on a porch. He could see it in her eyes, clear as day. His hard-won wisdom, the very truth that held the pieces of him together, was as useless as a key for the wrong lock. It could not open a mind so eager, so willing, to believe in a fairy tale.

His gentle, direct approach had failed. Spectacularly, a bitter echo of his attempts with Vivi and with Kevin. These kids were all so hungry for an escape hatch from their own lives. They would not recognize the bars of a pretty cage if the warden himself were standing right there, rattling the keys.

"No," he said flatly. "Not from a play."

He offered her a small, tight smile that didn't reach his eyes and retreated from the doorway. As he backed away down the hall, the door to the costume shop was ajar. He caught a glimpse of shimmering ball gowns on a rack, their fabric catching the light like spun sugar—a confection, a sweet trap—and she was walking right into it. The hum in his ears rose to a triumphant shriek, a sound of victory that wasn't his. The first part of his job was done. He had a threat, a target, and a location. But the second part, the intervention, had failed before it could even begin. He could not do this alone.

He watched from the landing as Zoe, humming a bright tune from the show, practically floated down the hall to her dressing room. She looked happy. Blissful. As she closed the door behind her, the hum in Malcolm's head snapped into focus, no longer a vibration but a pure, ringing note of immense power. She was in there with it now. The door was closed, and she was alone with it.

He turned, his heart, a heavy stone in his chest. He looked out over the vast, shadowed expanse of the main stage. And there she was. Cate stood beside the ghost light's solitary glow, watching him. She had seen it all. She had seen him try, and she had seen him fail. He met her gaze across the empty rows of seats, and in that silent look, everything was said. The understanding between them was absolute.

They were out of time for gentle warnings. They were out of time.

CHAPTER

FIFTEEN

FAIRY TALE ROMANCE

The lies bloomed easily as kudzu, and that was the most terrifying thing of all. What began as a single, guilt-strangled text to miss a rehearsal had grown into a whole cultivated wilderness of deception, its vines wrapping tight around her days. Zoe, a woman who had always worn her honesty like a comfortable old sweater, now found herself the careful groundskeeper of a garden filled with half-truths and well-tended excuses.

Lunch breaks, once a hurried affair with a protein bar, stretched into two-hour "migraine naps" taken in the driver's seat of her car. The thirty minutes between blocking a scene and a music call became a sacred "meditation session" she absolutely had to have, to connect with her character's truth. She'd started scanning the theater's prop lists for inspiration, telling a stagehand she needed to track down a specific vintage teacup for character research, all to buy herself another fifteen minutes. Her phone, once a simple means of communication with her friends, had become her primary tool of misdirection. Its glowing screen was a constant ledger of her own quiet downfall. The minor brass key to her dressing room, dangling from its simple ring in her pocket, felt heavier each day, its metal a hard promise of the cage she was building for herself.

The guilt was a single, sour note played constantly beneath the soaring symphony of her new reality, a dissonance she was becoming frighteningly good at tuning out. Because every stolen hour, every carefully constructed excuse, was a small tax paid for the world that waited for her on the other side of the looking glass. For Adrian.

The mirror finally placed her in a glittering gown at "The Ball," where he promptly fell in love with her. They danced and kissed until midnight. But the story took a twist, and instead of her clothes turning into rags, they began to disappear.

Zoe stood gasping in the shadows of the garden, moonlight draping her bare skin in silver. The fountain splashed nearby, the only sound besides the pounding of her own heart. She raised her arms instinctively to cover herself. Still, the shimmer of enchantment had already stolen her gown, every jewel, every stitch, leaving her revealed as if the night itself demanded her honesty.

Adrian staggered into the garden behind her, his breath ragged. When his eyes found her, his composure shattered. A man raised on courtly restraint suddenly burned with raw, unfiltered hunger. "Zoe..." His voice cracked, half-plea, half-prayer.

He stripped off his coat, his hands frantic, as though

fabric itself were an insult between them. Boots, tunic, every layer fell away until the prince who had danced with a vision stood as bare as she. The fountain caught him in its silver spray as he crossed the marble lip and pulled her into the water with him.

Cold rivulets raced over her skin, but his heat seared her instantly. His mouth found hers with desperation, kissing her like a man drowning, and she clung back as though he were the only solid thing in the world. Her back arched against the stone edge, droplets sliding down the curves of her breasts as his lips trailed lower—neck, collarbone, the soft swell he tasted with reverence before giving way to hunger.

Zoe gasped, threading her fingers into his wet hair, tugging when his mouth closed over her nipple and sent a shiver of fire straight through her. The garden dissolved into sensation—the thrum of her pulse, the insistent grind of his hips, the fountain's cascade masking the sounds of her moans.

"Mine," Adrian whispered against her skin, the single word fierce, possessive, worshipful.

Her laughter caught, breathless, daring. "Then take me."

He did. With the fountain splashing around them, with the stars as their only witnesses, Adrian pressed into her with a groan that echoed through both their bodies. Water lapped over them, cool and wild, but the heat of their joined bodies eclipsed everything. Each thrust was desperate, reverent, as the prince unraveled into the woman fate had dressed in silver to bear to him.

And when Zoe came undone around him—crying out his name, as though the garden itself held its breath. Adrian followed, shuddering against her, surrendering every ounce of himself into the woman who had stolen midnight.

Afterwards, they lay in the fountain's shallow pool, tangled and trembling, water still cascading over their bodies. Zoe's head rested against his chest; her lips curved in a smile that knew she had rewritten a fairy tale.

Adrian kissed the crown of her wet hair, his voice hushed and awed. "Not even magic could turn you back from me now."

The moment she knew she was in too deep came on a Tuesday afternoon. Cate stopped her by the green room door; her face carved with a quiet concern that made Zoe's stomach clench. "You've been pushing yourself to the bone, kiddo. Let's get out of this place for a bit. I'm buying you a real lunch, not whatever's in that vending machine."

The offer was so kind, so genuinely full of care; the warmth of it struck her with the force of a forgotten memory. For one shimmering second, Zoe saw another path unfold before her. A sunlit cafe, an honest conversation with a friend who saw her, the simple, grounding pleasure of a life lived in the light. But the pull of the mirror, the silent, seductive promise of a world without worry, was a gravity she no longer had the strength to fight.

Zoe manufactured her brightest, most grateful smile, a performance worthy of the main stage. "Cate, which is the sweetest thing I've ever heard. But I'm feeling so preoccupied about the role. I need to sit in my dressing room and run some Meisner repetitions, just me and the mirror. To be ready for the evening show." She placed a hand over her heart, a gesture of performed sincerity that felt both practiced and profane. "For the work."

The lie was designed to spare Cate's feelings, to paint her withdrawal as the dedication of a serious artist, not the symptom of a secret she could never share. It worked. Cate's worry softened into a fond, understanding sigh. "Alright, kid. But don't burn yourself out. We need you."

"I won't," Zoe promised, and the words were nothing but ash in her mouth.

The moment Cate turned the corner, Zoe didn't walk to her dressing room; she fled. A wave of relief washed over her that was so sharp it almost cut. She locked the door behind her, leaning against the solid wood with her eyes squeezed shut, her heart hammering a wild rhythm against her ribs. The low hum of the real world, the distant sound of stagehands and call times, faded away. The intoxicating, silent summons of the portal replaced it.

Stepping through was as if finally coming home after a long, weary journey. The shimmering, watery curtain of the mirror parted without a sound, and she was in Prince Adrian's world. She spent hours there, perhaps a whole lifetime, lost in a romance so perfect that it seemed more like a painting. They rode snow-white horses through an enchanted forest, where the sunlight fell in perfect, golden coins on the path but never dared to cast a shadow. The leaves on the impossibly green trees never rustled, poised forever in a state of perfect, silent beauty, as if held in place by a master set designer. They attended a grand ball in a glittering castle, dancing a waltz, moving as one under crystal chandeliers. At the same time, a distant orchestra played a melody that never, ever ended.

He was the storybook prince in every sense. His hand was always there, a steady pressure at the small of her back. His smile was a constant, adoring sunrise meant only for her. His compliments were poetry whispered in a voice that was both melodic and deeply familiar. He made her feel she was the most beautiful, most cherished woman in any world he could conjure, and everything she had ever let herself dream of was a flawless performance.

The fantasy reached its peak in his private tower, a circular room with tall, arched windows that overlooked the whole glittering kingdom. The space was overflowing with flowers. Thousands of white roses and lilies crowded every surface, their sweet, heavy perfume coating the back of her throat and making the candlelight swim. Soft, golden candlelight shone steadily from every surface, bathing the room in a warm, honeyed glow. This romantic tableau was so perfect it became a memory of a dream, a scene painted by a master who knew every secret yearning of a fairy-tale heart.

He led her to a bed piled high with silk pillows and sheets that whispered against her skin, cool and impossibly smooth, liquid moonlight. His movements were fluid and confident, a choreographed dance of seduction he knew by heart. He undressed her with reverence that was a form of worship, his impossibly handsome face, a mask of earnest, noble passion.

"You are more beautiful than any star in my sky," he whispered, his voice a rehearsed, resonant sound that filled the quiet room.

As he lay her back against the pillows, Zoe's mind was a spinning vortex of triumphant validation. *This is real*, she thought, a fierce joy rising in her. *This is my reward for always, always believing.*

His lovemaking was like his waltz, technically perfect. Every touch was gentle, every kiss placed with unerring, practiced precision—an art form, a symphony of romantic gestures performed by a master. He moved with a steady, metronomic rhythm, his body a flawless machine designed to deliver an experience. But as the moments stretched into a long, silent eternity, a strange and unwelcome thought surfaced from the depths of her mind, a tiny crack in the facade.

Quiet.

There was the soft rustle of silk, the distant, ever-present music from the kingdom far below. But there was no heat between them. There was no scent of him, no smell of sweat or warm skin or anything human. He smelled of nothing at all, as clean and sterile as the marble statues in his courtyard. There were no ragged breaths, no fumbling, no awkward, endearing sighs. There was only this beautiful, silent motion.

And in that sterile perfection, her mind, unbidden, betrayed her. It threw an image at her so sharp and jarringly real that it made her flinch. A memory of her disastrous first date with Tyler. She saw him so clearly, sitting across from her in that noisy restaurant, a smudge of red wine on the collar of his shirt where he had gestured too enthusiastically and sloshed his glass. He had not been smooth or princely. He had looked down, seen the stain, and let out a short, self-deprecating laugh, his eyes crinkling at the corners with a genuine, clumsy, unscripted humanity. The memory was so warm, so real.

The contrast was a physical shock. Adrian's body moved against hers, a specimen performing an ideal act of love. But the man in her mind's eye, with his rumpled blazer and his cynical, crinkling eyes, felt more present, more real, than the man in her arms. Adrian was a poem she had memorized. Tyler was a song she couldn't get out of her head, messy and real and stubbornly alive.

The realization was a hairline fracture in the flawless porcelain of her perfect world. This wasn't the messy, breathless thing called passion, but rather pageantry, beautiful and silent.

As if he could feel the shift in her, the sudden draft of reality in their room, Adrian's movements stilled. He looked down at her, his face a study in romantic concern, an expression he had worn a thousand times before. "Is it all to your liking, my lady?" he asked, his voice full of that same rehearsed sincerity.

The moment of clarity was shattered, shoved down, and swept away by a frantic wave of denial. A frantic NO screamed through her mind. She would not let the gray, clumsy truth of the real world stain this perfection. This was what she wanted. This was what she had earned.

"Everything is perfect," she whispered, forcing the truth from her mind and heart.

The rest of the encounter was a blur of aesthetic beauty and a deep, profound emotional emptiness, like being made love to by a magnificent, beautiful statue. Afterwards, she lay in the sea of flowers and silk, a hollow ache spreading through her chest that all the beauty in the kingdom could not fill. She had lived her ultimate romantic fantasy, the one she had held in her heart for years, and she felt nothing at all.

Her awareness of the fantasy's flaw, this passionless core, was a terrifying new piece of knowledge she could not unlearn. But the addiction was a hungrier, more powerful force. The hollowness didn't make her want to leave. It made her desperate to stay, to try again, to work harder, to force the feeling she was supposed to have. The compulsive need for this safe, escape now completely overrode her own body's quiet truth, her own heart's protest. Emptiness was another problem to be solved, another imperfection to be perfected.

Adrian propped himself on one elbow, a single lock of golden hair falling perfectly across his brow. He smiled down at her, a flawless, adoring expression that held no real, readable emotion.

"Nothing in your world could ever compare to this, could it?" he asked, his voice a soft, possessive murmur. This wasn't a question but was a statement of fact, a declaration of ownership.

A dread uncoiled in her stomach, a serpent in her perfect, sun-drenched garden, a truth and a lie all at once. Nothing in her world could ever compare to the visual perfection of this place. And nothing in this world could ever compare to the clumsy, warm reality of a single, genuine laugh.

She was terrifyingly aware that she believed the first half of that statement far more than she should.

She forced a smile, the gesture feeling brittle and fragile on her lips. "Nothing at all," she lied, and the words hung in the silent, flower-scented air between them, the final click of a lock sealing her in.

CHAPTER
SIXTEEN
MISSING DINNER

Time in Adrian's kingdom was a slow, sweet river of honey, the kind that dripped from a spoon on a humid summer afternoon. It had no sharp edges, no jarring turns. The perpetual golden hour hung in the air, a soft, hazy light that melted seamlessly from one perfect moment to the next. Zoe rode with him through an orchard where the trees had spun silver leaves and the air was thick with the scent of blossoms that never wilted or fell. The sweetness of it coated her tongue, a flavor she could almost taste. She danced with him in a pavilion made of moonlight and cool marble, the music a melody that felt both impossibly new and as familiar as a memory from a dream.

Every second was a polished gemstone, flawless and shining, and she was blissfully unaware as they strung themselves together into a necklace that wrapped around her throat, a beautiful weight that grew heavier with each passing hour.

She existed in a state of serene, uncomplicated joy. There were no missed cues in this world, no lines forgotten under the heat of the stage lights. There were no worried glances from Cate, her eyes sharp with a concern Zoe could never quite decipher. There were no cynical, probing questions from a journalist who seemed to think happiness was a puzzle box he needed to crack open to see how it worked. Here, there was only Adrian's adoring gaze and the beautiful, simple logic of a story where she was the cherished heroine, the one for whom the entire world stopped and smiled. This was the happily-ever-after she had practiced for, a performance so complete it had become her whole reality.

This phantom vibration from another world finally tore a hole in the tapestry. A faint, insistent buzz against her thigh, a tremor that didn't belong. She'd forgotten to take her phone out of her jeans pocket before she stepped through the glass.

The sensation was alien here, a piece of sharp, ugly machinery in a world of handcrafted beauty, the grating sound of a zipper in a silent church, a rude interruption to a sacred peace. She tried to ignore it, to will it away, to let the honeyed river of time wash over the disturbance. But it came again. And again. A frantic, rhythmic pulsing that was impossible to disregard, a desperate heartbeat from a life she had left behind.

"Is something amiss, my lady?" Adrian asked. His brow furrowed with an ideal mask of concern, an expression of flawless empathy that felt as scripted as his every other word.

"No," Zoe said, the word coming out a little too sharp, a shard of glass in the soft air. "Nothing at all."

But the spell was broken. The gentle river of time suddenly slammed into the hard concrete dam of reality. A sickening realization washed over her, a wave of icy water that extinguished the golden light. Dinner. Tyler. She had promised to meet him at seven. A simple promise, an easy thing, a real thing. She glanced at the sky, but the sun hung in its permanent, lazy descent, a useless, beautiful liar.

"I have to go," her voice tight with a panic that felt foreign and unwelcome in this peaceful land. The emotion was a weed, ugly and tenacious, sprouting in a perfectly manicured garden.

Adrian's smile didn't falter, not for a second. It remained as fixed and bright as the stars that never moved in his sky. "But you have only just arrived."

"No," she whispered, scrambling to her feet, the silken fabric of her borrowed gown feeling suddenly like a costume. "No, I've been here too long."

She fled the serene landscape, blurring into a smear of gold and silver as she ran. She ran back toward the shimmering gateway, her heart hammering a frantic, clumsy rhythm against her ribs. The phantom buzz of her phone became a shriek now, pulling her, dragging her back to a world she had so effortlessly, so cruelly forgotten.

Tyler stared at the two sweating glasses of water on the table. The ice in his own had vanished ten minutes ago, leaving behind a lukewarm disappointment. He had memorized the menu, from the fried green tomatoes to the pecan pie. He had traced the overlapping ghost rings of condensation on the red-and-white checkered tablecloth. He had conducted a silent, one-sided conversation with the guttering candle, its small flame a lonely spot of warmth in the cooling evening. 8:15. She was an hour and fifteen minutes late.

He wasn't angry. Not yet. He was adrift in that strange, hollow space between hope and disappointment, a lonely shoreline he knew all too well. He'd been stood up before, certainly. But this felt different. This felt wrong in a way that had nothing to do with his own bruised ego. Zoe wasn't cruel. She was, if anything, almost pathologically considerate, a woman who seemed to carry sunshine in her pockets to hand out to strangers. For her not to show up, not to send a text with a hurried excuse, felt less slight and more like a signal flare. Something was wrong.

His mind, a relentless engine of inquiry that never truly shut down, started building scenarios. Car trouble on a back road. A sudden family emergency she couldn't text her way out of. A debilitating migraine had her lying up in a dark room. He cycled through the logical explanations, the plausible reasons, but none of them fit the shape of the silence on the other end of his phone. A little part of him, the part that had started to hope, felt like a fool. Hope was a dangerous thing, a weed that grew in the cracks of a broken heart, and he'd been letting it run wild.

He pulled out his phone again, his thumb hovering over her contact photo. Her smile in the picture was so bright and genuine that it became a painful counterpoint to the empty chair across from him. He had already called twice, the calls echoing into an empty void. He had sent three texts.

Hey, are you on your way?

Everything okay?

And finally, the one that felt the most desperate.

Zoe, call me.

The silence was the only answer he got.

He finally signaled for the check, the knot of simple, human hurt tightening in his stomach. The journalist in him was quiet for the moment, pushed aside by the man who had worn his best shirt and felt a spark of something real. The waitress, a kind-faced woman with tired eyes, had been throwing him sympathetic glances all evening, refilling his water glass with a gentleness that was almost worse than being ignored. He paid the bill and left her a generous tip for her unspoken pity, then walked out into the cool breath of the night air.

Under the buzzing neon sign of the little Italian place, its cheerful glow now feeling mockery, he tried her number one last time. He let it ring, and ring, and ring, the sound of a lonely, unanswered question in the dark. He was about to hang up, finally surrendering to the quiet, when, to his shock, she answered.

"Tyler?"

Her voice was a ragged whisper, breathless and

panicked. It sounded like she had been running a marathon.

"Zoe? My god, are you okay? I was worried sick." Relief washed through him, so potent it almost buckled his knees, but immediately followed by a sharp spike of irritation.

"Oh, god, Tyler, the time! I'm so, so sorry. I completely lost track of everything."

"It's okay," his voice softened against his will at the sheer panic in hers. "What happened? Are you alright?"

There was a pause, a hollow silence that vibrated with unspoken things, with the frantic search for a plausible story. On the other end of the line, he could hear a faint, ambient echo, the sound of a vast space—a place with high ceilings and old wooden floors—the Meridian.

"Rehearsal," she finally said, the word tumbling out in a rush, a little too fast, a little too practiced. "It ran... it ran super late. Cate was on a tear about the finale, and we kept going and going. My phone was on silent. I'm so, so sorry."

The lie was a lead balloon. It didn't float or drift. It fell between them, heavy and obvious and loud in its impact. Tyler, a man who had spent a decade interviewing politicians, lawyers, and world-class con artists—a man with a finely tuned ear for the subtle architecture of deceit—felt an almost professional sense of offense, a terrible amateur's lie.

His journalistic brain, which had been dormant and sulking, sparked to life. *Lie detection 101: Too many unnecessary details. Vague but weirdly specific. Blaming a respected third party.* He knew Cate Hart by reputation. She was a perfectionist, yes, but she was also a fierce protector of her actors' time and energy. She didn't run them into the ground without warning or reason. And Zoe's breathless panic didn't sound like the bone-deep exhaustion of a long rehearsal.

A hot flash of suspicion instantly cauterized the hurt from being stood up. This wasn't a simple mistake. This wasn't a forgotten date. This was a cover-up. An amateurish, clumsy, and therefore deeply revealing one.

"Right," he said, and his voice was flat, all the warmth draining out of it. An analytical focus replaced it, he knew well. The voice he used for work. "Late rehearsal. Got it."

"I am sorry, Tyler. I feel awful." Her voice was small, pleading.

"Don't worry about it," he said, and the lie was his own now, a sharp, clean piece of professional misdirection: a tool, not an emotional failure. "We'll do it another time. Get some rest."

He hung up before she could say more, before she could spin another thread of her flimsy, insulting story. The fragile, budding personal trust between them had been severed. The woman he was starting to fall for, the one with the sunshine smile and the honest eyes, had been replaced by a subject. A source. A mystery he was now compelled to solve.

The moment the call ended, Zoe dropped her phone as if its plastic casing had burned her skin. It clattered onto the gritty floor of her dressing room, the sound obscenely loud in the silent, cavernous space. The lie she had told echoed in the quiet, ugly, and profane. She had lied to him.

A direct, blatant, and clumsy lie, and she had heard in the sudden, chilling flatness of his voice that he had known it. The warmth was gone, as if he had flipped a switch.

A wave of self-loathing so powerful it made her dizzy washed over her, hot and suffocating. She saw his face in her mind, not the cynical journalist she'd first met, but the man at the restaurant, his eyes soft with a hopeful, vulnerable light that she had carelessly extinguished. She had hurt him. She, Zoe Reeves, the girl who had built her entire identity on being kind, on being the sunshine, on fixing things for everyone else, had been careless and cruel and thoughtless.

The guilt was a physical thing, a heavy weight pressing down on her chest, crushing the air from her lungs. She curled into a ball on the threadbare, floral rug, her forehead pressed against the grimy floorboards. The smell of old wood and the ghosts of a thousand different perfumes filled her nostrils, a stark, punishing contrast to the cloying scent of phantom blossoms she had been breathing moments before. On the corner of her dressing table, a half-eaten bag of gummy bears, a silly gift from Tyler last week, seemed to mock her.

She was a disappointment. She was a liar. She was a terrible person.

The thoughts were a vicious, repeating chorus in her head, a soundtrack to her shame. The pain was a sharp, unbearable ache. And there, at the edge of her vision, was the only escape she knew.

The mirror.

It shimmered softly in the dim light, a silent,

beckoning promise of a world where she was none of those things. A world where she was perfect. Adored. A world where she could never disappoint anyone because disappointment didn't exist.

Her retreat wasn't a choice, but a desperate, pathetic crawl. Sobbing, she dragged herself across the floor, her hands reaching out for the cool, smooth surface of the glass. She didn't want the perfect romance now. She didn't like the adoration of a handsome prince. She wanted oblivion and quiet. She wanted to feel as if she wasn't the monster her own actions had revealed her to be.

Her fingertips touched the glass, and the grimy, lonely dressing room dissolved into a wash of brilliant light.

Tyler walked the dozen city blocks back to his apartment, the hurt and confusion of the evening solidifying into something hard inside him. His personal disappointment had been a fleeting, useless emotion—a fog that was now burning off under the harsh light of professional scrutiny. That suspicion was a tool; actionable and something he could use.

He let himself into his quiet apartment, the familiar, organized clutter a strange kind of comfort. He didn't turn on the lights. He walked straight to his desk in the dark, the ambient city glow from the window enough to see by. The screen of his laptop cast a pale blue light on his face, illuminating the corkboard above it—a chaotic yet meticulously organized tapestry of his investigation into the Meridian Theatre, all covered in names, dates, and faded news clippings, all connected by a web of red yarn.

He stared at the name he had pinned in the very center weeks ago. *ZOE.*

He had been approaching this all wrong. He had been digging into the past, looking for a ghost story, a historical oddity to write about for a Sunday feature. He had been looking for whispers and rumors about the theater itself. However, the story wasn't a ghost story, but a missing person's case, and the individual had not yet been officially reported as missing.

He sat down, his movements sharp and precise. He opened a fresh document on his laptop, the click of the keys unnaturally loud in the silent room. The cursor blinked on the stark, white page, a steady, patient pulse.

He typed a single heading, the letters appearing stark and black. *ZOE REEVES.*

He hit enter. The hurt was gone. The confusion was gone. All that remained was the clean clarity of a job to do.

He typed his first line of inquiry. Verify rehearsal schedules for the Meridian Theatre over the past 48 hours.

The investigation was no longer about a historical pattern, but about a clear and present danger.

SEVENTEEN

KEVIN'S DIRECT APPROACH

The hallway outside Zoe's dressing room was a churning river of noise and hurried energy. Stagehands, their faces tight with focus, rushed past with racks of glittering ballgowns, the plastic coverings whispering secrets of the ghosts of performances past. From the main stage, the muffled thrum of the Cinderella score pulsed up through the floorboards, a cheerful, relentless heartbeat that felt a world away from the grim purpose that had settled deep in Kevin's bones. Here, standing before her door, a pocket of heavy silence had formed all around him, a storm cloud in a sky determined to be blue.

He stared at the star-shaped nameplate, ZOE REEVES, its bubbly font a cruel joke against the task at hand. Vivi's phone call had been a short, sharp crack in the carefully constructed calm of his own day. Her words came back to him now, stripped of all theatricalities, echoing in the quiet chambers of his mind. *She deflected. Smiled right through it. She thinks it's healthy, Kevin. She's building a fortress out of sunshine.*

The strategy session with Marc had been a somber affair, a council of war where they all knew the weapons were inadequate. Vivi's gentle, empathetic approach, the one that should have worked, had evaporated against Zoe's bright denial. Now his turn. He was the next logical step, the heavy artillery they had to roll into place. His own escape had been into a world of Gothic romance, a shadowed place of beautiful suffering that, on its face, was a problem—a sickness. Zoe's was a world of light and hope, a cure that was the disease. He had to be the one to draw the parallel, to hold up a mirror of his own shattered past and show her that their two opposite worlds were different reflections of the same cage.

The thought of it made his stomach clench, a familiar knot of dread and memory. He had spent the better part of a year learning to walk away from that particular darkness, not to let the beautiful tragedy of it all define him. Now he had to willingly step back into its shadow, to unpack his own trauma not for healing, but as a strategic tool. Sarah's voice, a calm anchor from a therapy session weeks ago, surfaced unbidden. *Your scars aren't a weakness, Kevin. They're a map. The trick is learning to read it without getting lost in the old territory again.*

He took a deep breath, the air thick with the chemical sweetness of hairspray and the familiar scent of old wood and backstage anxiety. He was reading the map for Zoe. He raised his hand and knocked, the sound unnaturally loud, a single sharp report against the cheerful, muffled music.

The door flew open, and there she was, a supernova of determined brightness. Carmen was fitting her into her peasant costume, a simple dress that, on her, was the loveliest thing in the world.

Carmen studied the hem of Zoe's dress with unusual intensity. "You know," she said casually, "I've been finding the strangest things in the costume shop lately. Sand, of all things. In the middle of winter." She glanced up at Zoe, her eyes sharp behind her glasses. "Actors do bring the most interesting things back with them from their journeys into character."

Zoe laughed nervously. "That is odd."

"Yes," Carmen said, still holding Zoe's gaze. "Very odd. Almost like they've been somewhere... else." She smiled and returned to her sewing. "But then, this old theater has always been full of mysteries."

"Well, I think this is going to be beautiful on you. Can't wait to do the fitting for the ball gown," said Carmen as she left the room.

The counter behind her was a happy mess of brushes and open palettes, smudges of pink and gold powder dusting the surface. Hung on a hook by the wall, a confection of blue silk and shimmering tulle, the ballgown she would wear to meet her prince waited. The glare from the vanity mirror bulbs was a harsh, unforgiving light, illuminating the brittle edge of a smile that didn't quite reach her eyes. The mirror itself was polished to a brilliant, flawless sheen, a perfect, waiting surface.

"Kevin! Hey! What are you doing back here?" Her cheerfulness was a shield, a bright and gleaming thing aimed directly at him.

"Hey, Zoe. Got a minute?"

"For you, always!" She gestured him in, her movements a little too quick, a little too sharp. "The place is a mess, sorry. Pre-show chaos, you know the drill."

He stepped inside, the scent of her floral perfume and the hot lights closing in around him. She shut the door, and the soft click severed them from the frantic pulse of the theater. The room felt small, suffocating. He hated that he had to do this here, in her sanctuary, the very place that housed the heart of the thing he had to destroy. But there was no other choice, no other ground on which to fight this battle.

"We need to talk." He had to set the tone, bring the gravity of the situation into this bright, glittering space.

Zoe's smile tightened, the light in her eyes becoming watchful, guarded. "If this is about Tyler, I already feel awful. I promise I'm going to make it up to him."

"It's not about Tyler," Kevin said gently, though every instinct screamed at him to be anything but. "It's about you. It's about why you missed dinner with Tyler. It's about the mirror."

The name of it hung in the air between them, stark and undeniable. Zoe's face, for a split second, went utterly blank. The bright, performative mask she wore as a second skin fell away, and for a breathtaking moment, he saw the real girl underneath: scared, cornered, and so very young.

Then, as quickly, the mask was back, harder this time, more defiant.

"Vivi talked to you," she stated. Her voice had lost its airy, singing quality.

"Yes, she did. Because she's terrified she's losing you. Because I am, too."

He could see the path Vivi had taken, a gentle trail of breadcrumbs laid with love and concern. And he could see with painful clarity how Zoe had danced right over them, pretending not to notice. He couldn't afford to be gentle. He had to be a sledgehammer to a stained-glass window. He had to be the storm that broke the perfect, sunny day.

"I know where you're going, Zoe," he said with a conspiratorial whisper that was meant only for the two of them. "I know what it's like. That pull. The feeling that you've found a place that finally, finally understands you. A place that's better, more real, than this one."

Zoe crossed her arms, a thin wall of defense. "I don't know what you're talking about."

"Stop," he said, the word soft but absolute. "Don't lie to me. You're a terrible liar, Zoe, and it's one of the best things about you. I'm not here to judge you. I promise. I'm here because I think I'm the only other person on the planet who gets it. Not even Vivi gets it."

He took a step closer, closing the space she tried to keep between them, forcing her to meet his gaze. "My world was underground, damp, and it smelled of decay and wet stone. Full of torchlight and shadows and the most tragic opera you've ever heard. A beautiful, romantic tomb, built for me. And your world," he gestured to the shimmering mirror, "is a castle. It's full of sunlight and ballgowns and perfect princes who say all the right things. It's a beautiful, romantic fairy tale."

He paused, letting his words sink into the small, charged space. "Mine was dark. Yours is light. But they are in the same room, Zoe. They have different wallpaper. They're both prisons. And they will both kill you if you let them."

He laid his own story bare then, offering it to her as a fragile, priceless gift, both a warning and a key. He spoke of Christine, of the seductive, intoxicating allure of being told his pain was beautiful. He described the hollowness of the fantasy intimacy, making love to a reflection of his own sickness, a performance of passion that left him colder than before. He spoke of the lies he'd told, the rehearsals he'd missed, the trust he'd shattered with everyone who'd tried to pull him back to the surface. He was tracing his map for her, pointing out every dead end, every hidden cliff edge, every place he'd almost fallen for good.

Zoe listened, her expression unreadable. For a long moment, he thought he was getting through. He saw a glimmer of her genuine self, the empathetic, caring friend he knew was in there—as she spoke of her pain. But as he finished, her face hardened again, the soft lines of empathy rearranging themselves into something else entirely. Her expression shifted to pity. A gentle, conde-scending pity that made his blood run cold.

"Kevin." Her voice was soft and full of sadness, misguided wisdom that was more terrifying than any anger could have been. "I am so, so proud of how far you've come. I can't imagine how hard all that was to pull yourself out of a place like that."

She reached out and put a hand on his arm, meant to be a gesture of comfort, of solidarity—a dismissal, as if she were patting him on the head.

"But you have to see that you're projecting," she continued, her voice radiating a serene, unshakeable confidence that felt utterly alien. "You're seeing your darkness everywhere because that's what you know. My world isn't like yours. It's not a tomb. It's a garden. It's beautiful. It's inspiring." She looked past him; her gaze fixed on her own reflection in the mirror. "The music, the light, it all helps me find Cinderella's hope. It's not an escape, Kevin. It's part of my process. It's a healthy, positive source of creativity."

Her words didn't land a blow. They were worse. They were a fog, a sweet-smelling poison that seeped into the air and choked the truth. She wasn't deflecting. She was refraining. She was taking the very heart of his warning, the darkest and most vulnerable part of himself he had to offer, and twisting it into proof that she was right, and he was wounded. She was weaponizing positivity. She was using the language of healing to justify her own sickness.

And in that moment, the dawning horror of the situation became terrifyingly clear.

His addiction had been easy to spot, in the end. A world of darkness and depression is, by its very nature, a problem to be solved. Anyone could see that escaping to a place of romanticized suffering was self-destructive. But

Zoe's trap was a thousand times more insidious, more perfect. How do you convince someone they're in prison when the bars are made of sunshine? How do you save someone from a poison that tastes of honey and smells of hope?

Her perfect, happy escape had convinced her she wasn't escaping at all. She believed she was engaging in a radical act of self-care. She had taken the very tools of recovery—the language of inspiration and process—and built her cage from them. His personal appeal, the most powerful tool he had, was a complete and utter failure. He had shown her his map, and she had told him he was reading it wrong, that his own past broke his compass.

"Zoe," his voice was ragged with a new, clawing desperation. "That's what magic does. It finds what you want most and builds a perfect, hollow world out of it. For me, this was validation for my pain. For you, it's a happy ending. It's a trap. It's designed to be the most beautiful trap you've ever seen."

She pulled her hand away, her expression finally cracking into undisguised hurt and frustration. "No," her voice sharp as broken glass. "It's not a trap. It's beautiful. And I'm sorry you can't see that. I'm sorry that you can't imagine something being purely good." She delivered the final, killing blow. "Maybe you need to talk to Sarah about that."

The mention of Sarah was a deliberate, low strike, and it found its mark. She was casting his concern as a symptom of his own unresolved issues. She was putting him, the friend trying to save her, into the patient box. In her eyes, he was no longer an ally offering a lifeline. He was another case study in damaged goods. In that instant, she was no longer a victim of magic. She was its fierce, deluded advocate.

He had lost. The truth was a quiet, heavy certainty in the center of his chest.

"I think you should go," she said quietly, turning away from him to face the mirror. Her reflection looked back at her with a calm, reassuring smile that was a chilling parody of her own. She was comforting herself.

Kevin stared at her back, at the rigid, unyielding set of her shoulders. There were no more words. He had fired his only shot, the most powerful one in his arsenal, and it had dissolved against her shimmering wall of denial. He felt a profound sense of failure, but no anger. Just a deep fear. He had been so sure his direct, parallel experience was the key. But he was limited. He was a survivor, not a professional. He was a man with a map to a place she refused to believe she was going.

He turned and walked to the door, his movements heavy with the weight of his defeat. He paused with his hand on the knob, the metal cool against his skin. "I love you, Zoe," he said to her back, his voice rough. "And I'm not giving up on you. Even if you've given up on yourself."

She didn't answer. Of course, she didn't. She was already gone.

He stepped out into the noisy hallway and shut the door behind him. The muffled, cheerful music from the stage, some soaring ballad about wishes coming true, was a personal mockery. He leaned his head against the cool, painted brick of the wall, the frustration and fear a bitter taste in his mouth. A stagehand hurried by with an armful of props, not glancing his way. In the sudden quiet that followed, he heard another dressing room door down the hall click shut, a sound that amplified his own stark solitude.

He had failed. Vivi had failed. Peer support, the very thing that had helped pull him back from the brink, was useless against this. Zoe's delusion wasn't a symptom of her addiction but the engine, fueled by light, hope, and everything good. They needed a new strategy. They needed someone who could dismantle the engine without getting blinded by the light.

He pushed himself off the wall, his own resolve hardening from despair into a grim clarity. He pulled his phone from his pocket, his thumb moving with numb precision as he scrolled through his contacts. He stopped on Sarah's name, her photo a small, warm beacon of sanity in chaos.

His thumb hovered over her contact for a long, heavy moment. He was about to break his own hard-won rule of not mixing his recovery with his relationship, a boundary he'd built as carefully as a stone wall. But this was bigger than his rules. This was life. This was Zoe's life.

"Okay," he muttered to the empty hallway, his voice a low, defeated growl that was swallowed by the theater's cheerful pulse. "She won't listen to a friend." He looked back at Zoe's closed door, a fresh wave of fear washing over him. "Let's see if she'll listen to a shrink."

He pressed the call button.

EIGHTEEN

PERFECT STAGNATION

The heavy wooden door of her dressing room swung shut with a soft thud, and the noise of the theater died away, like closing the lid on a jar of agitated honeybees. Vivi's somber, disappointed face. Kevin's intense, pitying eyes. Their words still buzzed in her ears, a chorus of concern that tasted exactly like judgment. *Projection. Darkness. Trap.* They didn't understand. How could they? Their escapes were born of sorrow and shadow. Hers was a sanctuary built from light itself.

A stubborn defensiveness rose in her throat, warm and tight. She was exhausted by their relentless worry, by being seen as a project that needed fixing. She turned to the only one who truly saw her. The one who never judged, who never questioned, who never looked at her and saw something broken.

The antique mirror on the wall seemed to breathe, its surface shimmering with a soft, pearlescent glow that was a silent invitation home. She didn't hesitate. This wasn't an escape from guilt, not the way it had been before. This was a righteous retreat. She was choosing joy. She was selecting a healthy, positive source of inspiration, and if they couldn't see the goodness in that, well, that was a burden for them to carry, not her.

With a defiant lift of her chin, she stepped toward the cool, liquid surface, feeling it give way like dipping her hand into a spring-fed creek on the hottest day of summer.

The world that greeted her was now an immediate balm to her frayed spirit since she landed at the castle. The air was warm and hung thick with the scent of honeysuckle and sun-warmed stone, a constant, heady perfume that smothered all other thoughts. Prince Adrian was there, of course, waiting for her in the manicured palace gardens. His smile was a perfect, adoring crescent, crafted for her.

"You can't keep leaving," Adrian told her, his face showing the first signs of frustration. "The ball is tomorrow. You must be there."

"I have a job in the real world."

"This IS the real world. That other place is where you go when you're not needed here."

"My love," he said with the noble timbre of every hero she had ever imagined from the pages of a storybook. "I feared you would not return."

"I'll always return to you," she promised, and for a blissful, eternal afternoon, the promise felt as true and solid as the ground beneath her feet.

This visit stretched longer than before. She let the

world's flawless routine wash over her, a gentle tide pulling her further and further from the rocky, uncertain shores of her own life. The days bled into one another in a seamless montage of storybook perfection. They rode alabaster horses through an enchanted forest where the leaves were always caught in a breathless sigh of autumn gold but never fell to the ground. They dined at a banquet table laden with glistening roasts and towering, impossible cakes, a feast for the eyes. Still, she was noticing that everything, from the savory meat to the sweetest confection, tasted vaguely of the same mild, sugary flavor, day after day, the lovely, flat taste of a photograph of a feast.

In the evenings, a chamber orchestra played a gentle, looping score as they waltzed alone in a grand ballroom. She began to recognize the exact moment the cello would repeat a phrase, as well as the precise, soft intake of breath from the flutist before the melody resumed. Outside the arched windows, the stars in the deep cerulean sky were fixed in their constellations, and unchanging diamonds pinned to velvet.

Adrian was a flawless partner. He complimented the jewel-toned gowns that appeared, pristine and pressed, in her wardrobe that morning. He recited poetry as they walked along the marble terraces, his words as beautiful and predictable as the sunset that never truly set. He was attentive, devoted, and utterly focused on her happiness —everything she had ever dreamed a romance could be: a perfect, sun-drenched paradise.

And a hollowness was beginning to grow in the very center of it all.

The first real crack in her world appeared during a picnic by a stream so clear it looked like liquid glass. The sunbeams struck the same spot on the water they had yesterday, the light dancing in a pattern she now recognized. The blanket was the same shade of royal blue. The wicker basket held the identical, red apples and flawless cheese. The apples were a shade of crimson that didn't quite exist in nature, perfectly round and smooth, with no blemishes, no stems, no sign a living tree had ever borne them. Adrian was in the middle of a familiar, beautiful speech about her eyes, how they held more light than all the stars in his sky.

A sudden, messy, and intensely real memory surfaced, unbidden and sharp. She and her dad, years ago, crammed into their little kitchen, trying to make her grandmother's apple pie for the first time—flour coated every surface as a fine layer of snow. The warm, sharp scent of cinnamon hung in the air, a smell so real she could almost taste it now. Their laughter echoed off the chipped Formica countertops as the crust crumbled apart in their hands. It had been a glorious, lopsided disaster. The pie was a burnt-edged mess. But it had been their mess. They had made it together.

On impulse, Zoe turned to Adrian, interrupting his poetic flow. "What if we made something?" she asked, the idea a bright, unexpected spark in the placid landscape of her mind.

Adrian tilted his head, his handsome face a mask of noble confusion. "Made something, my love?"

"Yes. We could cook in the castle kitchens. I have this

recipe for apple pie that my grandmother used to make. It's messy and complicated and probably won't turn out right the first time, but it's so much fun."

He smiled, a gentle, dismissive curving of his lips. "But why, my dearest? The royal chefs prepare the most divine feasts for us. Why would we seek imperfection when we have this?" He gestured around them, at the flawless scene, the pre-packaged perfection.

The word hung in the humid, sweet air. *Imperfection.* To him, this was a flaw, a thing to be avoided at all costs. To her, in that moment, it was freedom. The bright spark of her idea fizzled out, doused by his serene, bottomless incomprehension.

"You're right," she said. "A silly idea."

But the crack had widened. She started to watch him with a new, critical eye. She tested the boundaries of his script, a quiet rebellion taking root in her heart.

"What were you afraid of when you were a little boy?" she asked him one afternoon. They sat by a fountain where the water arced in the same perfect, repeating pattern, the splash as rhythmic and constant as a clock.

"A world without you in it," he answered smoothly, taking her hand in his. A beautiful line, the kind of thing a girl dreams of hearing. But not an answer.

"No, before me," she pressed, a knot of unease tightening in her stomach. "What was your biggest dream? Not as a prince, just as a boy."

"My only ambition has ever been your happiness, my love," he replied, his gaze as adoring and as empty as a doll's.

Every question she asked, every attempt to dig beneath the prince's surface, was met with a beautifully crafted, romantic platitude that rerouted the conversation back to his adoration of her. He had no past before she arrived. He had no fears that weren't about losing her. He had no desires that weren't for her. He wasn't a person. He was a mirror. A flawless, beautiful mirror built only to reflect her own idealized desires at her.

The realization wasn't a sudden crash but a slow, creeping horror that coiled in her gut. The perfection she had craved, the flawless adoration she had seen as the ultimate good, was a cage. A beautiful, glittering, sun-drenched prison where nothing ever changed, nothing ever grew, and nothing was ever truly alive. This lovely place wasn't a sanctuary but more a gilded cage where joy went to die. The positive, healthy escape she had defended so fiercely to Kevin and Vivi was a stagnant pond. Safe, but dead.

She allowed herself to feel the profound, sickening unease. She didn't fight the thought. She didn't double down on the fantasy to chase away the dissonance. For the first time, she let the brutal, disillusioning truth settle in her bones. Her friends weren't wrong because they were mired in their own darkness. They were right. This place was a trap.

She played along for the rest of the day, her smiles feeling brittle on her lips, her laughter sounding hollow and strange in her own ears. She danced with him in the ballroom, moving through the familiar, practiced steps while her mind raced. He was a program, running a perfect, romantic loop. And she was the guest in a single-player video game.

That evening, she told him she was tired and wished to retire early.

"Then I shall dream only of you until tomorrow, my heart's delight," he said, kissing her hand with the same elegant flourish he always did.

She knew that tomorrow would be identical to today. And the day after. And the day after that. Eternal, blissful, maddening stagnation. Hope was a dangerous thing, a weed that grew in the cracks of a broken heart, but this place offered no cracks for it to grow.

She had to get out, not with the guilt-ridden panic of before, but with an urgent need to breathe real, imperfect air. She found her way back to the portal, the world of flawless beauty now feeling sinister. She stepped through, a new, terrifying goal forming in her mind. She had to come back, not for escape, but for research. She had to understand the rules of this beautiful, empty prison.

Zoe stumbled back into the close, imperfect reality of her dressing room. The air was stale, thick with the scent of old fabric and hairspray. The harsh glare of the vanity bulbs felt more honest and more accurate than the perpetual golden hour she had left. A half-eaten bag of pretzels sat on the counter, a wonderfully mundane reminder of real-world hunger. She felt a wave of relief so profound it almost brought her to her knees.

She sank onto the small, worn stool, her body trembling with the aftershocks of her realization. She was a fool. A happy, optimistic, deluded fool who had built her own beautiful prison and called it a paradise.

She looked up, her gaze landing on her own reflection in the mirror she had exited. Her face was pale, her eyes wide with a mixture of fear and dawning clarity. She stared at herself, the girl who wanted fairy tales to be real so badly she was willing to ignore the truth.

For a fleeting, horrifying second, the reflection wavered, the image of her own face melting. Her own disillusioned face didn't look back at her. It was Prince Adrian's. His features were sculpted, his smile adoring, his eyes loving.

And utterly, terrifyingly blank.

Zoe cried out and scrambled backward, her stool toppling over with a loud clatter that echoed in the silent room. She fell hard onto the floor, her heart a panicked fist beating against her ribs. She stared at the mirror, at her own reflection again, her face a mask of pure terror.

The vision was gone. But the image burned into her mind.

CHAPTER

NINETEEN

DRESS REHEARSAL DISASTER

The memory of Tyler's face was seared onto the back of her eyelids, a photograph of analytical dread from the night before, right before she'd slammed her dressing room door on the questions in his eyes. He knew. They all did—Vivi, her face a painting of sad, quiet disappointment. Kevin, with that grim, knowing pity that was somehow worse than anger. They were all watching, a silent jury waiting for her to finally, irrevocably crack.

"What is that smell, Zoe? You smell like... lye?" Marc said, confused.

"New shampoo," Zoe said quickly, desperately trying to scrub the servant smell off her hands. "Very... traditional."

Her skin prickled with a fresh and potent paranoia, a thousand tiny needles of awareness. She smoothed the heavy blue silk of her Cinderella ballgown, the fabric a calm, indifferent river against her trembling fingers. The

144

gown felt more real than her own skin, a beautiful blue shell to hide inside. Out in the vast, dark ocean of the theater, she could feel them. Cate, a hawk-like silhouette perched at the tech table, a predator in her nest. Tyler, a lone, brooding figure in the back row, his notepad a weapon and his gaze a verdict.

The only way through was to be perfect. She had to be so dazzlingly, undeniably brilliant that their concern would curdle into foolishness, their suspicion rendered baseless. She would perform with such heart that they would have to believe her. She had to prove that her source of inspiration was a wellspring of strength, not a sickness of the mind.

But the seed of doubt planted during her last visit to the kingdom had taken root in the soft soil of her heart. The memory of Adrian's eyes, so blankly adoring, and his smooth, untroubled inability to answer a simple question about his own past, was a splinter working its way deeper into her thoughts. It made his love feel fragile, a breath-taking sculpture of blown glass that might shatter into a million pieces if she dared to look at it too closely. This war inside her made her desperate for his validation. She needed the comforting, uncomplicated warmth of his gaze to burn away her fears. She had to see him, to feel his adoration wash over her and silence the whispers that now echoed in her own voice.

The orchestra swelled, the familiar, soaring notes of the royal ball fanfare rising to fill the theater. This was her moment. The pivotal scene. Her cue was coming, a bright flag on the horizon. She had to wait for the Royal Herald to announce her grand entrance, to call her into being.

She waited.

The music held on a triumphant, expectant chord. And it held. The note stretched, thinning until it became a wire of pure tension. A horrifying, cavernous silence opened up on the stage, right where the Herald's booming, cheerful voice should have been. Her scene partner, the young actor playing the prince, shot her a look of raw, panicked confusion. From the corner of her eye, she saw the choreographer in the wings, her arms making frantic, questioning shapes in the dim light.

She had missed her entrance. Lost in the quiet, bloody war inside her own head, she had missed the most important cue of the entire show.

A wave of shame, hot and prickling, washed over her from head to toe. The faces of the cast, all assembled for the grand ball, blurred into a single, monstrous stare of accusation. She could feel Tyler's journalistic focus sharpening, a lens in the darkness, could almost hear the low, barometric drop of Cate's fury as the storm front built. They were right. All of them. She was a fraud. She was failing.

Panic, sharp and clawed, scrambled up her throat. She needed him. Not the idea of him. She needed *him*. Now.

Desperate, her gaze flew upward, sweeping past the bewildered face of the boy on stage, past the ornate, painted flats of the ballroom set, and up into the high, steel-beamed darkness of the lighting grid. And she found him.

The grimy, workaday reality of the stage dissolved. The hot, metallic scent of the lights, the smell of rosin and old velvet, the bone-deep fear—all vanished. Up there, where a single, blinding spotlight should have been, the grimy steel of the lighting grid melted away. It reformed into the elegant curve of a white stone balcony wreathed in ivy that glittered with dew under a perfect, heavy moon. A gentle breeze, scented with night-blooming jasmine and the cool stone, seemed to drift down, a stark contrast to the hot, stagnant air of the stage. And on that balcony, bathed in a soft, impossible glow, stood Prince Adrian. He was dressed in his royal finery, his handsome face a portrait of pure, unconditional love. He wasn't confused. He wasn't angry or disappointed. He was looking down at her, only at her, his eyes full of the perfect, uncomplicated adoration she craved.

The relief was so potent it made her head swim. This was real. He was real. The rest of this, the missed cue and the staring faces, was a bad dream she was having.

A slow, genuine smile spread across her face, easing the tension in her jaw. The lines, which had become ash in her mouth only moments before, now came to her. They were imbued with a profound, real meaning she had never felt before. They weren't for the confused boy standing a few feet away. They were for Adrian.

She took a single, gliding step forward. Her voice rang out, not with the practiced projection of an actress, but with the fragile, trembling clarity of a whispered confession full of love that no one else in the room could see.

"I knew I'd find you," she declared, her voice shaking

with an emotion that was all too real, her eyes locked on that space in the rafters.

The effect on the stage was immediate and catastrophic. Her partner froze, his mouth hanging slightly open. The ensemble of dancers, poised for a waltz, shuffled to an awkward, collective halt. A frantic, panicked whisper erupted from the wings, a sound like dry leaves skittering across pavement. The world was breaking. The script was torn to shreds.

"Zoe," her prince's voice, a low, urgent current of sound meant only for her. "What are you doing? Your line is to *me*."

But she couldn't hear him. She was lost, blissfully adrift in the warm glow of Adrian's smile. She delivered her following line, a romantic and heartfelt promise of eternal devotion, to the empty air high above her.

A sharp, amplified voice cut through the theater like a shard of glass.

"Hold!"

The single word from the tech table shattered the world. The castle balcony vanished in an instant. The warm, loving glow was once again a harsh, blinding stage light. Prince Adrian was gone. There was only the empty steel of the grid and the dust motes dancing in the beam.

And the horrifying, absolute silence of a hundred people staring at her.

For one terrible second, the shame was absolute. It landed as a physical blow, knocking the air from her lungs and leaving her gasping. The real world rushed in with the force of a tidal wave. She saw it all with perfect, horrifying clarity. She could smell the faint, powdery scent of her scene partner's stage makeup, heard the nervous squeak of a ballerina's shoe on the Marley floor behind her. Tiny, insignificant details that screamed of a reality she had tried to obliterate. She saw the bewildered hurt on her partner's face, the open-mouthed shock of the ensemble. She saw the furious, tight-lipped expression on Cate's face at the tech table. A wave of pure shame, so intense, washed over her. She realized what she had done, how she had failed them all, how she had taken their trust and thrown it away for a dream. The honest Zoe, the girl who loved the theater and valued professionalism above all else, was trapped inside this strange, broken version of herself, screaming in silent, humiliating agony.

Then the denial slammed back into place, a thick, protective wall of brick and mortar that was her fault. They had pushed her to this. Their judgment, their suspicion, their complete lack of faith. They didn't want her to be happy. They didn't understand. Only Adrian understood.

Cate's voice, amplified and stripped of all warmth, crackled through the speakers again. "Zoe. Eyes on me."

Zoe slowly and reluctantly tore her gaze from the lighting grid and looked out into the yawning darkness of the house. She could make out Cate's rigid form, a general in her command post, a silhouette of pure, condensed fury.

"That was your entrance cue, which you missed,"

Cate's voice was dangerously calm, each word a carefully placed stone. "And your focus is not up in the grid. It is on your scene partner. On this stage. In this reality. Do you understand me?"

The words in *this reality* struck a chord with Zoe. Cate knew. She was mocking her. The humiliation curdled instantly into a hot, defensive anger; easier to be angry than to be ashamed.

"I'm fine," Zoe's voice brittle as spun sugar. "I was ... feeling the moment."

A collective, disbelieving sigh seemed to ripple through the wings, a soft gust of wind through a graveyard.

"Feeling the moment?" Cate's voice was now laced with ice. "Zoe, you delivered one of the most romantic speeches in the history of musical theater to a PAR can. I need you to get your head out of wherever it is and back into this production, or we are all going to have a very long, very unpleasant night."

The public nature of the rebuke, the professional dismissal of her feelings, was more than she could bear. This world was cruel, judgmental, and unfair. She looked at her stage partner, searching his face for some sign of solidarity, some flicker of understanding. He looked away, his expression a tight mask of frustration and embarrassment. Her friends, the other dancers in their glittering costumes, refused to meet her eyes, suddenly fascinated by their own shoes. She was utterly, completely alone on an island of her own making.

Her reputation, the one she'd polished and protected

like her grandmother's finest silver, lay shattered on the floor, and no one was helping her pick up the pieces. She felt a hundred pairs of eyes on her, dissecting her, judging her. Her professional world, the one thing that had always felt solid beneath her feet, had collapsed into ruins. And in those ruins, only one thing felt safe. Only one person offered unconditional acceptance.

The stage manager's voice crackled over the god-mic, a flat and impersonal sound cutting through the tension. "Holding for ten minutes. Places from the top of the ballroom scene."

The announcement was a starting pistol. As Cate called the hold, Zoe saw them. They were all converging on her, a closing net woven from pity and concern. From the wings, Vivi and Kevin were moving toward her, their faces etched with that dreadful, familiar worry she could no longer stand to see. And from the back of the house, a lone figure stood up. Tyler. He was no longer a passive observer in the dark. He was walking with a sharp, determined purpose down the central aisle, straight toward the stage.

Trapped. Humiliated. Exposed.

A primal animal instinct to flee took over her body, bypassing thought entirely. She couldn't face them. She couldn't endure their quiet questions, their gentle pity, their righteous I-told-you-so.

With a small, choked sob that was torn from her throat, Zoe turned and ran.

She fled offstage, the heavy silk of her gown whispering around her legs. She pushed past a startled stagehand, ignoring the calls of her name from Vivi, from Kevin, from the stage manager. She didn't look back. She ran, the delicate glass slippers of a fairy-tale princess slapping against the unforgiving concrete of the real world. Taped lines marking forgotten shows crisscrossed the floor. She wasn't running away from them. She was running *toward* the only sanctuary she had left.

The one place where she was always perfect, always loved, and never, ever a failure.

Her dressing room. And the mirror was waiting for her inside.

Zoe fled the stage, her glass slippers clicking against the floor. She ran past Vivi's outstretched hand, past Kevin's concerned shout, past Tyler, who was already rising from his seat in the back of the house. She couldn't face them. Not yet.

She burst through the stage door into the alley, the humid night air hitting her like a wall. For a moment, she stood there, gulping oxygen, trying to calm the hurricane in her chest. The stage makeup was already running in rivulets down her face.

I destroyed everything. I hurt everyone. They were right about me.

But as the guilt threatened to drown her, another voice whispered seductively in her mind: *Adrian would never judge you. Adrian understands. Adrian is waiting.*

She had to choose. Face the people she'd failed or return to the one person who would never see her as a failure.

Drawing a shuddering breath, she walked back into

the theater through the side door. The cast was dispersing, some heading to the green room, others lingering in the wings. She could hear Cate's voice, low and authoritative, giving instructions to Danny about damage control.

Zoe slipped past them all, a ghost in a ball gown, and locked herself in her dressing room.

CHAPTER

TWENTY

CATE'S REVELATION

She didn't make it ten feet down the backstage corridor.

A firm hand closed around her arm, stopping her flight with an authority that felt absolute. The grip wasn't meant to cause pain, but was unyielding all the same, an anchor of muscle and bone chaining her to the awful reality she was so desperately trying to outrun. Zoe didn't have to look. She knew that grip. She knew that scent, a strange and specific blend of old books, dark coffee, and something else that was nothing more than pure force of will.

Cate.

Wordlessly, the director turned her around. The pressure on her arm was a silent command, propelling her down the hallway not toward the cool night air of the exit, but deeper into the theater's labyrinthine heart. Zoe stumbled along in her ridiculous glass slippers, a condemned woman being led to her final judgment. The overwhelming shame from her public failure was a physical thing, a thick, smothering cloak so heavy she could barely draw a breath. Every averted gaze from a passing stagehand, every face that quickly turned away, was a fresh wound, a small nick on a soul already bleeding out.

Cate steered her up a narrow flight of stairs, the kind that groaned with the building's age, and directly into her office, a cramped space. Books and scripts were piled high on every available surface, monuments to past productions and future battles. A bank of small security monitors on the wall cast a shifting, ghostly blue light across the room, each screen a silent, watchful eye. The air hung thick and stale, heavy with the ghosts of burnt coffee and the dry, sweet scent of old paper. Cate guided her to a single, unforgiving chair and then stood before the door, her arms crossed, her face a grim, unreadable mask. She was a sentry. She was a jailer.

Zoe was trapped.

The next few minutes were an agonizing blur. The air in the little room hummed with a tense, waiting silence, punctuated only by the soft thud of her own heart against her ribs and the sound of quiet knocks at the door. One by one, the others arrived, summoned by some invisible signal, some summons she hadn't heard. Vivi and Marc were the first to enter, their faces a perfect mirror of shared, anxious concern. They moved as one, a single unit of worry. Then came Kevin and Sarah. Kevin's expression was a thundercloud, dark and brooding, while Sarah's radiated a calm, professional worry that somehow felt more damning in its gentle assessment.

Then Tyler. He didn't look worried, not in the same way. He looked like a man who had connected the final, terrifying dot in a story he never wanted to believe. He walked in with his reporter's notebook already in hand, the worn leather a familiar extension of his arm. He took a seat without a word, his sharp, analytical gaze fixed on Cate. He was here for answers, not comfort.

They were all here. The jury. Her accusers. The very people she had lied to, disappointed, and fled from, all of them assembled in this suffocating little room to witness her final disgrace. Zoe shrank in her chair, a physical curl inward, wishing the floorboards would part and swallow her whole. This was it. The professional reprimand she knew she deserved. The lecture on responsibility. Maybe even her dismissal from the show, a quiet and final severing. She braced herself, waiting for the impact of the words that would surely tear her apart.

Cate waited until the door clicked shut behind Tyler, the sound sealing them in. The silence stretched, growing thick and unbearable, a heavy blanket pressing down on all of them.

"Thank you all for coming. I know this is unorthodox," Cate said.

Tyler let out a short, humorless scoff, the sound sharp as breaking glass. "That's one word for it."

Cate's eyes narrowed at him for a split second, a warning flicker in their depths, before her gaze returned to the group. "What happened on that stage tonight wasn't a case of nerves but a lapse in professionalism." She paused, letting the weight of her words settle. "A symptom of a disease this theater carries."

Zoe's head snapped up. She had steeled herself for anger, for disappointment, not for this. Not this bizarre, winding metaphor that made no sense.

"I'm going to tell you all a story," Cate continued, her voice going utterly flat, stripped of every ounce of the theatricality that was her trade. "And you're not going to believe it. At first."

She paused again, her gaze sweeping over their confused, unsettled faces, lingering for a heartbeat on Vivi, then on Kevin. "I am not from this world. My name is not Cate Hart. That is a name I chose, a fiction I built to survive." Her voice was a monotone, a simple recitation of impossible facts. "I was born in a place of thunder and lightning, of foul weather and fair words. I was one of three sisters who served a king on a blasted heath."

The room was utterly still.

Cate's voice grew quieter, dropping to a near whisper, and her eyes took on a distant, haunted quality, as if she were looking at a memory only she could see. "I was there when the hurly-burly was done, when the battle was lost and won. But for me, the curtain never fell. The play ended, and I was left here." She took a breath, a slight, painful sound. "Trapped in a world without iambic pentameter to give it shape. Left in the silence. The cold of this place felt different, a quiet chill that seeped into the bones, so unlike the wild, storm-thrashed cold I had known."

Zoe's breath caught in her throat, not a metaphor or a

story. She was being literal. *She's insane,* the thought screamed through her mind, loud and panicked. *Our director is having a complete psychotic break right in front of us.*

The claim was so patently absurd, so completely unhinged, that a bubble of wild, hysterical laughter almost escaped her lips. A witch? One of the weird sisters from *Macbeth*? This was the most ridiculous, impossible thing she had ever heard in her entire life.

Just as Tyler opened his mouth, the cynical journalist in him was ready to voice the skepticism they were all feeling when the office door clicked open again.

Malcolm stood in the doorway, his large, solid frame filling the space. He was holding two steaming mugs, their warmth sending plumes of fragrant steam into the tense air. His kind, weathered face was calm, a bastion of solidity in a sea of chaos. He looked from Cate's rigid posture to the stunned faces of everyone in the room, and his sad, knowing eyes seemed to take in the entire impossible situation at a single glance.

"She's telling you the truth," he said. His voice was a deep, resonant timber, like the low, grounding note of a cello, and it left no room for argument or doubt. "Every word of it."

He stepped into the room, his presence a comforting weight. He handed one of the mugs to Cate, their fingers brushing in a gesture of quiet, familiar comfort that spoke volumes about years of shared history. The steam rising from the cup smelled of ginger and chamomile, a sharp, earthy scent that was startlingly real. "I was there, too,"

Malcolm added softly, his voice full of an old, settled sorrow. "I was the son of a murdered king, meant to take back a throne I never wanted. We escaped that world of blood and madness together."

The impossible words landed in the small room, and Zoe felt the floor drop out from under her. The quiet certainty in Malcolm's voice, the utter lack of drama or performance in his confession, was more convincing than any wild-eyed rant could ever be, a simple, tired statement of a man recounting a fact. The room tilted on its axis. The air grew thin and sharp in her lungs.

The beautiful, sparkling world she had found. The prince who adored her. Her secret sanctuary, her font of pure inspiration. Not a figment of her imagination, but a product of her own longing. Not an artistic tool either, but seemingly real. And if Cate and Malcolm's impossible story was real, then her world, her prince, her fairy tale, was real too.

And a trap.

The tiny seed of doubt that had been planted in her mind, the one she had so carefully ignored, blossomed in an instant into a monstrous, thorny vine of pure horror. Her prince wasn't a hollow reflection of her desires. He was a known predator. Her magical escape wasn't a secret garden for her alone but a cage, and the door had been left open for her deliberately. Her prince, Prince Adrian, was a smiling face on a repeating loop, a doll waiting for the next girl to come along and play.

The shame that had been choking her was swept away by a wave of sickening terror that was a thousand times worse. She wasn't special. She wasn't the chosen one. She was the latest victim in a long, silent line.

Her gaze darted from Cate's grim, determined face to Vivi, who was staring down at her own hands, her expression a mask of remembered pain. Then, to Kevin, whose jaw was clenched so tight that a muscle jumped in his cheek, his knuckles were white where he gripped the arms of his chair. They had tried to warn her. In their own broken ways, they had tried. They had used words like 'trap,' 'darkness,' and 'losing yourself,' and she had dismissed them, wrapped in the self-righteous, sunny glow of her own optimism.

She had been so, so wrong. So arrogant in her happiness.

Her own voice was a cracked, desperate whisper when she finally spoke, the sound raw and broken in the heavy silence. She looked from Vivi's pale face to Kevin's shadowed one, her last shred of denial pleading for a reprieve she knew in her bones would not come.

"Was it like that for you?"

Vivi flinched as if the words had been a physical blow. She wouldn't meet Zoe's eyes at first. Marc's hand found hers instantly, his thumb stroking her knuckles in a gesture of fierce, quiet protection. When Vivi finally looked up, her clear gray-blue eyes were swimming with unshed tears, her composure utterly gone. "Illyria," she whispered, the name of her beautiful world. "Beautiful. The sun was always setting; the sea was always warm. And a prison." Her voice broke. "He was... perfect. And he was empty. Just lines from a play, over and over."

Zoe's world, already cracked, shattered into a million irreparable pieces. At Vivi's confession, she saw Marc's face slacken with a dawning horror, the broken pieces of Vivi's past, the lies and the withdrawals, finally clicking into place for him in the most awful way imaginable.

Then Kevin spoke, his voice rough and low, scraped raw. *"The Music of the Night."* His words were laced with self-loathing so profound it made Zoe's stomach clench. "She promised me my darkness was beautiful. That pain was a gift." He chanced a look at Sarah, his expression stripped bare, raw with a new, terrifying vulnerability that had never been there before. "A beautiful, seductive lie to keep me drowning in the dark."

Sarah's professional composure crumbled. Her face went pale as she finally understood the trustworthy, supernatural source of the deep depression she had helped him fight. A parasite that fed on his suffering.

Zoe felt the truth of their words resonate in her own bones, a sick, echoing chime. Illyria. The Opera House. The Fairy Tale Kingdom. Different sets, different characters, same predator. Same beautiful, gilded trap.

She had been walking willingly, happily, into a monster's jaws, convinced of a lover's embrace. The realization was a physical agony, a knife twisting deep in her gut. She let out a small, choked sob, the sound torn from her throat, and buried her face in her hands. The heavy, magical silk of her ballgown, which had been a dream an hour ago, was now a shroud.

The silence that followed was different, no longer tense and expectant but heavy, weighted with shared trauma and the impossible new reality they all now inhabited. This secret wasn't Cate's anymore. But theirs. They were all in this together, bound by the theater's terrible, beautiful secret.

Everyone in the room looked from Zoe's shattered, sobbing form to Cate, the woman who had brought them all to this breaking point. She had risked everything, her credibility, her career, to force this moment of painful truth. Now they needed to know why. They needed to know what came next.

Tyler was the first to speak. He flipped to a clean page in his notebook, his pen hovering above the paper. The cynical journalist was gone, vanished in the face of an impossible truth. In his place sat a grimly focused investigator facing a story he could never write, an assignment he could never have imagined. His voice was steady, practical, a small, solid rock in the swirling chaos of emotion that filled the room. The familiar scratch of his pen against the page was the only sound.

"Fine," he said as his gaze locked on Cate, his eyes clear and sharp. "Let's say I'm on board. Let's say I believe all of this." He took a breath. "What, exactly, is this thing? And how do we fight it?"

TWENTY-ONE

TYLER'S ACCEPTANCE

The six words settled over the cramped air of Cate's office, a question that felt more like a stone dropped into the deep, still water of their shock. *What, exactly, is this thing?*

Tyler's world had come undone. The whole structure of it, built on a foundation of verifiable sources and hard evidence, had been carefully and completely dismantled in the space of an hour. Witches pulled from a play. Actors snatched out of reality. Magic, a real and hungry thing, living in the very bones of this old theater, a story he would have killed on principle, a lead so impossible it defied belief. And yet, he now understood with a certainty that settled deep in his gut, it was a fact. A journalist, when faced with a new, terrifying fact, didn't have the luxury of freezing. He opened his notebook.

The insistent scratching of his pen was the only sound that dared to move. It cut through the thick, shared atmosphere of disbelief and stale coffee, a small engine of order in a world gone mad. His fingers curled around the familiar, worn leather of the notebook's cover, a smooth, solid anchor in the swirling chaos. Where a stunned paralysis seemed to grip the others, a grim, familiar focus descended on him. He would treat the impossible the only way he knew how. He would treat it like a source—a hostile one.

"Okay." He was no longer the bewildered boyfriend, the cynical observer. He was the investigator, landed in the middle of a case with no precedent, no files, anything. He looked at Vivi, then at Kevin, his expression scrubbed clean of pity with the look of a man gathering intelligence before a storm. "Walk me through it. The entity. Orsino, Christine, whatever it wants to call itself. It's a predator. Predators have patterns. They have a hunting ground, a preferred prey, a method."

Vivi flinched, her arms pulling tight around her body as if to hold herself together. The question was a clinical instrument, probing a wound that was still bleeding. Marc's hand found hers, his knuckles white, his body a silent, solid wall between her and the memory.

Seeing the fresh ripple of terror on her face, the way her breath hitched, Tyler felt a shift inside him. The strategist took over from the interrogator. "Vivi." He held her gaze, his own firm but stripping away the clinical distance, making it a connection instead of an examination. "Your job isn't to go back there. Your job is to be an expert witness to what it did to you. Please tell us how it works so we can determine the best method for disassembling it. We're the ones who will get our hands dirty. Can you do that for us?"

The change in his approach was subtle, yet it rearranged the atmosphere in the room. He hadn't called her a victim, a survivor, or any of the other words that would have made her smaller. He'd called her an expert. He saw the slightest flicker of strength return to her eyes, a straightening of her spine. The terror didn't vanish, but it receded enough to let a grim purpose find its footing. She gave a single, sharp nod.

"It feeds on desire. For me," Vivi confessed, "desire for a perfect, painless romance. The kind you only read about. It gave me exactly what I thought I wanted."

Tyler's pen flew across the page.

Desire = Bait

He turned his attention to Kevin, who sat hunched in his chair, his shoulders curved under a weight only he could feel. His face was a thundercloud of self-loathing. "Kevin?"

Kevin didn't look up from his study of the floorboards. "It validated my pain," he rasped, the word scraped raw from his throat. "It told me my depression was beautiful. That all that suffering was art. It never offered happiness. It offered a better, more romantic kind of misery."

Psychological validation.

Tyler wrote it down; the words were stark on the clean, white page. He drew a hard line under them twice. This thing was clever. It didn't just offer a generic heaven; it custom-built a paradise from the pieces of a person's specific hell. He looked back at Vivi, pressing forward now that she had a foothold.

"You said it was a garden," his voice regaining its analytical edge. "A perfect, sun-drenched coast. Did anything ever change? Or was it the same day, on a loop?"

"The same day," she confirmed, a tremor working its way through her. "The stars never moved from their spots in the sky. The music from the ballroom never changed its tune on a loop. A perfect, beautiful loop."

Static environment. Repetitive loop.

Good. That was a system limitation. That was a crack in the facade—a vulnerability.

He pivoted back to his brother. "You said your mirror was in the basement. It became a cage. What were the bars made of? Metaphorically."

Kevin finally lifted his head. His intense blue eyes were dark with a remembered horror, a place Tyler had never been allowed to see. "A labyrinth. It felt safe when I first found it. Comforting, even. But the longer I stayed, the more I realized I was getting increasingly lost. The bars were my own isolation. It promised me a sanctuary from the world, but a prettier prison cell."

Isolation as a control mechanism.

Tyler's pen scratched furiously, a makeshift map of this impossible territory taking shape on the page. He drew two columns, one for Vivi and one for Kevin, and began listing the parallels—the pieces of the puzzle that fit together.

Bait: Tailored desire. Environment: Perfect, static loop. Method: Isolation and validation. Weakness: Cannot create, only reflect. It's hollow.

The words seemed to glow on the paper.

"It can't improvise," Vivi added, her voice gaining a measure of strength. She was reclaiming her own power, one observation at a time. "When I asked Orsino a question that wasn't in the script of *Twelfth Night*, he couldn't answer. He'd repeat a line of poetry. He was an echo."

"Christine was the same," Kevin agreed, a grim understanding dawning on his face, chasing some of the shadows away. "She could only talk about beautiful sorrow. Anything outside of that, anything normal, and she had no response."

"So, it's a parasite that uses the source material of the play as its script," Tyler murmured, the pieces clicking together in his head. He was thinking aloud now, the journalist building his thesis. "It can't generate original content. It can only perform." He drew a sharp circle around the words *PERFORMANCE* and *HOLLOW*. "That's its weakness. It's a lie. Reality is the one thing it can't replicate. Reality is imperfect. It changes. It's messy."

Sarah nodded from her corner, her therapist's mind finally latching onto a workable framework. "Its power is in the victim's willing participation," she clarified, her voice calm and clear. "It creates a feedback loop. The more you believe in the fantasy, the more real it feels, and the more you isolate from the very things that could break the spell. Things like genuine, complicated human connection."

"And it's tied to a physical object," Tyler added, tapping his pen on the page with a sharp, definitive click. "The mirror. Vivi, you broke yours. Kevin, you broke yours. And the connection was severed." He looked straight at Vivi. "How did you break it?"

"With the roses Marc gave me for opening night," her voice soft now, full of a meaning that had nothing to do with strategy. She glanced at Marc, and a whole universe of feeling passed between them in a single, silent look. A real-world symbol of imperfect, hard-won love, used to destroy a fantasy one.

"And you?" he asked Kevin.

"I smashed it," Kevin said. "With my fist."

Physical destruction severs the connection.

He underlined it three times. This was their kill condition.

"Not here."

Cate's voice, low and humming with command, cut through their frantic theorizing. She had been standing by the door the whole time, a silent, imposing guardian of the threshold. Now she pushed off the wall, her eyes burning with a new, urgent intensity that made the hair on Tyler's arms stand up.

"This is all theoretical," her gaze sweeping over them, lingering for a moment on the frantic scribbles in Tyler's notebook. "We are talking about strategy in a war room a mile from the front. It's useless. We need to be at the scene of the crime."

A fresh wave of fear and sharpness washed over the room.

"Cate, no," Vivi pleaded, her voice cracking with the memory. "Not her dressing room. The mirror is active. You can feel it from the hallway."

"Exactly," Cate's expression was grim as a winter sky. "This entity is escalating. It has Zoe. We aren't going to sit up here and let it get comfortable. We are going to take the fight to it. Now. All of us."

The command was absolute, leaving no room for argument. The transition was immediate, a silent, grim procession filing out of the small office and into the hallway. Their footsteps on the old wooden stairs were a somber, uneven rhythm, the house groaning under the weight of their new, terrible purpose. Tyler put a hand on Zoe's shoulder, where she was still curled into herself on the worn sofa. Her body was trembling with silent sobs, her spirit lost somewhere in the wreckage of her new reality. She was in no condition to walk.

"I've got her," Tyler said to Cate, his voice low. Without another word, he scooped Zoe up into his arms. She was shockingly light, a fragile bundle of silk and despair. She buried her face in his chest, her tears immediately soaking the fabric of his shirt, and he held her tight, a fierce, protective instinct surging through him like a current. He followed the others, his steps sure and steady as he descended the stairs.

Zoe's dressing room was a sacred space that had been violated. The air was thick with the scent of her life, a mix of floral perfume, the faint chemical tang of hairspray, and the lingering sweetness of the powder that dusted her vanity. On a rack, her clothes hung in a riot of bright, cheerful colors. A pair of worn-out dance shoes was tucked into a corner, their soles scuffed from hours of hopeful work. It was a room that vibrated with optimism, a stark, painful contrast to the predatory object that dominated the far wall.

The mirror.

It looked like a mirror, an ornate, gilded antique that could have been a prop from any number of plays. But now, they all saw it for what it truly was. A predator's lure. A monster's mouth, open and waiting to swallow its prey whole. The air near it felt colder, thinner, humming with a silent, hungry energy that prickled the skin. A half-finished mug of tea sat on the vanity, a cheerful cartoon cat on its side, its contents now forgotten. A small monument to a life interrupted.

Tyler gently set Zoe down in her vanity chair. She remained there, a pale spectator to the fight for her own soul. He stood beside her, his hand resting on her shoulder, a silent, anchoring promise.

The group gathered in the cramped space, a strange coalition of the walking wounded—a lighting designer whose art was based on revealing truth. A therapist trained to navigate the labyrinths of the mind. Two actors who had survived this monster's embrace. A journalist who was rewriting his entire understanding of reality. And two survivors from a different kind of violent play, their past a dark map of this place's dangers. Reflected in the glass, they looked like the cast of a play no one would ever believe, a strange, desperate army getting its first look at the enemy.

Tyler opened his notebook to a fresh page, the practicalities of his nature a shield against the creeping dread that emanated from the glass. He drew a series of boxes, organizing their fear into a flowchart.

"Okay," his voice low and steady, pulled their focus away from the hypnotic glass and onto him. "Here's the plan. We have to treat this like a deprogramming. An intervention. But for a supernatural entity." He assigned their roles, giving each person's fear a specific function, turning their terror into a tool.

"Vivi, Kevin." He looked at them both, seeing not the survivors but the soldiers. "You two are our primary witnesses. You've been inside. You know the terrain. Your job is to tell us every detail about how the fantasy feels, what its hooks are. What specific, real-world thing broke you out of it?"

He looked at Cate and Malcolm, the theater's haunted guardians. "You're the historical experts. You know the magic of this place better than anyone. You know its history, its rules. Any information on weaknesses, on how to fight back, that comes from you."

He turned to Sarah, whose calm, analytical presence was a balm in the tense room. "You're the profiler. Your job is to analyze the psychological tactics. It's preying on Zoe's need for perfection and validation. We need a counter-strategy. How do we arm her, psychologically, to resist it from the inside?"

Finally, his gaze fell on Marc. "Marc, you and I are logistics. We plan the operation. We figure out the tools. The timing. How to get Zoe out and how to seal the gate behind her for good."

A start. A tangible, multi-step action plan laid out in black ink, a fragile shield against the raw, consuming terror of a moment ago, but a shield, nonetheless. They were no longer victims cowering in an office. They were a task force.

Tyler stood in front of the ornate mirror, his notebook held firmly in his hand. He looked at the faces reflected alongside his own, this strange, impossible family bound together by a shared, terrible secret. He could see Zoe's reflection in the glass, a pale, haunted ghost of the vibrant woman she was, her eyes wide and lost.

He tapped his pen on the page, the sound a sharp, definitive click in the tense, humming silence.

"Okay." His voice was low and steady, as if addressing his troops before the first battle. "Phase one, intelligence gathering, is complete. Phase two is containment. That starts now."

His gaze was fixed, not on his own reflection, but on the empty, shimmering space in the mirror where a prince used to be, a vacancy that was waiting.

CHAPTER

TWENTY-TWO

THE FAIRY TALE TRAP

The voices were a low, urgent hum around her, a swarm of anxious honeybees that had forgotten how to make anything sweet. Tyler's was the one that cut the deepest, sharp and practical, slicing their shared nightmare into a neat, numbered list he probably saw on a whiteboard in his head. *Containment. Deprogramming. Logistics.* His words were meant to build a fortress of logic and reason around her, but to Zoe, they were just another kind of cage. Her skin crawled, the heavy silk of her ballgown feeling less like a costume and more like a straitjacket woven from their good intentions. In their loving, worried eyes, she was no longer a person. She was a problem to be solved, a tactical objective—a broken thing.

Zoe remained in the vanity chair, a ghost in her own wake, watching her friends, her jury, all reflected in the gilded surface of the mirror. Vivi's face was a mask of painful empathy, her actress's training failing to hide the raw sorrow in her eyes. Kevin's expression was a grim mirror of his own dark journeys, a recognition that scared Zoe more than anything. And Cate's was a familiar, haunted intensity, the look of a general who knew this battlefield all too well. Their concern was a physical thing, a thick, suffocating blanket of Southern humidity that promised to choke the air from her lungs. They had taken her beautiful, secret world—a world that felt more real than this one—and painted it black. They had twisted her prince, her Adrian, into a monster.

And the worst part, the part that gnawed at her insides with teeth of ice, was that she believed them. A small, treacherous part of her believed every single word.

But belief was a feeling, a vapor. But no proof.

A tiny spark of defiance, stubborn as a dandelion in a sidewalk crack, pushed its way through the ashes of her humiliation. This was her dream; they were maligning it. Her love. She couldn't let their bitter, broken histories be the final word on her own. She had to know, for herself. She couldn't spend the rest of her life wondering if they were right, living with this shred of hope, this splinter of doubt lodged deep in her heart. She had to go back, one last time. Not as a willing princess swept up in a fairy tale, but as an executioner. She would ask the hard questions, push against the flawless walls of her world, and find out for certain if it was a home or a prison. She had to give Adrian one last chance to be real. This was the only way she could ever truly leave him, or the only way she could ever truly stay.

"Stop."

The word was a choked whisper, brittle as a dried leaf,

but it cut through Tyler's strategy session like a shard of glass. Every head turned to her. Seven faces, a constellation of pity and alarm, all fixed on her, the broken star at the center of their universe.

"Please," she begged, her voice finding a sliver of strength with the same tone she used to use on stage for tragic heroines, but this was no performance. "... stop. I'm currently unable to do this. I need to be alone."

Tyler's pragmatic mask slipped, crumbling to reveal the raw, desperate worry underneath. His face was a roadmap of fear for her. "Zoe, that's the last thing you need. We're not leaving you alone with... with that thing." He gestured at the mirror, his hand a tight fist, as if he wanted to punch the reflection itself.

"It's my dressing room," she said and pushed herself to her feet, the movement clumsy and graceless in the heavy gown. It felt alien to her now, a costume for a part she no longer knew how to play. Next to the mirror, on the corner of the vanity, sat a cheap plastic tiara from a community theater production of a forgotten musical she'd done years ago, its fake rhinestones dull under the bare bulbs. That felt more real, more her, than the diamond-bright promise in the glass. "And it's my life. You've all had your say. Now I need to think. Please. Just go."

A silent, frantic argument passed between them, a current of unspoken words and shared history. Cate's jaw was tight, a clear veto hardening her lips. She had seen this magic turn deadly, and her entire being screamed against leaving a soldier alone on the field. But Sarah, the therapist, ever the calm center, gave a nearly imperceptible nod. She understood. You couldn't force someone to accept a truth they weren't ready to see. You could only walk with them to the door and pray that they chose to open it.

Cate saw the nod, and the fight seemed to drain out of her. Her shoulders slumped in a rare admission of defeat. "Fine," she clipped out, her voice tight with suppressed fear. "Ten minutes, Zoe. That's it. Then we're coming back in. Don't you dare do anything foolish."

They filed out, a reluctant, protective rear guard, their backward glances heavy with unspoken warnings that became weights on her shoulders. Tyler was the last to leave. He paused in the doorway, his handsome, cynical face a mess of love and terror that almost broke her. "Zoe..."

"I need a minute, Tyler," she whispered, turning away so he couldn't see the lie blooming in her eyes. "I promise."

The click of the door closing behind him was the loudest sound she had ever heard, a final, definitive snap that separated her from their world and left her in her own.

Alone. The silence of the small, cluttered room was a relief and a terror all at once—a messy, imperfect space— and she breathed it in like clean air after a storm. It smelled of spilled setting powder, stale coffee, and the faint, comfortable scent of old fabric. A half-eaten bag of barbecue potato chips sat on her counter, forgotten. A single, sad-looking bobby pin lay on the floor near her worn-out sneakers. Real. Messy. Flawed.

And for a moment, she couldn't bear it—the sheer, unvarnished reality of agony.

Her gaze, helpless as a moth to a flame, snapped back to the mirror. The air around was still; the ornate, gilded frame an invitation to a place where there were no half-eaten bags of chips, no scuffed sneakers, and no lonely bobby pins on the floor. This was it. Her last chance to prove them all wrong. Her last chance to save the one perfect, beautiful thing in her life. This wasn't an act of addiction, she told herself fiercely, trying to drown out the voice that called her a liar. This was an act of faith.

Or maybe this was an act of self-destruction. At this point, standing on the precipice, she wasn't entirely sure there was a difference.

Taking a deep, shuddering breath that was tearing her apart, she walked toward the glass. Her reflection walked with her, a pale, determined woman in a fairy-tale dress. She didn't wait for it to shimmer, for the invitation to be extended. She was done waiting. She closed her eyes and plunged her hand forward, bracing for the familiar, cool surface.

But there was no surface. The transition was instantaneous and absolute. One moment, the scent of her own life, of powder and chips, was in her nose. Next, it vanished, replaced by an overwhelming, cloyingly sweet perfume of a million roses—a scent as powerful as a physical presence. The muffled, ordinary sounds of the theater —the creak of the building, the hum of the lights—gave way to the soaring notes of a string orchestra playing a waltz she knew by heart.

She was no longer in her cramped dressing room. She was standing on a vast marble balcony under a sky of impossible, twilight purple, a color that didn't exist in the real world's palette. Below her, a garden of blood-red roses, each one flawless and without a single thorn, stretched to a horizon that never seemed to get any closer. The ballgown, which had felt so heavy a moment ago, was now light as air, its silk whispering against her skin like a lover's promise. It shimmered with an inner light, a perfect, pristine garment that would never wrinkle or stain.

And he was there.

Prince Adrian stood by the balustrade, his back to her, looking out over his perfect, unchanging kingdom. He turned, a slow, practiced movement she had seen a hundred times, and his face lit up with that familiar, breathtaking smile, a smile of pure, uncomplicated adoration, a smile that had healed every wound she'd ever had. For one heart-stopping moment, all her fears, all her friends' warnings, melted away like snow in the sun. This was her Adrian. This was her love. They were wrong. They had to be.

"My princess," he breathed, his voice the deep, poetic baritone she had fallen for over and over again. "You have returned to me. I knew your heart could not stay away for long."

He glided toward her, his movements impossibly graceful, each step a note in a ballet. He took her hands in his, his touch warm and firm, his skin impossibly smooth. It all felt so real. The last tendrils of doubt receded, burned away by the warmth of his gaze.

"Adrian," she began, her own voice trembling, thick with a hope that felt dangerous. "We need to talk."

His smile didn't waver, but was as constant as the twilight stars in the purple sky. "Of course, my love. We can speak of the stars, of the music of our souls, of the eternity we shall spend together in this moment."

The first crack in the flawless facade. The script. It was a line she had heard before. She pushed past the sudden chill that pricked her skin.

"No," she said, gently pulling her hands from his. The movement was a rebellion. "I want to talk about... about a future. A real future."

A brief, subtle wavering passed through his perfect blue eyes; it wasn't exactly confusion, but rather a kind of blank incomprehension, the look of a machine encountering a line of code it couldn't process. For a split second, the perfection of the sky behind him seemed to lose its depth, becoming flat and painted.

"But our future is this, my love," his voice recovered its melodic cadence as he gestured with a graceful sweep of his arm to the flawless garden and the glittering castle beyond. "This moment, this love, forever."

"But people don't live in moments," she insisted, her heart starting to pound a frantic rhythm against her ribs. This was the test. "They live in days and weeks and years. They face challenges. They make mistakes. They... they grow old." The words were profanity here, a vulgarity spoken in a holy place. "What will we do when my hair has turned silver? When have we faced our first great trial and carried the scars of it on our hearts?"

Adrian's smile remained, but was now a fixed, beautiful, terrifying thing. It didn't reach his eyes. The light of understanding, of genuine consideration, wasn't there. He was a statue carved from living marble, breathtaking and completely inert.

"My love for you is a constant flame that time cannot quench," he recited, his voice full of a practiced passion that now sounded hollow, rehearsed. "Your beauty is a star that will never fade from my heavens. There are no trials in this kingdom, my darling, only joy. There are no scars, only perfection."

The words, which once made her swoon, now stung like hailstones. He wasn't answering her question. He was deflecting with poetry, offering her another pretty, empty box. He couldn't answer her. The dread that had taken root in Cate's office returned, wrapping its icy tendrils around her heart. Vivi was right. He was an echo. An echo of a story, nothing more.

Zoe took a step back, the movement involuntary, a retreat from a beauty that had suddenly become grotesque. "What if I want scars?" she whispered, the question a desperate, final plea for him to be real, to be more than the lines he was written to speak. "What if I want to build something new with you? Something that isn't already here? What if," and the word caught in her throat, the most forbidden concept of all in this world of eternal courtship, "what if I want a child?"

At that, his programming seemed to shatter. The handsome, beloved face went utterly blank. The smile vanished. The poetic light in his eyes died. For a terrifying second, there was nothing behind them at all, just a void. The orchestra, which had been playing its endless waltz, faltered, a single sour note hanging in the air like a question before the melody clumsily resumed.

Then, as quickly, his programming seemed to reboot, defaulting to its core function. His expression shifted, not to understanding or tenderness, but to a look of intense, predatory focus. He had registered her hesitation, her pulling away, not as a question to be answered, but as a flight risk to be managed.

His response wasn't verbal but physical.

He closed the distance between them in a single, fluid motion, the most graceful, romantic, and utterly terrifying movement she had ever seen. His hands came up to cup her face, his thumbs stroking her cheekbones with a mechanical precision that sent a shiver of horror through her.

"You are overwrought, my love," he murmured, his voice a low, hypnotic croon designed to soothe and pacify. "You speak of sorrows and shadows that do not exist here. Let me remind you of the only truth. The only reality."

This was it. The perfect seduction. The final weapon in the fantasy's arsenal.

His lips descended on hers. The kiss was flawless, technically perfect—a masterclass in romance taught by a phantom professor, hitting every note of passion, tenderness, and desperate longing that a storybook could describe. But it was utterly, completely hollow. There was no response to her own trembling uncertainty, no gentle query in his touch, no give and take. A kiss was performed *at* her, not shared *with* her. His hands moved from her face to her shoulders, then slid down her back, pulling her flush against him. His touch was firm, possessive, a cage of flawless technique designed to overwhelm and subdue.

She was a doll being expertly maneuvered by a master puppeteer. The overwhelming scent of his sterile cologne and the suffocating perfume of the thornless roses filled her senses, thick and cloying. She was drowning in perfection, suffocating in a dream that had become a nightmare.

With a surge of panicked adrenaline born of pure terror, she pushed against his chest. "No."

The beautiful dream shattered into a million sharp, glittering pieces of glass. This wasn't a prince but a trap. This wasn't a kingdom but a gilded cage. And the man holding her, the man she had loved with all her broken heart, wasn't her soulmate.

He was the warden.

With a raw, terrified scream that tore from her throat, she shoved him with all her strength. The force of it broke his hold, and he stumbled back a single, graceful step, his balance perfect even in retreat. The mask of passion fell away completely, replaced by that same blank, uncomprehending stare. He was waiting for his next cue, a beautiful machine paused in its function.

Zoe didn't wait to give it to him. She turned and fled. She scrambled back toward the spot on the balcony where she had entered, her breath coming in ragged, sobbing gasps, the heavy silk of her gown tangling around her legs. Behind her, she heard his voice, no longer seductive or poetic, but now a flat, monotone command, the machine showing its true face at last.

"Return," it said.

She threw herself backward, into the invisible seam in the air, praying it was still there. For a horrifying, heart-stopping second, she felt a resistance, a thick, syrupy pull as if the world itself was trying to hold her, to drag her back into its perfect, airless prison. Then, with a wrenching pop that tore her soul in two, she was through.

She stumbled and fell, landing hard on the worn carpet of her own dressing room. The scent of spilled powder, stale chips, and old fabric filled her lungs, the most beautiful, most wonderful smell in the entire world. The silence was absolute, a blessed, imperfect quiet that was all her own.

Shaking uncontrollably, she pushed herself up and looked in the mirror. Her own face stared back at her. Pale, tear-streaked, her mascara running in black rivers down her cheeks. Her ballgown, once shimmering and pristine, was now rumpled and sad, a gaudy costume for a tragedy. She was no longer a princess-in-waiting. She was a woman who had woken from a beautiful, terrible dream. A woman who had escaped a prison she had willingly, lovingly, built for herself.

The perfect love was a lie.

And now, she was utterly, terrifyingly alone with the ruins of her life and the messy, imperfect, frightening reality she had no choice but to face.

TWENTY-THREE

REAL VULNERABILITY

The green room was a pocket of weary silence deep in the heart of the theater, a stillness so heavy as the humid air before a summer storm. Its shabby comfort seemed to know all her secrets and judge none of them. This was a room made for the messy, imperfect business of being human, and right now, Zoe had never hated a place more.

Tyler had convinced the others to give them space, promising to check in after the ten minutes Cate had allotted had long since passed.

She sat curled on the sofa, a small knot of misery lost in the folds of her magnificent ballgown. The iridescent silk was a cruel joke in the isolated glow of the single lamp someone had left burning. The fantasy had shattered. The prince was a program. The castle was nothing but a cage. She had pushed against the bars of that world and found them unyielding, had looked for a soul and found only a script. The escape she'd felt from Adrian's hollow perfection had been a short, sharp spike of triumph. Now, back in the plain, honest reality of the theater, there was only the crushing weight of what came after. The terror was gone, and in its place was a vast, hollow ache. She had nothing. Not the flawless dream, and indeed not the courage to face the waking world.

The hum of the hallway vending machine was a low, mournful drone, the only sound in her drab, purgatorial existence. She'd fled her dressing room and the unblinking eye of the mirror, only to end up here. She didn't know how long she'd been sitting there, listening to the thin sound of her own breathing, when a quiet noise from the doorway pulled her back from the deep.

Tyler stood there, his tall frame a silhouette against the dim hallway light. He wasn't carrying a sword or a scepter. He was holding two steaming, styrofoam cups. Vending machine coffee. The most mundane, real, and unimpressive offering in the whole world. He walked in, his steps soft on the tired carpet, and sat on the far end of the sofa. He left a careful, respectful ocean of space between them. He nudged one of the cups across the coffee table in her direction. The styrofoam felt warm and slightly pliant in her cold hand, a flimsy anchor in the swirling chaos of her mind. And yet, this was an anchor.

"It's probably burnt," he whispered. "That machine sounds like it's on its last legs."

She didn't move. She stared at the steam curling from the cheap cup like a fragile prayer.

"I talked to Vivi." his voice was now stripped of its usual cynical armor. "And Kevin. They told me what it's like. The... the perfection. How easy it is. How it gives you exactly what you think you want, so you never have to do any of the work."

Zoe flinched. The word *work* struck her with a dull, heavy force.

"I can't compete with that," Tyler said, and his honesty was so raw it felt almost brutal. He leaned forward, resting his elbows on his knees, his gaze fixed on the worn patch of carpet between his feet. "I can't give you a fairy tale, Zoe. I can't promise you a world without consequences, bad days, or silences that feel too long. I'm all tangled up inside. I'm cynical, and I'm difficult, and half the time I'm not sure I'm worthy of the kind of light you carry into a room."

His confession hung in the air between them, a fragile and terrifying thing. He finally looked up, and she saw the same fear churning in his eyes that she felt in her own gut. He was as scared as she was.

"All I can offer you is the messy, complicated, real thing," he went on, his voice thick with an emotion she had never heard from him before. "I can offer you arguments about whose turn it is to take out the trash, and burnt coffee from a dying vending machine, and me, being terrified that I'm going to screw this all up. I can offer you the work. However, I will work *with* you. I love you, Zoe. And that's the only real thing I have to give."

Those words shattered the last fragile piece of her composure. A raw, ragged sob tore from her throat, the sound of a lifetime of performance cracking right down the middle. Tears streamed down her face, hot and fast, smearing the last of her stage makeup into a mess of black and pink.

"I don't know how," she wept, the words ripped from the most hidden, hollow part of her. "Tyler, I don't know how to be real. I only know how to perform. Happy Zoe. Optimistic Zoe. The perfect girlfriend, the perfect Cinderella. It's all I am. Underneath it... There's nothing there. I'm a costume on a hanger."

She expected him to argue, to reassure her, to tell her she was wrong.

He didn't.

He listened, his expression softening with a deep, aching tenderness that hurt more than any judgment ever could. When her sobs finally quieted into ragged, hiccupping breaths, he spoke, his voice so gentle, almost a whisper.

"Then we can stop," he said. "Right now. I'll walk you to your car, and you can go home. You don't have to do or be anything you're not ready for. This is your choice. All of it."

That was it—the moment of truth. Adrian had never offered her a choice. He had provided only a single, perfect, predetermined path. Tyler was offering her an exit. He was handing her the key to her own cage. He was telling her it was okay to be afraid, OK to be a mess, and okay not to be ready.

Her choice.

Slowly, deliberately, she uncurled herself from the tight, protective ball she had made of her body. The silence stretched out, filled only with the sound of her own unsteady breathing and the soft patter of rain that had finally begun against the high windows. He didn't move. He waited, his gaze steady, his heart laid bare, giving her all the space and all the power in the world.

She reached out a trembling hand and laid it on his knee. The contact was a jolt of simple, solid reality. The rough texture of his jeans, the warmth of his body underneath. It wasn't magic; this was ... real.

And then, with a surge of courage she didn't know she possessed, she closed the distance. She slid across the worn velvet of the sofa and pressed her mouth to his.

The kiss was a clumsy, beautiful wreck, wet with her tears and his unspoken relief. Her nose bumped into his. His hand, when it came up to cup her face, was hesitant and uncertain, nothing like Adrian's flawless, practiced passion. But this was a thousand times better. Truly.

He responded not with the smooth confidence of a prince, but with the fumbling, earnest gratitude of a man who had had his most desperate prayer answered. His lips were soft, questioning. His hand trembled slightly against her cheek.

"Zoe," he whispered against her mouth, a question and a plea and a prayer all in one.

"It's okay," she whispered back, giving him the same permission he had given her. "I want to try. I want to learn how to do the work."

His other hand came up to frame her face, and his next kiss was deeper, surer, but still so incredibly gentle. There was no algorithm here. No script. Just two terrified people choosing to be brave together.

The journey from the sofa to the floor was a tangle of awkward limbs and rumpled silk. Her ballgown, designed for grand entrances, was a clumsy, impossible barrier—a button on his worn cotton shirt caught on the shimmering fabric, and instead of a smooth, graceful disrobing, a fumbling, patient process ensued, punctuated by whispered questions that felt more intimate than any touch.

"Is this okay?"

"Yes."

A moment of hesitation, a breath held. "What about this?"

A shaky, breathless laugh escaped her lips. "Yes, Tyler. Yes."

He was so careful, so attentive to every shift in her expression, every catch in her breath. He wasn't performing seduction. He was asking for access. He was checking in. He was ensuring she was still making this choice, choosing him, every single step of the way. When his skin finally met hers, the contact was warm and solid, a grounding heat against the lingering, sterile cold of the fantasy. The room was hazy with dust motes dancing in the single beam of lamplight, each one a tiny world oblivious to the others.

He wasn't a chiseled statue. He was a real, living, breathing man. His body was lean but solid, with the faint shadow of ribs under his skin and a soft scattering of hair on his chest. There were no soaring violins, only the sound of their own ragged breathing and the frantic, beautiful rhythm of their hearts.

Awkward. Messy. The old wool rug smelled of time

and countless footsteps. At one point, his knee bumped a stack of scripts, sending them sliding to the floor with a soft whoosh of paper. They both froze, then looked at each other, and a small, genuine laugh bubbled up out of her. He smiled back, a real, unguarded smile of pure, unadulterated joy. In that moment of shared, imperfect reality, she felt a connection more profound than a thousand of Adrian's perfect, empty declarations.

When he finally moved inside her with slow, deliberate care, there was a question in itself. He watched her face, his eyes searching hers, waiting for her confirmation. She gave it with a nod, a whispered "yes," and the tightening of her arms around his back, feeling the solid grain of the old floorboards through the thin layers of fabric and memory between them.

This wasn't a fantasy. This was work and communication. This was slow, patient, and sometimes a clumsy process of two people learning each other's rhythms, of finding a shared tempo in the dark. This was tender and hesitant. Then, as trust built between them like a vine finding purchase, it became searching, hungry, and breathtakingly real. A discovery, not a performance. And it filled the hollow, empty spaces inside her with something warm and solid and trustworthy.

Afterward, they lay tangled together on the floor, her ball gown pooled around them like a defeated, shimmering cloud. His arm was a warm, heavy weight over her waist. Her head was pillowed on his chest, and she could feel the slow, steady beat of his heart against her ear, the most beautiful music she had ever heard.

He was real. This was real.

She stared up at the water-stained acoustic tiles of the ceiling, a cracked and imperfect map of past storms. She felt the solid, living warmth of the man beside her. She had touched something real, something that demanded her presence, her vulnerability, and her work. And all was beautiful.

But in the humming stillness of the green room, another thought crept into the edges of her mind, a seductive whisper. This had been beautiful. But it had also been hard. Adrian was easy. Adrian was perfect. Adrian asked for nothing at all.

She had chosen the work. But was she strong enough to keep picking it, day after day?

The answer came in the form of a crash into the mirror.

CHAPTER

TWENTY-FOUR

OPENING NIGHT CRISIS

The five-minute call echoed through the backstage corridors, a lonely sound promising an end to something, or maybe a beginning. Zoe stood in the wings, feeling the magnificent pull of her Cinderella ballgown, a shroud of glitter and bone-deep dread. A damp chill had settled in her palms, and her stomach was a tight knot of sour worry. Beyond the heavy velvet curtain, the house lights were down. A two-hundred-seat theater held its breath, a single dark lung waiting for the magic she was supposed to deliver.

All she felt was the hollow ache of a lie.

Her skin was still a map of memory from Tyler's touch, a real and imperfect warmth that was both a balm and a quiet accusation. She had chosen him. She had selected the work, the beautiful and terrifying mess of real life. But as the first optimistic notes of the overture soared, the strings became a siren song from a country she no longer lived in. This music was from a world of easy answers and happiness that came with a guarantee. A little whisper of doubt, like a snake in the summer grass, moved through her veins. Had she made a mistake? Was she strong enough for the life she had chosen?

The curtain rose. The stage lights bloomed, a wall of manufactured sunshine that felt blindingly false.

From her place in the wings, she watched the opening scene unfold. The stepsisters wore their garish costumes, their voices sharp against the painted backdrop of a dreary kitchen. Everything was so perfect, every line and movement a testament to weeks of practice. A frantic pulse beat against her ribs. She caught a glimpse of Marc in the lighting booth high above, his face a mask of focus, his gaze darting between his board and the stage below. She saw Cate at the back of the house, a dark, still sentinel keeping watch. She knew Tyler was out there too, a warm presence somewhere in the velvet dark, watching her, trusting her.

Her cue was coming. Her entrance as Cinders, the girl whose hope was a stubborn, unkillable weed. Performance. That was a country she still knew by heart. She could do that.

She drew a long breath, borrowed a smile from a girl she used to be, one who believed in wishing on stars, and stepped into the light.

For the first fifteen minutes, the old magic of the stage held. The muscle memory of a hundred rehearsals took control of her limbs. She swept the prop hearth with a familiar grace, sang her wistful song about dreams with a voice that didn't betray the tremor in her soul, and hit every single mark. Her voice was clear, her movements fluid. The audience was a quiet, captivated sea. In the front row, a critic for the *Westgate Chronicle* scribbled a note in the dark, the faint scratch of his pen barely audible. *Reeves embodies a luminous, almost supernatural optimism.* He circled the word *mystical*, his brow furrowed in thought.

Backstage, in the humid, close-packed darkness smelling of rosin and hairspray, was where the real world tore at the seams.

A high, sharp scream cut through the dimness, slicing through the muffled swell of the orchestra, and was choked off quickly. Zoe, waiting for her next cue, caught a movement in her peripheral vision. One of the large, antique mirrors lining the backstage hallway, the one the dancers used to check their makeup, bloomed with a sickening, poison-green light. A young ensemble member stood before it, lipstick in hand, half changed for the next scene. For one horrible, stretched-out second, the mirror didn't show the dancer's reflection. It showed a place of wrong angles and screaming colors that hurt the eyes to see. A collective gasp rippled through the nearby crew. Then, as if a switch had been thrown, the mirror was a mirror again. But the dancer, Amelia, was gone. Her lipstick clattered to the floor, the slight sound unnaturally loud as it rolled to a stop by a discarded cable.

Danny Kim, the stage manager, whose face was ashen, was already speaking frantically into his headset. "We have a problem. Stage right. Amelia is..." His voice broke, strangled by a disbelief that was turning to horror.

Another pulse of light, this time from the opposite wing. An actor, dressed as a royal footman and waiting for his entrance, vanished in a silent flash of corrosive yellow. He was there one second, a solid, breathing person, and the next he was ... gone. His prop trumpet hit the concrete floor with a hollow clang. A strange, chemical smell filled the air, like ozone and sugar left too long on a hot stove.

Panic spread through the backstage crew like a fever.

Onstage, Zoe's carefully built performance fell apart. She could hear the frantic, terrified whispers cracking over Danny's headset, could see the wide-eyed terror on the face of a crew member peeking through the wings. The world was tilting on its axis. The solid ground of performance she had stood on her entire life was turning to soft, pulling mud.

Then the chaos bled through the curtain and onto the stage.

The enchanted pumpkin coach, a masterpiece of whimsy and stagecraft, unraveled. It shimmered, its solid form dissolving at the edges like a photograph left out in the sun, its cheerful orange bleeding out to a dead, pixelated gray. For a breath, the painted vines along its side seemed to twist into thorny, grasping things. The orchestra faltered, a single violin screeching a painful, untuned note as the conductor glanced backstage, his face pale with a confusion that was quickly souring into alarm.

A low murmur rolled through the audience, a wave of whispers that rustled through the darkness like dry leaves. The critic in the front row frowned, then jotted down another note. *Bold, deconstructionist technical effects. A bit much?* The woman beside him leaned toward her husband, her voice a tense whisper. "This seems broken."

A prop vase on the mantelpiece, filled with silk flowers, shattered. It didn't fall. It simply exploded outward in a spray of ceramic dust, a minor, violent punctuation to the growing dread. A shard of the broken prop skittered across the stage, its sharp edges glittering under the lights as it came to rest near the toe of her glass slipper.

Frozen mid-line, Zoe stared at the piece of debris on the floor. And in its small, dark, reflective surface, she didn't see the chaos of the stage lights or the panicked faces of her fellow actors. She saw a perfect, sun-drenched ballroom. She saw glittering chandeliers and graceful couples waltzing to a flawless orchestra. She saw Prince Adrian, standing at the far end of the hall, his face serene, his arms held open in a silent, patient invitation.

The truth didn't crash. It seeped into her, a flood that filled her lungs until she could not breathe, a weight that settled deep in her bones and threatened to splinter them.

This wasn't a random failure. This wasn't some terrible coincidence. This was a consequence. This was the bill for her secret world, arriving with payment demanded in full. The magic of the theater was an interconnected system, a single living body, and she had poisoned it. Her repeated, selfish journeys into a perfect, static world had introduced a sickness, a rot that was destabilizing the whole thing from the inside out. Or worse. This wasn't some delayed reaction, but a retaliation, a tantrum. A spurned prince, a spurned thing, was lashing out because she had chosen another. He was tearing her world apart piece by piece to get to her.

Her choices. Her secret. Her perfect, beautiful dream was a weapon, and she had pointed it at the heart of her own community. Amelia was gone because of her. The footman was gone because of her. The audience, now stirring from confusion into a very real alarm, was in danger because of her.

Her internal conflict wasn't about Tyler versus Adrian anymore. Her own selfish wants were set against the lives of her friends. This debt of guilt was so profound it felt bottomless.

This is because of me.

The thought wasn't a whisper, but a brand, burned into the softest part of her soul.

The spell of the performance was broken beyond repair. Onstage, the actor playing the prince finally broke character, his handsome face a mask of pure, unscripted fear. "Stop," he breathed into his mic, his voice shaking and thin. "Something's wrong."

As if summoned by the word, a stagehand, a kid barely out of high school, burst from the wings, his eyes wild with a terror that was utterly real. He ran to the center of the stage, right into the middle of the frozen, broken fairy tale.

"Lights up! Stop the show!" he screamed, his voice cracking with a panic so raw it echoed in the high, dark space above the stage.

That was the final confirmation. This wasn't a story anymore. This was a wreck. The critic in the front row dropped his pen with a soft thud. The audience gasped, a single, unified sound of dawning horror. A woman screamed. People rose from their seats, a dark mass of bodies stirring, getting ready to run.

Frozen on the chaotic stage, Zoe could only stare at the shard of broken ceramic. The ballroom shimmered within its surface, a beautiful, damning mirage. The weight of what she had done was a physical thing, pressing down on her, a crushing force that promised to break her into a thousand pieces.

From the wings, two figures burst through, their faces pale in the harsh, sudden light. Tyler and Cate. They had seen it all from the back of the house and had come running.

As they cleaned up the backstage area, Carmen appeared with a broom and dustpan. She swept up what looked like ordinary stage dust, but Tyler noticed she was carefully separating certain particles into a small envelope.

"What are you doing?" he asked.

Carmen looked at him steadily. "Collecting evidence," she said. "I've been doing it for thirty years. Little things that don't belong. Sand from beaches that don't exist. Flower petals in colors that nature never made." She sealed the envelope and wrote a date on it. "Someone needs to remember. Someone needs to keep track."

She patted his shoulder and walked away, leaving Tyler staring after her in dawning comprehension.

"Zoe!" Tyler shouted, his voice raw with a terror that tore through her.

Just as she looked up, her eyes meeting his across the disastrous stage, a final, overwhelming pulse of golden energy erupted from the very spot where she stood. This wave of pure gold heat blew her hair back from her face and made the very air sing a single, deafening note.

And a voice, not in her head, not a whisper on the wind, but amplified, booming through every single speaker in the Meridian Theatre's sound system with the whole, possessive force of a god, spoke with chilling, unwavering love.

"My princess. The real world is hurting you. It is time. Come home, forever."

TWENTY-FIVE

THE UNITED FRONT

A scream was tearing the soul out of the Meridian Theatre with a sound that had a shape, a high, keening shriek of magic let off its leash, a vibration that hummed deep in Vivi's bones. It harmonized with the audience's earthly terror, a panicked flood of people clawing for the exits. On the stage, time itself had broken. The actors were frozen like figures in a snow globe, their eyes wide and hollow, caught forever in a single gesture beneath the pulse of sickeningly colored lights. The air, thick with the electric tang of ozone and the smell of singed velvet, tasted of chewed-on foil.

This was pure chaos, but Cate Hart's voice sliced through the noise like a piece of sharpened flint. "Storage! Now! The ones we pre-staged in the west corridor closet!" she yelled, her face a taut mask of fierce, wrangled fear. Malcolm was already a blur of motion, a ring of old brass keys appearing in his hand as he bolted toward the back-stage corridors.

Marc's hand found hers, and his grip was a lifeline, a solid, grounding weight in the disorienting storm. His presence was the only thing that kept her feet on the floor as the familiar, honey-sweet whisper of Illyria seeped from a nearby prop mirror. An impossible coastline shimmered into view, painted over the distorted reflection of fleeing stagehands. Cate had called it a narrative feedback loop, a serpent swallowing its own tail. Zoe's desperate reach for perfection had fractured the theater's delicate system, and now its magic was scrambling to fix the error, trying to trap every soul inside their own perfect, permanent story.

"Amelia and Jon are gone," Danny Kim's voice cracked, his headset hanging crooked against his pale face. "The mirrors took them."

"We'll get them back," Cate said, leaving no space for doubt. She turned her laser focus on Vivi, Kevin, and Zoe, who were clustered near the ruined stage like a small, sad gathering of ghosts from traumas past and present. "This ends tonight. The loops have to be cut at the source. You three are the only ones who can do it. You have to go in, face them, and reject the lie. Out loud. With everything you've got."

Malcolm returned, his breathing labored, his arms filled with three ornate mirrors crusted with the grime of long neglect. Their surfaces swirled with a faint, sickly light. One held the image of a sun-drenched marble terrace. The second offered a glimpse into a candlelit cavern. The third held a glittering, flawless castle that seemed to hum with terrible perfection. Two weren't the originals, which had been destroyed, but similar antique replacements Cate had locked away, fearing they might one day be needed again. The cold from the glass seemed to leech the warmth from the air, and Vivi saw a thin film of condensation bead on the gilded frames, as if they were sweating with anticipation.

"Your partners are your anchors," Cate commanded. "Do not let go. This magic knows you. It knows the song your heart used to sing. It will offer you the one thing you thought you couldn't live without. You have to choose this world, out loud, where we all can hear you."

Marc squeezed her hand, his warmth a living shield against the promise of the past. She looked into his eyes and saw not a flicker of doubt, only a deep, unwavering trust that felt more real than the solid floor beneath her feet. She gave a slight, firm nod. She hadn't clawed her way out of Illyria's beautiful cage to watch its shadow swallow her friends whole.

"We're first," her voice more solid than the tremor in her heart. Marc helped her carry the Illyrian mirror, setting it down in a clear space amid the backstage wreckage. The others formed a tight, protective circle around them, their faces drawn and grim.

As she faced the glass, the shimmering landscape inside sharpened into focus. The marble terrace overlooking an impossible sea, the air thick with the scent of saltwater and the sweet perfume of oleander. And then there was Duke Orsino, his beauty a perfect, painful ache, his face a sculpture of tragic, pleading love.

His voice was a silken thread winding its way directly

into her mind—my Viola. Please do not leave me to this loneliness. Their love is work. It is painful. Mine is perfect, eternal adoration. Come back. Let me worship you.

The pull was a physical thing, a deep, resonant chord of memory that vibrated in her soul with the promise of being cherished without the messy effort of being known, of being loved without the terrifying, uncertain labor of it all. This lie she had nearly traded her life for was the story she had dog-eared with the promise of returning, only to find she'd lost the book somewhere along the way.

She felt Marc's grip tighten, a solid, real pressure against her palm. She felt the slight roughness of a callus near his thumb, a small imperfection that spoke of real work, of a life lived in a world of texture and substance. She looked from Orsino's flawless, unchanging face to the beautifully imperfect worry on Marc's. His love wasn't worship from a pedestal but a foundation, poured and set with every early morning coffee, every shared joke, every choice to show up, again and again.

Vivi lifted her chin, her voice ringing through the back-stage clutter, carrying the undeniable force of a hard-won truth.

"You aren't love," she declared, speaking to the perfect man in the mirror. "You are a cage. A beautiful, empty cage. I am not an object to be worshipped. I am a person to be known." She drew a sharp breath, her voice gaining a strength she didn't know she had. "I reject your cage. I chose the work. I choose him."

For one heart-stopping moment, Orsino's expression of pleading sorrow curdled into a mask of pure, reptilian rage. Then, with a sound like a thousand wine glasses shattering at once, the image imploded. The light inside the mirror winked out, leaving only a dark, empty surface. The scent of the sea was gone, replaced by the familiar, honest smell of old rope and stage paint.

A collective breath of relief rippled through the circle. It had worked.

The air that clung to the second mirror was smelling of damp earth and the sweet, cloying decay of roses left too long in a vase. Kevin felt the pull of it before he saw the image, a familiar, seductive ache that settled deep in his marrow. The lure of beautiful suffering was the lie that his pain made his depression a holy wellspring for his art. Sarah's hand was a small, warm anchor in his, her steady presence a quiet denial of the melodrama he had once mistaken for life itself.

In the glass, the Phantom's Lair shimmered, the black water of the underground lake reflecting a constellation of candlelight. Christine wasn't there in form, but he could feel her presence, a promise of validation for the darkest, most self-destructive parts of his soul.

Her voice wasn't in his mind. It seemed to bleed from the mirror itself, a sound like black velvet. Maestro. Do not forsake your gift. Their world is shallow. Their happiness is a flimsy thing. Your sorrow is a cathedral. Your art requires it. Return to the beauty of the dark. Return to me.

His knuckles were white where he gripped Sarah's hand. The temptation was a siren song aimed at the part of him that still romanticized his own illness, the part that missed the intoxicating relief of letting the darkness be his entire identity. It promised an escape not from pain, but from the complex, unglamorous work of getting better. The cold radiating from the glass was more than a draft; it seeped into his bones like a familiar winter sorrow, a chill he used to wrap around himself like a favorite coat.

Then he looked at Sarah. Her face was calm, her expression holding a quiet, unwavering faith that humbled him. She wasn't offering to fix him or promising to banish his darkness. She was just here. Holding his hand. A witness to his fight, not its judge. Her love didn't demand that he be happy. It only asked that he be present.

Kevin faced the mirror, his own reflection a pale, determined ghost against the backdrop of the glittering lair. His voice, when it finally came, was low and rough, but it held no whisper of hesitation.

"My pain is not a gift," he said, the words a direct defiance of the lie that had nearly drowned him. "It is an illness. And my art is not an escape. It is a voice." He squeezed Sarah's hand, drawing strength from the simple, solid contact. "I reject your beautiful suffering. I choose the messy, complicated truth. I choose to heal."

The mirror flared with a sharp, violet light. The haunting echo of a grand organ chord swelled and then shattered into a discordant crash. The image vanished. The second mirror went dark. The scent of decay was gone, leaving only the clean, sharp smell of ozone. Two down.

Every eye in the small circle turned to Zoe. She stood trembling, the weight of her guilt a physical cloak, heavier than the magnificent silk of her ballgown. Her mirror was the last, the epicenter, the wounded heart of the plague she had unleashed. Cate's hand settled on her shoulder, a gesture of grim, urgent support.

"Zoe, this will be the worst one," Cate warned, her voice low and tight as a guitar string. "The backlash will be violent. He will not let you go easily. Do not break contact with Tyler. No matter what you see, no matter what you hear, you hold on."

Tyler was at her side in an instant, his face carved with such profound fear that it made her own heart clench. He took her hand, his fingers lacing through hers. His palm was clammy like her own. He was terrified for her. The brutal, beautiful reality of his fear, of his love, was a truth she couldn't hide from.

Together, they turned to face the final mirror.

The glass didn't shimmer. It detonated with light. The glittering ballroom wasn't a reflection anymore. It became an overwhelming, immersive reality that seemed to push out from the frame, pressing against the backstage air. The scent of a million perfect, suffocatingly sweet roses flooded the space. The sound of a flawless orchestra swelled, drowning out the last, distant shouts from the front of the house.

And Prince Adrian was there. He stood on the other side of the glass, more real and radiant than he had ever been. But he wasn't smiling. His face was a mask of wounded, desperate possession.

His voice was a boom inside her head, a sound of pure, disbelieving rage. You would choose him? An imperfect, cynical mortal? Would you choose burnt coffee, arguments, and the ugliness of real life over this? Over me? Over-perfection?

Behind him, the ballroom twisted and broke. The waltzing couples dissolved into screaming, distorted figures of smoke. The crystal chandeliers shattered, raining down diamonds of hard light. The castle was finally showing the furious, chaotic magic that held it together.

"Don't listen, Zoe," Tyler pleaded, his voice a desperate rasp right beside her ear. His arm wrapped around her waist, holding her tight as a physical wind blew from the mirror, whipping her hair and the silk of her gown around them. The wind carried the chill of an empty, forgotten castle hall.

I gave you everything! Adrian roared, his voice now laced with the shriek of tearing metal. A world without pain! A love without consequence! You are nothing without me! You are a fraud, a costume! You will come back!

His hand pushed through the surface of the mirror, impossibly stretching the glass like a sheet of liquid silver. It reached for her, his fingers long and perfect and utterly terrifying.

The lie. The lie he was screaming at her was the same one she had whispered to herself in the dark her entire life, that she was nothing without the performance. That beneath the smiles and the bright colors, she was hollow.

She squeezed Tyler's hand, the solid reality of his bones a declaration against the lie. He was real. His fear was real. The messy, complicated love he offered her was real. This wasn't a fantasy but a chance—a chance to be real, too.

Zoe looked at her prince, her beautiful monster, dead in the eye. Her voice, when it came, was a choked whisper, but it carried across the unnatural silence with the force of a shifting continent.

"I am not a princess," she said. "And you're not my prince."

She took a ragged, tearing breath, her gaze finding Tyler's, her anchor, her choice.

"You are a beautiful, beautiful lie," she told the furious face in the mirror. "And I choose him. I chose the work. I choose... me."

As the last word left her lips, she felt Tyler yank her backward, shielding her with his body. The mirror erupted. It wasn't a quiet implosion like the others but a violent, silent detonation of pure white light that bleached all color and sound from the world. A wave of force, immense and colder than a grave, slammed into them, throwing them across the floor.

The magic snapped. The unnatural hum that had vibrated in their bones ceased. The frantic, overlapping whispers from every reflective surface in the theater died.

The silence that fell over the Meridian was sudden, absolute, and profound.

In the center of the backstage chaos, the three mirrors stood inert, their surfaces now ordinary, darkened glass. Onstage, the frozen actors stirred, blinking slowly, touching their own faces, looking around with the dazed confusion of people waking from a long and baffling dream. A disoriented Amelia, her lipstick smeared, stumbled out from behind a rack of costumes, her eyes unfocused and lost.

The theater was safe. The magic was quiet. The catastrophe was over.

Zoe lay on the gritty floor, tangled up with Tyler, his arms a protective cage around her. The silence pressed in, a heavy blanket after the hurricane. The immediate, world-ending danger was gone.

She pushed herself up, her gaze meeting Tyler's. The frantic terror in his eyes had receded, replaced by a quiet, raw, and bottomless relief. The noise was gone. The crisis was averted. There were no more monsters to fight, no more worlds to save.

There were only the two of them, in the sudden, echoing stillness of the aftermath. And in his eyes, a single, silent, terrifying question.

And now?

TWENTY-SIX

ADRIAN'S LAST STAND

After a long moment, Tyler had helped her to her feet, and she'd retreated to the silence of her dressing room, needing to be alone. The silence in the room was the loudest thing Zoe had ever heard, a deep, ringing quiet that had settled over the Meridian Theatre, the kind of stillness that comes after a thunderclap has shaken the whole house. The audience's screams, the piercing shriek of raw magic, and the urgent voices that had crackled over headsets—all of it had been soaked up by this thick, weary quiet. Zoe sat on the small, wobbly stool before her vanity, her reflection looking back like a stranger in the stark circle of lights. Her Cinderella ballgown was a ruin, the shimmering fabric smudged with grime from the stage floor. A tear ran through the bodice, a dark line showing where Tyler had thrown himself in front of her.

Her dressing room had become a map of the evening's wreckage. Smudged makeup wipes were strewn across the counter, small white flags of surrender. The bouquet of sunflowers Tyler had brought her for opening night was already giving up, their bright heads drooping heavily on their stalks. Their once-sweet scent was turning thick and cloying, the first soft perfume of decay. A half-eaten protein bar, a relic of a life that felt a hundred years old, sat forgotten next to a water bottle. The air itself was a stale cocktail of sweat, hairspray, and the distinct, age-old smell of the theater—a mixture of old velvet and settled dust that always reminded her of secrets. This mess was real. And some deep, cowardly part of her wanted to run from it all.

The guilt was a physical thing, a smothering heat in her chest that had nothing to do with the humid summer air outside. Amelia and Jon, the two ensemble members, were safe. They had been returned, looking as if they'd woken from a confusing dream, but they were safe. The audience was gone. The disaster had been stopped. But this was a disaster she had caused. Her secret, her selfish need for a perfect escape, had nearly unraveled her entire world. That knowledge was a shard of ice pressed against her soul.

She squeezed her eyes shut, the harsh bulbs of the vanity searing a pattern of light against the back of her eyelids. All she wanted was a single moment of darkness, a second of relief from the sight of her own tired, guilty face.

And there, in that quiet dark she had made for herself, the temptation came.

It didn't come from the mirror. The mirror was now a dark sheet of glass, its strange power gone. This temptation grew from inside her, a memory so clear it felt truer than the stool she was sitting on. The magic took its last breath, its final, desperate plea for her heart.

Prince Adrian's voice washed through her mind, impossibly smooth, a hypnotic balm. It wasn't the voice of his anger she remembered, but the voice of his first promise, now sharpened to a perfect, seductive point.

My dearest Zoe. Look what this world of yours has to offer. Chaos. Fear. Guilt. You tried to save them, and this exhaustion is your only prize—this pain. You carry the blame for their terror, and they will blame you too, sooner or later. This is the 'work' you have chosen. A treadmill of struggle that never, ever stops.

The vision bloomed behind her closed eyes, a flawless projection onto the dark screen of her thoughts. His kingdom was more achingly beautiful than she had ever seen it. Streams of what looked like liquid light flowed through the gardens, the water never moving yet forever sparkling. Flowers in impossible shades of sapphire and emerald bloomed in a state of constant perfection, their petals never touched by blight or time. The air was a perfect, comfortable warmth, and the sky was a deep, cloudless twilight blue, the first stars beginning to prick through the velvet.

There is no guilt here, his voice whispered, a silk cloth over her raw nerves. There is no pain. There is no failure. No one ever gets hurt. No one is ever disappointed. Here, you're not the source of chaos. You are the source of all joy. It is a world built from my passion for you, and it is waiting. A life without struggle. A love without any cost. It is my final gift. A perfect, happily ever after.

For one dizzying, terrible moment, she felt herself leaning toward it. The thought of never feeling this gut-deep guilt again was a relief, but it became a pain of its own. The image of the sun-drenched kingdom was a sanctuary calling her home. It would be so easy. So safe. So perfect.

But then another image rose in her mind, uninvited and unwelcome.

With that thought, the vision in her mind changed. The beautiful, flawless kingdom didn't fade away. It grew sharper. And in its terrible, high-definition clarity, she finally saw the horror of it.

The crystalline stream wasn't flowing because it was frozen solid, a glittering, dead sculpture of water. The ever-blooming flowers weren't alive. They were intricate statues of silk and wire, their perfection born of a factory's sterile precision, not the chaotic, stubborn miracle of life. The people, the eternally smiling courtiers who waltzed in the grand ballroom, weren't happy. They were hollow. Their eyes were made of glass. Their movements were the flawless, repetitive motions of animatronics on a theme park ride. They were puppets arranged in a shoebox diorama, and Adrian was the one holding all the strings.

The castle was no longer a palace, but a museum exhibit—a beautiful, breathtaking, and utterly lifeless prison. The vision of Adrian, his arms held open in a promise of eternal adoration, was no longer tempting. He was a warden, and he was offering her the most beautiful, gilded cage ever made.

A wave of nausea and a suffocating closeness washed over her, so intense it made her gasp for air that wasn't there. The visceral feeling of being trapped, of being a doll placed on a shelf, was more terrifying than any magical explosion could be. A life without struggle wasn't peace. A life without the possibility of pain was a life without the possibility of growth. She would never learn another thing. She would never feel the thrill of overcoming a challenge. She would never experience the profound, resonating joy of connecting with another person through shared vulnerability. She would be a perfect, happy, and utterly dead thing.

She finally understood. Her whole life, she had believed "happily ever after" was the destination. The part of the story where all the problems were finally solved, and the princess could rest. But that wasn't the "ever after" part. That was "the end."

The real happily ever after wasn't an ending at all but a beginning. A messy, beautiful choice to start building a life with someone was the work. And the only thing that felt real.

She was saving her own future. She was choosing the woman she could still become over the perfect, finished doll Adrian wanted to keep on his shelf forever.

The vision of the kingdom, the last echo of the magic, still glittered in her mind's eye, a silent, breathtaking promise. The memory of Adrian's face, full of adoration and hope, waited for her answer. His world was a masterpiece, flawless in its construction, a monument to a love that demanded nothing.

And the most horrifying thing she had ever seen.

Zoe took one last look at the impossible, internal paradise. Then, she opened her eyes.

Her gaze met her own reflection in the plain, ordinary mirror. Her face was pale, and her eyes were red-rimmed. A smudge of dirt streaked across her cheek where a single tear had traced a clean path through the grime. She looked exhausted. She looked broken.

She looked alive.

She drew a long, steady breath, her lips parting to speak the truth finally.

TWENTY-SEVEN

CHOOSING GROWTH

The silence that settled in her mind was a fragile, newborn thing. Zoe opened her eyes, and the world rushed back, not in a flood, but in a slow, sticky trickle. Not the frozen, perfect world of Adrian's kingdom, but this one. This room, with its smudged makeup wipes on the vanity and the wilting opening-night flowers in their vase. This place, with the smell of old building dust and the damp chill that always seemed to live in the theater's bones, a scent of her own exhausted sweat layered over it all.

Her own reflection stared back from the dark, still surface of the antique mirror. She saw a stranger with hollowed eyes. A clean path carved by a single tear traced its way through the grime on her cheek. She looked like something broken and left in the dirt. She looked alive.

She had made her choice on the quiet battlefield of her own heart. She had seen the truth hiding behind the beautiful lie. Now, she had to find the strength to act on it.

As if it could feel her decision taking root, the mirror stirred. The darkness inside it pulled back, replaced not by a vision in her head, but by a physical one right in front of her. The glass, which had been inert and dead, now pulsed with a desperate, pleading light, a portal reopening for its final argument. The glittering kingdom reappeared, no longer a horrifying little diorama but returned to its full, seductive glory. And there he was. Prince Adrian pressed against the invisible barrier of the glass, his impossibly handsome face a mask of tragic desperation.

"Zoe, don't," his voice whispered. The sound was a melodic, magically enhanced thing that resonated in the very air of the room, not in her head, a sound engineered to bypass all reason and pluck at the strings of a girl's heart. "Don't throw this away. Don't choose the struggle. Don't choose the pain."

His eyes, the color of a Carolina summer sky, filled with what appeared to be tears. Each one was a perfect, glistening diamond. "I can give you happiness. Guaranteed. No fear of inadequacy, no terror of not being enough. You will be loved, perfectly and forever. Isn't that what you've always wanted?"

A siren song aimed straight at the oldest, deepest fear she owned. The fear that she was only lovable when she was a constant source of sunshine. That her authentic self, the tired and scared and sometimes sad girl from a town too small to hold her dreams, wasn't worthy of a happy ending. He was offering a permanent escape from that fear. A permanent performance where the applause would never, ever end was the ultimate drug, custom-made for her own private addiction.

Her heart hammered against her ribs. Some young, wounded part of her that still believed in fairy tales screamed for her to accept. To step back through the glass. To be the princess.

Knock. Knock.

The sound was solid, real wood on wood. So wonderfully mundane and out of place against the magical symphony of Adrian's plea, that it was a shock to her system.

"Zoe?" Tyler's voice came through the door, muffled and laced with an uncertain, genuine concern that was a whole world away from Adrian's flawless pronouncements. "Are you... Are you okay? We're all out here. We're waiting for you."

The choice crystallized then, a visceral, physical war being fought in the small space of her dressing room. Behind her was the door. A real, solid slab of painted wood, and behind it stood a man who had seen her at her absolute worst and still chose to knock. A man who offered not a guarantee, but a chance. He was the terrifying, uncertain potential for real growth before her was the mirror. A shimmering portal to a world of guaranteed, static perfection. A world where she would never have to be anyone but the smiling, beloved princess, forever and ever.

Her fear of being unlovable if she wasn't perfect rose; a choking tide of panic became saltwater in her lungs. To kick it out from under herself would bring the whole fragile structure of her identity crashing down around her. Who would she be without a smile? Who would love her without the performance?

She looked at Adrian's pleading face. He was beautiful. He was safe. He was an ending.

She thought of Tyler's messy, real love. He was a challenge. He was a risk. He was a beginner.

In a sudden, blinding flash of clarity, she knew. She wasn't choosing between two men. She was choosing between two versions of herself. The perfect, finished doll on a shelf, or the real, unfinished woman with dirt on her hands.

Her fear was still there, a knot pulling tight in her stomach. But beneath it, something new and hot was rising. Anger. A white-hot fury at the thing in the mirror that had sniffed out her most profound insecurity like a hound. It had used her desire to be loved against her. It had tried to lock her in a beautiful, gilded cage. Her entire life, she had run from complicated feelings. She had performed happiness to avoid conflict, to keep the peace, and to ensure everyone liked her. But the chaos of the last hour had burned that part of her away. She had caused this mess. Now, she would be the one to clean it up.

Her gaze fell upon the small, simple wooden stool tucked under her vanity, a heavy, solid one made of dark, unpolished oak that had been scarred and scuffed by decades of actors' shoes. This piece of the theater's history had nothing to do with magic and everything to do with work.

She didn't hesitate. She didn't give herself a single

second to think, to let the old, familiar fear reclaim her. With a guttural cry that was torn from the deepest part of her soul, a sound of rage and terror and sweet, sweet liberation, she moved.

She grabbed the stool, its rough-grained legs scraping loudly against the worn linoleum floor. The weight was a shock, a solid, grounding reality in her hands. She hefted it up, her arm muscles screaming in protest. The heavy Cinderella gown, a costume for a part she had finished playing, twisted around her legs like a beautiful trap.

For a final, frozen second, she met Adrian's horrified gaze through the glass.

Then, with all the force of her fear, her guilt, and her newfound, desperate hope, she swung.

The sound wasn't the delicate tinkle of fairy-tale glass but a violent, explosive crack that seemed to shake the very foundations of the room, a sound like a thunderclap caught in a bottle. The moment the heavy oak connected with the mirror's surface, there was an explosive flash of white light, and the entire pane of glass erupted. It detonated.

A spiderweb of cracks raced across the surface in an instant, and then the mirror blew outward in a shower of glittering, silver shards. The magical energy that had been trapped within it discharged with a high-pitched, metallic scream. A wave of force washed over her, and it smelled of sharp ozone and dead air, the scent of a winter storm on a starless night. The beautiful kingdom, Prince Adrian, his pleading face, all of it vanished, annihilated in a storm of broken glass.

The pieces rained down onto the floor. They skittered across the linoleum like a thousand tiny, sharp-edged stars. They held no reflections, no magic, no light. They were slivers of silver-backed glass, mundane and dead and harmless.

The stool clattered from her numb fingers, landing with a dull thud amongst the wreckage.

Silence.

A profound, absolute silence returned, a quiet so deep it seemed to weigh its own broken only by her own ragged, breathless gasps for air. She stood there, trembling, her chest heaving as she stared at the empty, splintered frame of the mirror. The portal was gone. The magic was gone. The temptation was gone.

She had done it. She had destroyed it. She had chosen.

A single, final piece of glass, dislodged from the top of the frame, tinkled to the floor. The sound was sharp and clear in the ringing stillness.

Then, a second knock. Softer this time, hesitant.

"Zoe?" Tyler's voice was right there on the other side of the door. Real. Close. Waiting. "Are you okay in there?"

She had destroyed the past. Now, she had to open the door to the future.

TWENTY-EIGHT

LEARNING REAL LOVE

The knock sounded again, a soft, hesitant rhythm that was the only thing keeping the world from flying apart at the seams. Zoe's ragged breaths were a storm in the sudden, ringing quiet of the dressing room. She had brought the beautiful lie of the past crashing down around her. Now, she had to find the courage to open the door to whatever came next.

She managed a single, shaky step. The sound of broken glass crunching under the sole of her flat shoe was a sharp, granular song of what she had done, a sound that seemed to scrape against her very bones. Her hand, trembling like a leaf in a high wind, closed around the cool, solid weight of the brass doorknob. She pulled the door inward.

Tyler stood there, his frame a solid silhouette against the dim hallway light. His face was a tangled map of emotions, relief, and fear warring with a bone-deep exhaustion that mirrored her own. His gaze slid past her to the devastation sparkling on the floor, a constellation of heartache where the splintered frame of the antique mirror and the heavy wooden stool lay in ruin. A low whistle, sharp and quiet, escaped his lips.

"Okay. So that happened."

His eyes found hers again, sharp and analytical as the journalist inside him took the reins. He looked her over, his gaze cataloging the saltwater tracks through her smudged makeup, the wildness tangled in her hair, the tremor that still shook her hands. "Are you hurt? Physically?"

Zoe shook her head, the motion feeling slow and disconnected, like it belonged to someone else. A powerful, childish ache rose in her throat. She wanted to fall into his arms. She wanted him to wrap her up and whisper that everything was going to be alright, to swaddle her in the safety of a storybook ending. She'd earned it, hadn't she? She had faced the dragon in its lair and somehow, miraculously, won. This was supposed to be the part where the prince kissed the princess and the credits rolled toward a guaranteed happily ever after.

"I'm okay," she said, forcing a smile on her face. This costume she could barely hold in place, a pale watercolor version of her usual sunshine, already cracked and peeling at the edges. "I'm good. We're good. Everyone's safe. We did it."

She reached for his hand, her fingers lacing through his, a desperate need to pull him into the room and into the future she was trying so hard to believe in. She wanted to steer them both directly into the happily ever after, to tie a neat, pretty bow on all the trauma and move on.

But Tyler wasn't moving on. He was processing. He was still scanning the room, the reporter in him already laying out the story, brick by painful brick. "The final energy spike coincided with a seismic tremor that the city's geological sensors picked up. Did you feel that when it blew?"

"I... I don't know," Zoe stammered, her forced smile starting to crumble. His question was chilly and precise. He was debriefing a source after a disaster, not holding a survivor. "Tyler, can we not?"

"We have to document this, Zoe," he insisted, his tone perfectly reasonable, which only made it feel firmer. He hadn't let go of her hand, but his grip was absent, his attention a million miles away, lost in the mechanics of the impossible. "Cate's theory about severing a narrative feedback loop was right. We have to understand how it works. What did Adrian say? What was the final trigger? Did you destroy the mirror cause the magical backlash, or was the backlash what shattered the glass?"

Every question was a tiny, sharp shard of glass pressing into a fresh wound. She had clawed her way out of a battle for her own soul, and he was treating the battlefield like a science experiment. The fairy-tale moment she craved was dissolving before her eyes, turning into a detached post-mortem. The warmth of his hand in hers suddenly became a memory.

"He said he could promise me forever," she whispered, her voice tight with unshed tears.

"A static loop," Tyler muttered, his mind already racing, a hound on a fresh scent, connecting her whispered pain to his logical framework. "Unchanging. A simulated eternity. It makes sense. That's the only way to guarantee something is 'perfect.' Did he offer any new information about the source of the magic?"

"No," she said. She pulled her hand from his, the small gesture feeling as final as a slammed door. The smile was gone now, replaced by a fragile, sharp edge to her voice. "He tried to convince me to stay. Can we please go? I don't want to be in this room anymore." The air was thick with the ghost of magic she never wanted to feel again.

"Of course." His focus finally snapped back to her face. The reporter receded, and the man she thought she knew returned, his eyes softening with concern. "You're right. We should get out of here. My car is downstairs. We can go back to my place."

The drive to his apartment on North Hemlock Street was a blur of thick, humming silence. The city lights smeared across the windows, painting the quiet car in strokes of red and gold. The honest, lived-in mess of his living space was a jarring splash of water after the magical opulence of Adrian's castle, and a starker contrast to the neat, curated optimism of her own apartment. Here, precarious towers of books and old newspapers leaned against every surface, threatening to collapse. A forgotten Chinese takeout container sat on the coffee table like a small, sad monument. A Ficus in the corner had surrendered to its neglect, its brown leaves a quiet testament to its priorities. The air smelled of day-old coffee, old paper, and the faint, grounding scent of him.

He switched on a single lamp, and a soft, intimate glow spilled over the chaos, making it feel less like a mess and more like a map of his life. He turned to her, and her heart sank when she saw him pick up his worn reporter's notebook from the kitchen counter. A black Moleskine, like the one Vivi always carried, but his was battered, its cover softened with use, and its pages bristling with little colored sticky notes.

"Okay," he said, all business once more. "Let's go over it one more time, from the top. When the mirror reactivated..."

And that's when she broke.

"Stop it!" The words ripped from her throat, louder and sharper than she intended, echoed in the small, cluttered room. "Just, for one single second, can you stop being a journalist?"

Tyler froze, notebook in one hand, pen in the other, his expression completely baffled. "What? Zoe, this is important. We have to understand what we're dealing with."

"*I* know what I was dealing with!" she cried, and the tears of frustration and exhaustion she had been holding back finally spilled over, hot and angry down her cheeks. "I was dealing with a monster who was promising me a beautiful life where I never had to feel this awful, crushing guilt again! A life where I didn't have to be me! And you want to talk about seismic tremors?"

"It's how I process things," he said defensively, the cynical armor falling back into place with a familiar, hollow sound. "I analyze. I understand. It's how I make sense of the chaos. You, of all people, should get that. You spent a month trying to escape into a world where everything made perfect, simple sense."

"That isn't fair!"

"Isn't it?" he shouted back, his voice rising to meet hers. "You wanted a fairy tale, Zoe, and when reality gets messy, you want to pretend it didn't happen. You want to skip to the 'happily ever after' without dealing with the blood and the broken glass."

"No!" she sobbed, wrapping her arms around her own waist as if to hold herself together. "I don't want to pretend. I want to feel safe! I just faced the absolute worst parts of myself, the ugliest parts, the parts that would sell out everyone I love for a pretty lie, and I chose you! I chose this! This mess! And I needed... I needed you to hold me. I needed you to tell me we would be okay. Don't ask me to diagram the magical physics of it all!"

Her confession hung in the air between them, raw and wounded. She felt the old, familiar instinct rise inside her, the desperate need to smooth it all over, to apologize, to be the person he needed her to be to make the fighting stop.

But then, something in Tyler stopped. He looked at her, truly looked at her this time, and the anger in his face dissolved, replaced by a dawning expression of horror at himself. He dropped the notebook onto a stack of magazines. It landed with a quiet, final sound.

"No, wait." He took a hesitant step toward her, his hands raised in a gesture of surrender. "I'm sorry. You're right. I'm being a bastard. That's not what you need right now."

That was it. That was the moment. His apology, so simple and so absolute, was the olive branch that gave her the courage to stop pleading and start demanding. Her anger, which she had always seen as an ugly, forbidden thing to be tamped down and hidden away, suddenly was a source of strength, the engine of her honesty, and she let it run.

"No, it's not." She didn't smile or offer him an easy out or try to make him feel better. "I feel like my entire soul was turned inside out and scraped raw, and the man I chose to do this with is treating me like a source for his next article."

The words were valid, and they struck him with the force of it. She saw the hurt flicker in his eyes, a deep, wounded shadow, but she held her ground. This was the work. This was the messy, painful, honest part of love they didn't write about in fairy tales.

He closed the distance between them, his expression stripped of all its usual irony and cynicism. He looked like a man who was terrified he had broken the most important thing in his life.

"I'm sorry," he said again, his voice thick with an emotion she couldn't name. "When I'm scared, I intellectualize. I hide behind facts and questions because feelings... feelings aren't my area of expertise. And watching you stand in front of that mirror, watching that thing try to take you... Zoe, I have never been so scared in my entire life."

His vulnerability stripped away the last of her fight, leaving her feeling open and exposed. He was as terrified as she was, and his armor was as thick as her performative smile had been.

"I need to know that choosing you wasn't a mistake," she whispered, the deepest, most secret fear she held finally given voice. It trembled in the space between them. "I need to feel safe *with* you. Not from the magic, but from... all of this." She gestured around at the messy apartment, at the beautiful, frightening reality of it all.

Tyler's hands came up to cup her face, his thumbs moving with a gentle hesitation to wipe away her tears. His touch was uncertain, but his gaze was steady and unwavering.

"My entire life, I've believed that happy endings were a naive fantasy," his voice went straight to the heart of her. "Something for other people. Something you write about with a certain professional detachment. But you... You're the first thing in a very, very long time that has made me want to be wrong."

He leaned in and kissed her. It wasn't a storybook kiss, not a passionate, sweeping crescendo, but clumsy and honest, salty with tears still wet on her face—a kiss of apology and acceptance.

When they broke apart, she rested her forehead against him, breathing in the simple, grounding scent of his t-shirt. The argument, their first real one, had been terrifying. It had threatened to prove that their deepest flaws were fatally incompatible, that his cynical realism could never coexist with her desperate hope. But they had navigated it. He had lowered his shield and, in doing so, had given her the courage to find her own voice. The fragile, tentative connection between them hadn't shattered. It had been forged in the fire of their honesty into something more substantial, something more resilient.

They didn't talk about the magic again that night. He ordered greasy, excellent takeout from the Thai place down the street, and they ate sitting on the floor of his living room, using a formidable stack of history books as a table. He put on some soft, instrumental folk music, a quiet melody on an acoustic guitar, and for the first time in months, she didn't perform. She didn't force a smile when she didn't feel it. She didn't pretend to be anything other than what she was: exhausted, fragile, and profoundly, intensely relieved.

Later, wrapped in the quiet intimacy of his arms in the soft, forgiving glow of the single lamp, she felt a sense of peace settling over her, deep in her bones. This wasn't the hollow, glittering perfection of the fantasy she had escaped. This was a deep, warm, and solid feeling of rightness. It was the feeling of being truly seen, flaws and all, and not being accepted for them, but being chosen because of them.

This was real. And for the first time in her life, she had something she was genuinely terrified of losing.

CHAPTER

TWENTY-NINE

CATE AND MALCOLM'S FUTURE

The silence that fell over the Meridian Theatre wasn't an absence of sound but a presence all its own. Hours had passed since the last frantic burst of energy had faded, since Zoe had been guided away by a shaken but steady Tyler, since the final crew member had walked out into the night with the dazed look of someone who had seen a ghost and wasn't sure they believed their own eyes. Now, a profound stillness settled over the house, a quiet so thick you could press your hand into it. The deep red velvet of the seats seemed to drink the shadows, row after empty row of silent witnesses to a war no one else would ever know was won.

Cate Hart stood in the wings, her arms wrapped tight around her middle. It wasn't a defense against any physical chill but a brace against the crushing weight of the quiet. The air, heavy and warm, still carried the sharp, clean scent of ozone, a spectral residue of the power that had nearly pulled the building from its foundations. This smell she knew in her bones, a fragrance that lived in the deepest parts of her memory, forever tangled with the metallic tang of blood and the damp stone of a world she had barely crawled out of alive.

Malcolm found her there. He appeared at her side with the same noiseless grace he always had, a comforting solidity in the echoing emptiness. He didn't speak, but he hadn't yet reached for her. He stood with her, his gaze following hers to the bare stage, a shared vigil in the hushed aftermath. For years, this had been their language, a conversation built in the spaces between words, a partnership welded together in the inferno of a shared, unspeakable past.

"They're gone," Cate said. Her voice was a low rasp, a sound that seemed to catch on the thick, waiting air. It didn't echo. The heavy velvet drapes and the worn fabric of the house seemed to absorb the sound, as if the theater itself were too exhausted to repeat it.

"They are," Malcolm agreed, his own voice a balm, a smooth, cool stone in the turbulent river of her thoughts. "Zoe made her choice. Tyler is with her. Vivi and Marc, Kevin and Sarah. They're all right where they ought to be."

They had won. Their theory, painstakingly assembled from the shattered mosaic of their memories and the secrets in Carmen's hidden archive, had proven true. A person could reject the fantasy, could sever the connection if they were anchored by a love that was real and true in this world; a victory, a monumental one, but it felt strangely hollow. The immediate danger had passed, and in the immense quiet it left behind, a question they had held at bay for decades finally had the space to take a breath.

"What now?" Cate asked, the words feeling clumsy and foreign on her tongue. For so long, the answer to that had been simple. Now, surviving the next day, getting through the next rehearsal, watching the next leading actor with the anxious, protective gaze of a hawk became the work.

Malcolm turned to her, his kind, weathered face carved by the stark light from the stage. "We could leave," he said, laying the option out between them as if it were a clean, simple map. "Sell our shares. Move somewhere with no stages, no scripts, no mirrors. Somewhere the weather actually changes, and the past is just the past." He spoke of it with gentle wonder, imagining the specific pleasure of feeling rain on his face or smelling the rich scent of damp earth after a storm—the imperfect gifts of the real world he had learned to cherish.

The offer was a tangible thing she could hold in her hands. A small house on a quiet coast. A life where the most dramatic event was a summer thunderstorm rolling in off the water. A future where they were just Cate and Malcolm, not the Witch and the King who had fallen out of a madman's tragedy, a vision of peace, of a final, earned rest. And it terrified her down to her very soul.

"Could we?" she whispered, the question scraped raw with a vulnerability she only ever let him see. "Is what we have, this thing between us, real if we walk away from this place? Or are we two ghosts, forever tied to the spot where we died?"

The question haunted her nights, the fear that coiled in her heart during the day. Their bond was absolute, forged in the crucible of a mad king's paranoia and the shared horror of a world built from ambition and blood. They had saved each other. They had pieced each other back together. But was their entire relationship a reaction to that trauma? Was their love a scar, intricate and deep, but a scar, nonetheless? A scar was proof of healing, a map of the damage, but it never let you forget the wound. If they left the source of that wound, would the very tissue that held them together dissolve into nothing?

Malcolm's hand found hers then, his calloused fingers lacing through her own. His touch was a familiar pressure, a grounding weight in the disorienting quiet. "I used to wonder about that," he admitted, his voice low and certain. "I used to think my love for you was a debt I owed for my life. That I was staying here to protect you from the memories that clung to this place like ivy. But tonight, watching you, watching all of them, I saw something different."

He gestured with his free hand toward the empty stage, toward the single watchful eye of the ghost light. "We weren't surviving tonight, Cate. We were guiding. We were teaching. What we have, what we *know* from what we went through, is not a wound. It's a qualification."

The word didn't strike her. It settled. It settled in the profound quiet of the theater with the gentle weight of a truth she had been blind to for twenty years—a *qualification.*

She had always seen their past as a stain, a brand of

madness that set them apart from everyone else. It was a curse that bound them to this place, forcing them to be forever vigilant, forever reliving the horror in the wide, vulnerable eyes of each new lead. She saw herself as a fearful survivor, a haunted warden of a beautiful prison. But Malcolm, with his steady, quiet wisdom, was turning the prism. He was showing her a different light. He was turning their most significant weakness into their most profound strength.

"All those years," she breathed, the idea taking root inside her, spreading through her chest like a slow, warming light. "All those years of watching, of worrying over them. The cryptic warnings they never understood. It wasn't fair talking." A realization bloomed, soft and startling. "Research."

"Experience," he corrected gently, his thumb stroking the back of her hand. "No one else in the world can do this. Vivi and Kevin now know the shape of their own cages. However, we are familiar with the architecture of the prison itself. We know how it thinks. We know how it seduces."

They could leave. They could run and find their own small measure of peace. Or they could stay, and in staying, transform the very foundation of their relationship. They could stop being two people defined by healing *from* the past and start being two people who were building a purposeful future. Their bond would no longer be a lifeline woven from a shared nightmare, but an anchor forged for a shared mission. To be guardians. To be the keepers of the strange, beautiful, and dangerous magic of the Meridian. To turn this place from a potential trap into a true sanctuary.

The choice was so clear and breathtaking. To leave would be to abandon others to a fate they had only narrowly escaped themselves. It would be a betrayal of every hard lesson their suffering had taught them. They had to take the ugliest, most violent chapter of their lives and use it to write a new story, a story of protection and of community.

As she looked out at the stage, the single beam of the ghost light no longer seemed lonely. It looked like a light-house, a solitary beacon meant to guide lost ships to a safe harbor. A small, genuine smile touched Cate's lips, the first she'd felt in what seemed like an eternity. "Guardians," she repeated, testing the weight of the word on her tongue. It felt right. It felt solid. It became a foundation on which they could build a life.

She squeezed his hand, her grip firm and sure, a silent affirmation that he felt all the way to his soul. They were no longer just survivors, clinging to the wreckage. They were protectors. Their partnership, once a desperate handhold in a sea of madness, was now an anchor for an entire community.

They stood there for a long moment, the silence of the old theater no longer feeling empty, but full of this new, shared purpose. From down the hall, the faint, stale aroma of old coffee drifted from her office, a grounding, real-world scent that was more beautiful than any perfume. Finally, Malcolm broke the quiet, his tone shifting from reflective to practical, a hint of a smile in his voice.

"Alright then, Guardian," he said. "Where do we start?"

Cate met his gaze, her own expression clear and focused, the haunted fear of the past two decades replaced by a sharp, unwavering certainty. She thought of Vivi's fragile perfectionism, Kevin's romanticized depression, and Zoe's desperate, blinding optimism. She thought of all the beautiful, deadly lies the mirrors told.

"Rule number one," her voice ringing with the authority of hard-won knowledge, echoing with the strength of a truth bought with blood and time. "The mirror is a liar."

THIRTY

THE NEW DYNAMIC

The main stage of the Meridian Theatre was an island of light in a deep and waiting sea of darkness. A single ghost light stood its lonely watch at the center of the stage, pouring a circle of white onto floorboards that had been worn smooth by generations of imagined lives. Beyond that quiet circle, the shadows pooled long and distorted, stretching into the vast, empty auditorium like the searching roots of an old cypress swamp.

The entire remaining company had been summoned to an emergency meeting. They were scattered among the two hundred plush, crimson seats, their faces anxious and pale in the strange glow of their phone screens. Tyler Bacon sat in the front row with the core group, the newly minted guardians. Zoe was beside him, her hand a small, warm weight in his. Her presence was a constant, grounding reminder of what was real. Next to her sat Vivi and Marc, then Kevin and Sarah. They formed a silent, unified front against the encroaching dark.

On the stage, caught in the unforgiving glare of the work light, stood Cate Hart and Malcolm. They didn't look like a director and her partner. They looked like two sovereigns about to deliver a grim wartime proclamation to a kingdom on the verge of collapse.

Cate cleared her throat. The sound, amplified by the theater's acoustics, sliced through the nervous hum of whispers. The house fell into a tense, echoing stillness.

"Thank you for coming," Cate said with none of the haunted fear Tyler knew was churning just beneath the surface of her composure. "What happened last night during the performance wasn't a technical malfunction. It wasn't a prank or mass hysteria."

She paused, letting her words hang in the air, letting their weight settle on every soul in the room. Tyler watched the audience, his journalist's eye taking inventory of the reactions. He saw confusion give way to impatience, then saw that impatience curdle into a ripple of fear. He saw a young woman from the wardrobe, her hands usually busy with thread and needle, now twisting a loose strand of her own hair around and around her finger until the tip turned white.

"The Meridian Theatre," Cate continued, her voice ringing with the authority of a truth she had carried like a stone for decades, "is magical. The building itself possesses a unique and dangerous power. Under the right circumstances, during an active production, it allows actors to physically access the fictional worlds of the plays we perform through the antique mirrors in this building."

The truth didn't land softly. It fell like a felled oak in a silent forest, a crash that shook the very ground they sat on.

A wave of choked disbelief washed over the assembled company. A few people laughed, a short, sharp, nervous sound that died almost as soon as it was born. Tyler saw a young lighting technician lean over to whisper frantically to the person beside him. The fragile calm they had all been clinging to since last night didn't just crack. It detonated.

"Last night, Zoe's deep connection to her role destabilized that magic," Cate stated, her voice cutting cleanly through the rising noise. "It caused a feedback loop that put everyone in danger. Two of our ensemble members, Amelia and Jon, were pulled into a void between worlds. We got them back. We stabilized the magic. But the secret is out. We are informing you of this now because you have the right to be aware of the risks associated with working here. You have the right to make an informed choice."

Chaos bloomed in the dark velvet.

The words hit Danny Kim. *Magical? Fictional worlds?* For a wild, untethered second, he thought Cate had finally and spectacularly broken under the pressure. This was the only explanation that made any sense. He gripped his stage manager's clipboard so hard his knuckles were white peaks against his skin. The neat schedules and contact sheets, his sacred texts of order and reason, suddenly were relics from a sane world he no longer recognized.

But then his eyes found the faces in the front row. His sister, Sarah, a Doctor of Psychology, wasn't looking at Cate with clinical concern. She was watching her with a grim, steady focus that spoke of shared knowledge. Vivi Asbury and Kevin Brooks, two of the most grounded and difficult actors he knew, sat like soldiers who had already seen the worst of the war. And Zoe, who had been at the very center of the whole disaster, looked fragile but terrifyingly lucid.

They knew. They all knew. They *believed* it.

The professional rage that followed that realization was immediate and sharp as a shard of glass. This wasn't just some shared delusion. This was negligence on a scale he could not comprehend.

"Are you serious?" Danny's voice, sharp and accusatory, sliced through the panicked babble. He was on his feet before he was aware of standing, the clipboard held out in front of him like a shield. He took the three short steps to the lip of the stage, glaring up at Cate, his shadow a hulking, angry thing thrown against the proscenium arch.

"Is this your explanation?" he demanded, his voice shaking with a fury that was part fear, part righteous indignation. "Magic? You're telling us this theater is an active supernatural hazard, and you've known? What about our insurance? What about liability? You're telling me that there's a line in my contract I missed about the risk of being, what, 'pulled into a fictional world'?"

His words, loud and pragmatic, gave the fear in the room a name and an anchor.

"She's right, this is insane!" a sound tech shouted from the back, his voice echoing in the cavernous space.

"I'm not getting eaten by a goddamn mirror for twelve-fifty an hour!" a young stagehand cried out, her voice cracking with pure terror. She scrambled from her seat and bolted up the aisle, her footsteps a frantic, lonely drumbeat in the stunned silence that followed. Another person followed her, and then a third person joined them. Three of his best crew members have just gone.

The meeting fractured. The solid block of fear was breaking apart into angry, panicked shards. Danny felt the entire operational stability of the theater, *his* theater, *his* show, collapsing in on itself like a house of cards. He was the stage manager, and his job was to manage risk, to keep people safe. And his boss was telling him Shakespeare haunted the building. He glanced toward the wings and saw a prop, a silver goblet from the ball scene, sitting innocently on a crate. The sight of it, so regular and so tied to the work they were supposed to be doing, sent a fresh wave of rage through him.

"This is an unacceptable workplace hazard, Cate!" he yelled, his professional restraint shredding into raw anger. "You had a duty of care! We need protocols, we need risk assessments, not ghost stories!"

The meeting was coming apart at the seams. Danny's pragmatic fury was a lit match in a room filled with the gasoline of panic, and the fear was the fuel. Cate stood her ground, her face a mask of stone, but Tyler could see the helplessness swimming in her eyes. You could not contain this kind of storm.

Just as the arguments were about to boil over into a full-blown mutiny, a single, shaky voice cut through the noise.

"It's true."

Every head in the theater turned. It was Jon, one of the two ensemble actors, who had vanished from the stage. He was standing in the fifth row, his body trembling so violently that it was visible from the front. Amelia, the other actor, was beside him, her hand gripping his arm for dear life, her own face ashen.

Jon swallowed hard, his eyes wide and haunted. He wasn't offering a theory. He was giving testimony, bearing witness.

"I don't know what it was," he whispered, yet it carried across the silent theater as if he had shouted. "One second, I was waiting for my cue in the wings. The next... I was somewhere else. So cold. And silent." His gaze was fixed on something far away, something none of them could see. "I was... trapped behind glass. I could see the stage, I could see all of you, but it was like watching a movie with the sound turned off. There was no sound. I screamed, but I couldn't make a sound." His voice broke on a raw, terrified sob that he choked back down. "I was just... gone. And then... then there was this light. And I was back. Lying on the floor backstage. My costume was covered in... frost."

His raw, undeniable terror was more convincing than any explanation Cate could have offered. It sliced through the practical arguments and the angry disbelief, laying a blanket of silence over the room. The fear was still there, a living thing in the air between them, but now it had a new and more terrifying shape. It had a human cost.

A hand went up in the back of the house. Carmen, the quiet, watchful costume designer, a woman who saw everything and said little. "The sand," her voice soft but clear as a bell. "For years, I've found sand in the hems of costumes. From *Twelfth Night*. And flowers I couldn't identify from *A Midsummer Night's Dream*. I kept them."

Another voice, this one from a veteran props master near the side aisle. "Remember the forest set for *Macbeth* two years back? The real moss we used was dead and dry by opening night. But every morning, we'd come in and find fresh spiderwebs on the prop trees. Perfect ones. Like they'd been spun overnight in a damp wood."

Then a sound tech spoke up. "We get phantom audio on the comms sometimes. Full conversations in iambic pentameter when all the mics are dead."

One by one, small, inexplicable experiences were offered up like confessions at a midnight revival. They were pieces of a puzzle no one had realized they were holding. The chaos was settling, hardening into a new, reluctant consensus forged from the shared, unspoken weirdness of working at the Meridian.

Then Marc stood up.

Tyler watched him, intrigued. Marc, the lighting director, was a man of quiet, artistic integrity. He wasn't a man for grand speeches. He was the kind of man who spoke with light, not words.

"I don't know what I saw last night," Marc said. His voice was calm and steady, a grounding force in the emotionally charged room. "I don't know anything about magic or fictional worlds. But I know what I felt. I felt this company, our company, pull together to save our people and our show against impossible odds. I saw people running towards the crisis, not away from it." He paused, and his gaze swept across the remaining faces, a quiet benediction. "Whatever the cause was, that response was real. That dedication was real. I'm not going anywhere."

His simple declaration of professional loyalty, of simple human solidarity, did more to quell the remaining fear than anything else had. He had not affirmed the magic. He had affirmed *them*.

Cate stepped forward again, her expression softening with a gratitude that seemed to take years off her face. She had regained control of the room. It wasn't the authority of a director but the trust earned by a leader who had weathered the storm alongside her people.

"Danny, you were right about one thing," her eyes finding his in the crowd. "We need protocols. We need new rules. And we will write them now. Together."

Danny stood there, the fire of his anger now banked to grim coals of purpose. He gave a slow, deliberate nod. He picked up his clipboard from where it had fallen. He was still a stage manager, and a new kind of show was to be run. A much stranger, more dangerous show. He clicked his pen, the sound small but decisive in the vast room.

The group, smaller now but stronger, collectively built a new reality. Three core safety protocols were established, born from shared experience and fresh fear. First, no one works alone in the theater after hours. A buddy system was now mandatory. Second, all antique mirrors were to be covered when not essential to a production. Direct, prolonged eye contact was to be avoided at all costs. Third, an open-door reporting system. Any strange experience, no matter how small, was to be reported to Cate or Malcolm immediately, without fear of judgment.

A new consensus had been forged, not despite the fear, but because of it.

Later, after the last of the company had filed out, their faces a mixture of exhaustion and a strange, newfound solidarity, Malcolm began his work. The shattered remnants of the mirrors from Vivi's and Zoe's dressing rooms were carefully swept up and boxed away like dangerous relics. Then, he methodically gathered the others. He collected the large, gilded mirrors from the upstairs dressing rooms, the tarnished one from the basement that had almost claimed Kevin, and a long, narrow one from a disused administrative office on the third floor.

He carried them one by one to the secure storage room in the deepest part of the basement, a space now fitted with a new, heavy deadbolt. As he carried the last one, the long, narrow mirror from the office, his hand brushed against a rough patch on the ornate, carved wooden frame. The feel was different, not the smooth, worn lacquer of the others but something sharp and intentional.

He set the heavy mirror down carefully, leaning it against the stone wall beside its fellows. He ran his fingers over the back of the frame, searching for the spot again, a splinter. It felt deliberate, etched into the wood. He turned the heavy piece over, angling it to catch the dim, naked bulb light from the hallway.

Scratched into the dark, aged wood was a small, unfamiliar symbol, a spiral, coiling tightly inward, bisected by a single, perfectly straight line.

He had seen the backs of dozens of mirrors in this theater over the decades. He had helped Cate research, document, and fear them. He had never seen a mark like this before, a maker's mark. It felt older, like a warning, or maybe a designation.

An unsettling whisper settled in the dark, a hint that the magic they had just agreed to manage might have rules or an origin they didn't yet understand at all.

THIRTY-ONE

VIVI AND MARC'S COMMITMENT

The city outside breathed a low, sleeping hum, a sound that rose and fell with the rhythm of a world still turning. From their window, the air conditioning was a calm balm against the memory of the day's humid press, Westgate was a tapestry of distant light against a dark velvet sky. A single lamp cast a pool of warm honey across the living room, making the shadows long and soft, and transforming the familiar corners of the room into something gentle and inviting.

Vivi's apartment had once been a stage set for a life of careful minimalism, a place as guarded and impersonal as she was. But Marc had moved through it like a season, slowly, without announcement, leaving behind the quiet evidence of his presence. A worn flannel blanket, soft as a thousand washings, lay over the arm of the sofa. A stack of his lighting design textbooks, full of stark angles and the physics of light, leaned against her own well-loved copy of Shakespeare, a silent conversation between two different worlds. This was no longer just her refuge. It had become their home.

She sat curled on the couch, the warmth of a forgotten mug of tea seeping into her palms, and watched him. He stood by the window, his frame a dark shape against the city's glow, the muscles in his shoulders drawn tight with a tension that the end of the crisis hadn't quite managed to unknot. The theater's new normal had settled over them all like a low-lying fog, a strange landscape of buddy systems and mirrors shrouded in thick canvas from the scene shop. They shared the unbelievable secret, but the tremors of what they'd survived still shook them in the quiet moments.

"It's so quiet. The theater, the city. Everything."

Marc turned from the window. The soft lamplight caught in the faint lines around his eyes, creases of worry that hadn't been there a few months ago. "Too quiet?"

"No," she murmured, shaking her head. "Just... quiet."

He crossed the room in a few straightforward strides, and the couch gave a familiar sigh as he sat beside her. He gently took the mug from her hands, setting it on the coffee table before gathering her fingers in his. His touch was warm, solid, a grounding weight that seemed to chase the last phantom chill of Illyria's perfect, sterile air from her bones.

"I'm not going to stand here and pretend I wasn't terrified I was losing you," he admitted, his voice low and a little rough, raw with an honesty that still had the power to stop her heart. He met her gaze, his own wide open, letting her see every last flicker of fear he held. "That kind of feeling doesn't just pack up and leave because the magic is stable for now. Some nights, I still wake up halfway, and for a second, I expect the space next to me to be empty."

His confession was a gift, a perfectly flawed, human offering that reached for her past all the walls she'd ever built. The old Vivi, the actress who had spent a lifetime behind layers of performance, would have deflected with a polished line. She would have offered a comforting lie, a pretty reassurance meant to smooth over the messy, inconvenient truth of his fear. But she wasn't that woman anymore. She had learned, through fire and fantasy, that real love wasn't about protecting each other from the truth but more about holding it together, with both hands, no matter how much it shook.

"I know," she whispered, her fingers tightening around his. "There's a part of me that still remembers the temptation of that escape. The silence. The pure and simple absence of pain." She took a breath, a deep pull of the real, tangible air in this room, forcing herself to give voice to the new foundation of her heart. "And I won't pretend that turning away from that temptation won't be a choice I have to make again and again. But it's easier now. It's so much easier knowing I'm not running *from* something but running *to* you."

That was it. That was the core of this new life, a commitment she was beginning to understand wasn't a place she had arrived, but a path she chose to walk every single morning when she woke up. Love wasn't a destination but a direction.

A slow, relieved smile spread across Marc's lips, a sweet warmth that smoothed the last of the tension from his face. He leaned in and kissed her, a soft, lingering press of his mouth that said more than words ever could. A kiss of gratitude, a homecoming, became a shared understanding that they had earned together.

"So, what does that look like now?" he asked, pulling back just enough to see her face. "For us. After everything."

"It looks like this," she gestured, taking in the quiet safety of their shared space. "But it also has to look like... more." The thought had been taking root in her mind ever since the meeting, ever since she saw the dawning horror and helpless recognition in Zoe's eyes. "We have a responsibility. To Zoe. To the next Kevin. To anyone who feels that pull and doesn't know what it is."

Marc nodded slowly, his expression growing serious. He understood immediately, the way he always seemed to. "That's a heavy thing to carry, Vivi. Mentoring someone through something like that... It's going to bring it all back up. The fear, the temptation. It could put a strain on what we've built right here."

"I know it could," her voice gaining a strength she didn't know it had. "But we can't just know what we know and stand by while it happens to someone else. Not after everything we went through. Not after what Cate and Malcolm did for us, what they're still doing." Her past was no longer just a source of her pain; it had become a kind of qualification, a hard-won knowledge they were now obligated to use. Their peace could not be bought with someone else's safety. "We have to be there for her. For all of them. Together."

She watched him, her breath held somewhere in her throat, knowing the shape and size of what she was asking. She wasn't just asking him to share a life with her. She was asking him to share a burden, a constant, watchful duty that would forever tie them to the theater's strange and dangerous magic.

He brought her hand to his lips and kissed her knuckles, his gaze steady and clear. "Okay, together."

The word settled between them, not like a promise but like a foundation stone being laid. It wasn't a vow that life would be free of fear or pain, but a pact that they would face all as a team. Their love, forged in the impossible heat of a supernatural crisis, was now being tempered into something more, a partnership with a shared purpose, a love that knew how to look outward as much as it looked inward.

A profound sense of rightness washed over Vivi, a warmth that had nothing to do with the cooling tea on the table. This was the very opposite of Illyria's hollow perfection. This was real. This was earned. This was the messy, complicated, and breathtakingly beautiful reality she had chosen, and would keep choosing, for the rest of her life.

She leaned into him, her hand sliding from his to cup the back of his neck, her fingers tangling in the soft hair there as she pulled him closer. "I love you," she murmured against his lips. The words were the most straightforward, most authentic truth she had ever spoken, stripped of all performance, all script.

"I love you," he breathed back, his voice thick with an emotion that vibrated through her.

Their kiss deepened, no longer just a quiet promise but a celebration. His hands moved from hers to her waist, strong and sure, pulling her from her seat and onto his lap. Her body molded against his with a rightness, a familiarity that was still new enough to send a thrill singing through her veins.

The low hum of the city faded to nothing. The ghosts of the theater, of Illyria, of her own past, all fell away, pushed back by the undeniable, grounding presence of him. His scent filled her senses, a mix of sawdust from the shop, the dark roast coffee he favored, and something that was uniquely, wonderfully Marc. The soft scrape of his stubble against her cheek, the solid strength of his arms around her, the way his breath hitched when her fingers tightened in his hair, every detail was a brilliant, imperfect piece of reality.

This wasn't the choreographed, passionless perfection she had known in a storybook. There were no rose petals strewn on silken sheets, no poetic declarations whispered in flawless iambic pentameter. There was just the clumsy, beautiful truth of two people learning each other's rhythms in the soft lamplight of their living room. There were fumbled buttons and the smooth, breathless laughter that followed. There were whispered questions and honest, vulnerable answers. So awkward and tender, it made her want to weep with gratitude.

He lay her back against the soft cushions of the couch, the worn flannel blanket tangling around them. The light from the lamp painted his face in gold and shadow, his eyes dark with a love that wasn't a performance, but a profound, soul-deep truth. In his gaze, she wasn't Viola, she wasn't a leading lady, she wasn't a collection of flawless techniques and memorized lines. She was just Vivi. And for the first time in her life, she knew this was more than enough.

Later, as they lay tangled together in the peaceful aftermath, their breathing slowly evening out, Vivi rested her head on his chest. She could feel the steady, reassuring beat of his heart against her ear, a rhythm that had become the new baseline of her world. Her gaze drifted to the large window, to the millions of distant lights that made up the sleeping city of Westgate. In the distance, she saw the dark, familiar silhouette of the Celadon Arts District, where the Meridian Theatre stood silent and waiting under the moon.

For the first time, the thought of that building, of the magic that pulsed within its old brick walls and the dangers it would always hold, didn't send a tremor of fear through her. It didn't trigger the old instinct to retreat, to perform, to hide behind a character. Instead, a quiet sense of purpose settled in her heart, a shared weight that was no longer a burden. It became an anchor, holding them fast in the real, wonderful world they had chosen to build. Together.

CHAPTER

THIRTY-TWO

KEVIN AND SARAH'S PARTNERSHIP

The quiet in Sarah's apartment was a language Kevin was only learning to speak. For most of his life, quiet had been a void, a roaring silence he'd been desperate to fill with the borrowed ghosts of characters or the sharp, jagged static of his own mind. This quiet, though, was different. This presence was as real and warm as the blanket draped over his legs, the soft gold of the lamp spilling across the pages of Sarah's book, turning them the color of warm butter. The steady, low hum of the refrigerator was a mundane yet beautiful anchor to a world that was real and here to stay. The sweet, clean scent of the chamomile tea she'd placed in his hands warmed into his palms like a promise.

He sat on her comfortable, worn sofa and just watched her. She was across the room at a small wooden desk, her brow gently furrowed as she looked over a draft of what they'd started calling the "Welcome Materials." It was

256

Cate and Malcolm's fierce attempt to distill their hard-won wisdom, a guide for new actors that felt less like a welcome and more like a survival manual, filled with cryptic, urgent notes about staying grounded and the razor-thin line between character and self. On the corner of her desk, a small, slightly shriveled succulent sat in a painted pot, a testament to her quiet, persistent hope for the smallest of living things.

Weeks had passed since the crisis, since Zoe had shattered her own reflection and chosen the messy, complicated reality with Tyler, and weeks had passed since the theater had settled into its new and strange rhythm. The company that remained, bound by a secret that was equal parts terror and trust, now moved with a quiet, watchful solidarity. The buddy system was law, and the once-alluring antique mirrors were now shrouded in thick velvet cloths, their dangerous songs muffled but not silenced.

Kevin's own recovery, once a desperate scramble from one day to the next, had settled into something more durable, now a low hum, like the hum of a refrigerator. The therapy sessions continued, the work progressed, but the breathless, drowning panic had given way to a profound, grateful peace. He had a future. He had *her*.

"You're staring," Sarah said. She didn't look up from the screen, but a small smile touched her lips.

"I'm admiring," he corrected, his own voice low and easy in the warm room. "The view's good from here."

She finally lifted her head, and her kind, intelligent

eyes found his. Behind her, the city lights blurred into a soft halo through the windowpane. "I was just reading Cate's first rule. 'The mirror is a liar.' It's poetic. And completely terrifying."

"It's the most honest thing she's ever written," Kevin said. He knew the truth of that statement in his very bones. He knew the seductive beauty of the lie the mirror told, the perfect, dark reflection of his own pain he had found in Christine—a ghost he no longer gave his breath to.

He set his half-empty mug down on a coaster. The quiet clink of ceramic on wood was a slight, solid sound in the stillness. "I was thinking about that," he said, the idea forming itself as he spoke the words aloud. "About what comes next. For us. For the theater."

Sarah swiveled in her chair to face him, her attention a gift he would never take for granted. "What were you thinking?"

"Vivi and Marc are stepping up. Cate and Malcolm are the guardians. But we have something they don't." He leaned forward, the energy of the idea making him feel more alive than any performance ever had. "You and I, we're bridges. Between magic and the mind. Between the sickness and the healing. I've lived it. You have the training. We could work together. We could be the first line of support for people who are starting to feel that pull."

He saw the future in that single moment, clear and bright as a summer morning. A partnership that wasn't just personal, but purposeful. He and Sarah, a team, were using their singular strengths to help others navigate the labyrinth he had only just escaped. It felt right, like the joining of his past and his future—a way to give his own suffering meaning that would last.

Sarah's expression softened with a warmth that made his heart give a gentle, happy ache. She stood and crossed the room to sit beside him on the sofa, her hand finding his.

"I love that," her voice full of sincerity. "I love that your first instinct now is to help. It's the most beautiful part of watching you heal, seeing you turn outward." She squeezed his hand, her thumb tracing slow patterns over his knuckles. Then she hesitated, a small, troubled line appearing between her eyebrows. "But there's a complication, Kevin."

He felt a phantom echo of defensiveness, a ghost of the old Kevin who bristled at any hint of a challenge. He met her gaze, his heart open and waiting. "Okay. What is it?"

"Me," she said. "My training. I can't be a therapist to my friends. I can't be a therapist to people in our immediate community, those with whom I have personal relationships. It's called a dual relationship, and it's one of the biggest ethical lines we're not allowed to cross. It blurs boundaries, it creates a power imbalance, and it can do far more harm than good."

The words were spoken gently, but they carried the weight of a closing door. The perfect, elegant vision he'd held in his mind of them working as a seamless unit, him sharing his story and her providing the clinical framework, dissolved. For a heartbeat, he felt a sharp sting of disappointment, a frustration that the world had to be so complicated, so full of rules that stood in the way of a good heart trying to do a good thing.

He saw the worry in her eyes, the fear that he would take this as a rejection, that he would retreat into that old, brittle shell. The old Kevin would have. The old Kevin would have seen this as just one more obstacle, another sign that the universe was conspiring against him.

But the old Kevin was a character he no longer played.

He reached out with his free hand, gently taking her other one. He held them both, anchoring them together. "You're right," he said clearly. "Of course, you're right. The last thing I'd ever want to do is help them but hurt us. Or to put you in a position that compromises the very principles that make you so damn good at what you do."

The relief that washed over her face was almost painful to witness. She let out a breath she hadn't realized she was holding. "Thank you for hearing that," she whispered.

"It doesn't mean we can't do it." His mind was already shifting, adapting. This wasn't a wall but rather a turn in the road. "It just means we do it differently. We redefine the roles."

The conversation that followed was the most important of their lives, quiet and focused, a masterclass in the kind of mature, collaborative partnership he had once dismissed as a naive fantasy. They didn't argue. They built something, right there on her worn sofa, their hands still clasped between them. This, he thought, was so much better than the tragic, beautiful arguments he used to believe were the only proof of love.

"My role isn't to give advice. It's not to be a therapist. I'm not qualified for that. My role is to be... a signpost. To be the guy who can sit down with someone who's feeling that pull and say, 'I get it. I've been there. You're not crazy, and you're not alone.' My value is my story." He looked at her, the idea solidifying into a core belief. "I can be a peer support. The first conversation. The one who makes it safe to admit there's a problem."

Sarah nodded, her eyes bright with an understanding and a pride that made him feel ten feet tall. "Yes. That's exactly it. You can de-stigmatize it. You can be the proof that there's a way through." She picked up the thread seamlessly, her voice gaining its own energy. "And my role isn't to be their doctor. My role is to be a liaison—the resource. I can't treat them, but I know dozens of incredible therapists in this city. I can be the one who vets them, who finds the right fit for the right person. I can make sure they get to a qualified professional who has no personal connection to the theater, who can give them a safe, confidential space to do the work."

They were no longer a single unit. They were two distinct, interlocking pillars. Kevin, the gatekeeper of shared experience. Sarah, the gatekeeper of professional help. This was stronger, more ethical, and built to last. It protected their friends, and just as importantly, it protected them. It built a necessary, healthy wall between their life together and the work they would do for the people they cared about.

This, he realized with a quiet surge of clarity, was the practical application of his recovery. This was about *being* better and about his ability to hear a boundary, to validate it without a fight, and to collaborate on a solution. This was the ultimate proof that the healing was real.

"So that's our partnership," he said, a slow, genuine smile spreading across his face. This future he could believe in, built on a foundation of respect, boundaries, and a purpose they could share. He squeezed her hands. "I commit to that."

"I commit to that, too," her voice full of a love that was both tender and fiercely proud.

The conversation was over. A new silence settled in the room, but this one was filled with the quiet, powerful energy of a vow just made. He pulled her closer, and her head found its familiar place on his shoulder. He breathed in the scent of her hair, a clean, simple fragrance that smelled like home. With his free hand, he gently traced the woven pattern of the sofa's fabric, a small, grounding act. This was his reality. This imperfect, beautiful, tangible gift he had chosen over a perfect, empty darkness.

Just then, a sharp buzz vibrated from the coffee table, cutting through the stillness.

Kevin's phone screen lit up the dim room. A text message. He glanced at it, and his heart gave a slight, strange lurch.

The screen showed a name and a message that was both an interruption and a beginning.

> Tyler Bacon: Hey, Kevin. You got a minute? I need to talk to someone who gets it.

Sarah saw the look on his face, the shift in his stillness. "What is it?"

He turned the phone and showed her the screen. She read the words, and a look of profound, gentle understanding passed between them.

Their work had already begun.

THIRTY-THREE

TYLER'S ARTICLE

The blue-white glow of the laptop was a lonely island of light in the sea of darkness that had swallowed Tyler Bacon's small apartment. It was three in the morning, that hollow hour when doubt creeps in like a stray cat, hungry and persistent. Outside his window, the city of Westgate held its breath, the humid air thick and still, waiting for a storm or for the sun. The only sound was the soft whir of the laptop's fan, a mechanical sigh against the profound silence. The blinking cursor on the blank document was a patient, accusing pulse, a quiet metronome counting down the beats to his deadline.

The air in the room was a heavy cocktail of stale coffee and the sharp, electric tang of a machine worked too hard for too long. His desk was a testament not just to a story, but to a war fought within himself, a landscape of the battle, littered with interview transcripts and pages torn from his reporter's notebook, the ink on them hurried and frantic. Ghostly rings from a dozen coffee mugs mapped the long hours, including one cheap ceramic one from a gas station that read *World's Okayest Brother*, a gag gift years ago that was a punch in the gut tonight.

His editor at the *Sunday Arts Magazine* wanted a feature on the Meridian Repertory Theatre. A nice little human-interest piece. Something good about the resilience of local arts in a world that was forgetting how to care about them.

Tyler had something better. He had a truth so sharp and so heavy it could crack the foundation of the world.

He had a story that could carve his name into the annals of journalism. A tale that smelled like a Pulitzer. A story that would, without question, be an act of arson for the new and fragile life he had just started to build. It would burn his world to the ground, and it would salt the earth where it had stood.

His fingers hung suspended over the keyboard, trembling just enough to notice. He was a journalist; more than a job title on a business card, and the very architecture of his soul. His entire life and identity were built on a single, stark principle that could be developed into a church. Find the truth. Print the truth. You don't comfort. You don't hide. You drag things into the light, even if the light makes them scream.

He drew in a long, shuddering breath that tore something loose in his chest, and he typed. The words came easily, the professional in him taking over, his fingers moving with a practiced efficiency that felt alien to the rest of his body.

The magic at the Meridian Repertory Theatre is not a

metaphor. For nearly a century, the historic playhouse in *Westgate's* Celadon Arts District has been a site of literal supernatural phenomena. During active productions, antique mirrors within the building become physical portals, allowing actors to step directly into the fictional worlds of the plays they perform. But this pipeline to inspiration is not without its cost. The *theater's* own archives, along with the recent testimony of its members, detail a chilling history of performers who have been lost to these fantasy worlds. Some for hours, some for days, and some, it is feared, forever.

The paragraph glowed on the screen, a clean and brutal thing. Factual. Sensational. And without a shadow of a doubt, the single best lead he had ever written. Irrefutable, sourced, and so explosive it would leave a crater where a small, beloved theater once stood. He could see it all unfolding. The immediate ripple effect was that the story was picked up by national news outlets, which were hungry for the bizarre. He saw the scientists and the paranormal crews, two sides of the same curious coin, descending on the Meridian like buzzards circling something wounded. He saw the ridicule and the rabid disbelief, followed by the obsessive, dangerous attention that would fix its unblinking eye on a small community of artists who had only just dragged themselves from the wreckage of a crisis born from that very secret.

He saw Cate's face, a mask of hard-won calm he had come to respect so deeply. He watched it shatter in his mind as she was forced to defend her life, her sanity, her family against a world that would paint her as a madwoman. He saw Malcolm, a man who had escaped a world of violence and found peace in the simple texture of reality. He saw that gentle, trauma-forged peace broken apart by the invasive curiosity of strangers who would never understand the price he had paid for it. He saw Vivi and Marc, their new love as fragile and beautiful as a spring frost, melting under the heat of a merciless public microscope. He saw Kevin and Sarah, their carefully built framework of recovery and support—a thing of such quiet courage—dismantled piece by piece by the casual cruelty of public scrutiny.

And he saw Zoe.

His breath caught. He saw her bright, beautiful, authentic smile, the one he had fought to see return to her face. He saw it wilting under the glare of a spotlight she had never asked for, a light far harsher than any Marc could rig on stage. He saw her, forced to recount her most profound trauma for a hungry, gawking public. He saw her story, her fear, her strength, all of it twisted into a tabloid headline designed to be consumed and forgotten. On his desk, next to the mess of notes, was a postcard of a ridiculously sunny beach she'd given him last week, a silly, hopeful thing. On the back, in her looping script, she had written,

Wish you were here, even though we're already here.

The thought of that simple, private joy being dissected by strangers made him feel physically ill.

The professional pride he was supposed to feel, the electric thrill of the ultimate scoop, was a phantom limb, an ache where a feeling used to be. In its place was a sick churning in his gut. A profound sense of betrayal that felt like swallowing mud. This wasn't truth-telling. This was a violation. This wasn't journalism but exploitation of the highest, most personal order.

He had walked into the Meridian a cynic. He was a man who saw the world in headlines and bylines, a man who believed love was a fairy tale told to children and fools. He had found a woman who taught him that happily ever after wasn't an ending you stumbled into, but a choice you made, every single morning, to show up and try. He had found a community that had looked literal monsters in the eye and chosen to heal together, to mend the broken places with trust and shared silence. He had declared his love. He had laid his cynical heart at their feet, and in return, they had trusted him. They had trusted him with their secret. They had trusted him with their lives.

Hope was a dangerous thing, a weed that grew in the cracks of a broken heart. Zoe had planted a whole garden of it in his. Printing this story wouldn't just be breaking a promise. It would be an act of profound self-destruction. It would mean erasing the very man Zoe had helped him become—the man he desperately wanted to be for her.

His hand, no longer trembling, closed over the mouse. The sharp plastic was cool under his palm. The click as he depressed the button was a slight, sharp sound in the quiet apartment, but it felt as loud as a gunshot. He dragged the cursor, highlighting the entire paragraph. The glowing words, his career-making truth, the story that would put his name on the map, shone for one last, tempting moment.

Then he hit delete.

The words vanished. The screen was a field of clean, patient white. The cursor pulsed quietly at the beginning of the void, waiting. He had just thrown away a Pulitzer Prize. He had never felt so relieved in his entire life.

A heavy sigh escaped him; a sound of such finality it seemed to draw all the knotted tension from his shoulders and release it into the air. He wasn't just a journalist anymore. He was one of them. A guardian. His duty, he now understood, wasn't to expose but to protect.

But the story still had to be written. The deadline was a stubborn fact of life. He reached for his coffee, took a sip of the bitter liquid, and grimaced. He set the mug aside, a small dismissal of the man he used to be. He had to find a different kind of truth. The real truth. Not the what of their magic, but the why of their humanity.

He opened his reporter's notebook, a worn leather-bound thing whose spine was cracked from years of being shoved into back pockets. He flipped past the chaotic, frantic notes from the night of the crisis, past his own crude diagrams of magical feedback loops and transcribed testimony about shimmering portals. He kept turning pages until he got to the quieter interviews he had conducted since, the conversations that took place in the calm after the storm. He found a quote from Vivi, her voice so clear and articulate that he could hear it just by reading the words.

"Art isn't about escaping reality," she had told him, her hand resting on Marc's in a way that was both new and ancient. "It's about borrowing a different lens to see your own reality more clearly. I needed perfection. It turns out, I just needed to be seen, flaws and all."

He found Marc's words from that same conversation, the director's perspective a counterpoint to the actor's. "Directing isn't about control," Marc had said with his eyes on Vivi. "It's about creating a space safe enough for people to be vulnerable. The real art, the thing we're all chasing, only shows up when there's trust."

He found a line from Kevin, spoken with a quiet, hard-won authority that had replaced the brooding intensity he used to wear like armor.

"We romanticize the tortured artist," Kevin had said, Sarah nodding beside him, her presence a quiet anchor. "We think pain is a prerequisite for depth. But that's a lie. Real art, the real connection, starts when the healing does. You don't find truth in the darkness. You bring light to it."

He found the powerful, cryptic statement from Cate, spoken to the whole company during the meeting, that had changed everything. The words that had first started to chip away at his own cynical armor.

"A theater is a machine for empathy. It's the one place we can walk in another's shoes and come out changed. That power is real. It can be beautiful. But it demands our respect. It demands we stay grounded in the world we are trying to illuminate."

That was the story. That was the absolute truth. Not the supernatural mechanics of it all, but the human heart beating at its center. The magic of the Meridian wasn't in its reflective glass, but in its people - their breathtaking courage to face their own reflections and choose authenticity over performance, every single day. This transformative power of a community refused, fiercely and stubbornly, to let its members get lost in the dark.

His fingers found the keyboard again, and this time, they didn't hesitate. The sound of the keys was no longer a frantic race against a deadline.

The magic at the Meridian Repertory Theatre is not a metaphor. It is, however, misunderstood. It is not found in the ropes and pulleys of the fly system, nor in the carefully focused beams of light that drench the stage. The magic of the Meridian is quieter, more human, and far more profound. It is the palpable energy of a community that believes in the transformative power of art, not as an escape from reality, but as a crucible for forging a more authentic version of oneself.

He wrote for hours. The words flowed out of him now, not from a place of professional ambition, but from a place of deep, abiding love. He wrote about Cate Hart's fierce, protective leadership, framing her as the steadfast heart of a found family. He wrote about that family, about how the bonds forged in the shadows backstage were the proper foundation for the art presented in the spotlight. He wove Vivi's journey from technical perfection to raw, breathtaking vulnerability, portraying it as the ultimate triumph of an artist's courage. He used Kevin's words to craft a powerful, unvarnished narrative about mental health in the arts, about the courage to seek healing and the community that rises to support it.

He wrote about Zoe, carefully, protectively, as if his words were a shield. He described her as an actress of such profound and stubborn optimism that she dared to believe in happy endings, and in doing so, inspired a cynical journalist to believe in them too.

He didn't mention mirrors, portals, or princes from storybooks. He told the truth. The most actual truth he had ever written. He honored their stories. He protected his family.

As the first pale fingers of dawn crept through his window, casting long shadows across the room, he typed the final sentence. The distant rumble of the city's first garbage truck of the day signaled the end of the night. He read the entire article one last time, a sense of quiet, bone-deep satisfaction settling in his chest.

He attached the file to an email, typed **"MERIDIAN FEATURE"** in the subject line, and, with a final, steadying breath, hit send. The soft whoosh of the email leaving his outbox was a final, definitive choice—a door closing on one life, and another opening.

He leaned back in his chair, utterly exhausted but completely at peace. He had chosen them. He had chosen Zoe. He had chosen himself.

His phone buzzed on the desk, the vibration a sharp, intrusive sound in the quiet room. A second buzz followed almost immediately. He picked it up, his thumb swiping across the screen. He was expecting an automated reply from the magazine's server, a digital nod confirming receipt.

He got two messages. The first was the automated receipt, as expected.

The second was from his editor, a man not known for his speed or his brevity, a man who usually let emails sit for a day before acknowledging them.

Got it. This is... not what I was expecting. Call me first thing in the morning.

A knot of familiar, professional anxiety tightened in Tyler's stomach, a ghost of old fears he thought he had laid to rest. He had done the right thing for the people he loved. He had kept his promise to his own heart. Now, he was about to find out what it had cost him.

THIRTY-FOUR

CARMEN'S REVELATION

The low, familiar hum of the Meridian Theatre was a different creature in the basement. Down here, sunk deep in the foundation of the old building, it wasn't the sound of the theater breathing so much as the sound of it dreaming. The air, thick and cool, carried the scent of cedar from the moth-repelling planks lining the walls, a smell that mingled with the sweetness of decaying paper and the faint, mineral tang of damp concrete. In the single, stark beam of a bare work light, particles of settled history danced like fireflies, a swirling galaxy of everything the theater had held and forgotten. The light caught the faces of the Meridian's newly formed council, a strange and weary constellation of survivors, gathered among the towering ghosts of productions past.

Cate stood with her arms crossed over her chest, a posture of defense that couldn't quite conceal the exhaustion settled deep in her bones. Her intensity, usually sharp enough to cut glass, was softened now, worn smooth by a responsibility she had never wanted. Beside her, Malcolm was a quiet, solid harbor, his stillness a counterpoint to the nervous energy that thrummed through the room. Vivi and Marc were a single unit near a stack of painted flats, his hand resting on the small of her back in a gesture of such simple, grounding reassurance that it made Vivi's heart ache with its rightness. Kevin and Sarah sat on the edge of a heavy prop trunk, the one still bearing the stenciled label *Macbeth, 1989*. Their shoulders touched, a silent conversation of support passing between them at that small point of contact. Near the heavy metal door, Zoe and Tyler stood together, his arm a protective line around her shoulders. Her guilt remained a shadow in her eyes, a stain his love had not yet managed to wash away. And leaning against a flat painted to look like a forest, Danny Kim clutched his stage manager's clipboard like a shield, his headset a forgotten necklace around his neck. A tarnished prop crown, its paste jewels long since fallen out, sat on a crate nearby, its empty settings catching the light like hollow eyes.

"He killed the story," Tyler said into the quiet, answering the question that hung in the air among them. He met Cate's gaze. "And I quit."

They were tangled in a problem of language, trying to distill a century of lethal, beautiful magic into a few gentle warnings for the welcome packets. Trying to write a map for a country that lives inside the mind.

"The problem is the proof," Tyler's voice cut through the hushed debate. His journalistic instincts, the part of him that demanded facts and sources, were still sharp after everything he had come to believe. "We can tell them to stay grounded. We can start a buddy system. But until they feel it, until it gets its hooks in them, it's just a ghost story. How do we make it real for them *before* it's too late?"

A profound, listening silence fell over the small group. The hum of the theater seemed to deepen, pulling them all into its slow, dreaming rhythm. The question hung in the air, thick and suffocating with the weight of all the souls who had been lost because no one had an answer.

No one but Carmen.

She had been standing in a corner shrouded in shadow, a small, unassuming figure in her practical work blouse and slacks. For years, she had been a part of the theater's furniture, a fixture as reliable and over-looked as the worn velvet seats in the main house. She was the warm and watchful costumer, the keeper of needle and thread, the woman who mended what was torn. Now, she stepped forward, moving from the darkness into the single beam of light. The motes of sediment parted around her as if making way. Her hands were clasped before her, her face a mask of solemn purpose that transformed her familiar features into those of a stranger.

"Because a story isn't enough," she said. Her voice, usually as soft and melodic as a wind chime, held a new note, a quiet resonance that spoke of a secret kept for a lifetime. Every eye in the room turned to her, drawn by the unexpected gravity in her tone. "They need to see the evidence."

Cate's brow furrowed, her sharp gaze fixing on the

woman she had worked with for two decades. "Carmen? What are you talking about? What evidence?"

Carmen drew a long, slow breath, and Vivi could almost see a lifetime of secrets gathering behind her eyes, a flood tide held back by the thinnest of walls. "I had a friend. Her name was Clara. This was in... 1988. We were in rehearsals for *Hamlet*. She was our Ophelia. And she was brilliant. Luminous. The kind of actress who doesn't just play a role, she becomes it. But the part... the part began to consume her," she said.

"She started talking about the river," Carmen continued, her gaze turned inward, lost in a memory nearly forty years old. "Not a stage river made of painted canvas and light. A real one. She said the water was so clear, like swallowing stars. She described the flowers that grew on the bank, saying they were like nothing she'd ever seen before." Carmen's throat worked, a small, painful motion. "We all just thought... method. The way actors talk when a role gets under their skin. We thought just pretty words."

She paused, the memory of that willful ignorance tightening her expression. "The night she disappeared from the show, she left a note in her dressing room. It just said, 'I've gone to the river.' And on her dressing table, she'd left a small handful of wildflowers." Carmen's eyes met Vivi's, and the pain in them was sharp and fresh. "They were blue. A shade of blue I have never seen before or since. A color that hurts your eyes to look at. They wilted by morning, turning to a fine, grey powder, all except one. The one I kept was paper and velvet beneath my fingers before it, too, crumbled to nothing."

A collective, sharp intake of breath rustled through the small room, a sound like dry leaves skittering across pavement. The story of the lost actress, the face in the Green Room photograph that had haunted them all, suddenly had a name. Clara. She was Ophelia.

"I tried to tell the director," Carmen said, and a shadow of old hurt passed over her features, brief and sharp. "Mr. Albright. I told him what Clara had been saying. I showed him the dust from the flower. He just... he patted my hand." Her voice went flat, stripped of all emotion by the remembered condescension. "He told me actors were flighty creatures, prone to dramatics. He told me to 'stick to the sewing.' He reported her to the police as a runaway."

The raw injustice of it hung in the air, a poison that had been sealed in this basement for decades. Vivi glanced at Kevin, then at Zoe. She saw the same horrified understanding reflected in their eyes. They had all been Clara. Each of them had stood on the bank of their own river, just one choice away from stepping in.

"That day," Carmen's gaze swept over them, her quiet strength finally unveiled like a hidden blade. "I was given a new role. One I didn't audition for and didn't want. I became an archivist."

She turned and walked toward a shadowed corner of the room, to a tall, teetering stack of old, floral-patterned hat boxes. They looked like forgotten props from a bygone era, their paper surfaces coated in a thick film of grime, their colors faded to muted suggestions of rose and ivy.

"I couldn't stop what was happening," she

confessed, her voice thick with the burden of her long, lonely vigil. "I couldn't make anyone believe me. But I could watch. I could document. I could... help, in my own quiet way."

Her steady, wrinkled hands reached for the top box. With a soft scrape of cardboard on cardboard, she pulled it down. A peeling, handwritten label on its side, the ink faded to a watery brown, read: "Hats: Summer Stock '92." She placed it on a clear space on the concrete floor and, after a moment's hesitation, lifted the lid.

The group gathered around, their faces a collage of shock and awe in the stark, unforgiving light of the bare bulb.

The box wasn't filled with hats but with impossible things. A handful of coarse black sand that shimmered as if it were ground from obsidian, sealed in a small plastic baggie, and labeled with a piece of masking tape: *A Midsummer Night's Dream, '92*. A single, iridescent feather that seemed to drink the light, its barbs shifting from black to deep violet, marked *The Tempest, '97*. A small, intricately carved wooden bird, impossibly light, as if it still remembered how to fly, labeled *The Cherry Orchard, '03*. Each item was a ghost, a remnant, a piece of physical proof from a world that wasn't supposed to bleed into this one.

Vivi's mind flashed backward, a memory replaying with sudden, shocking clarity, from chapter fourteen of her own life, a scene she had thought was insignificant. Her first Viola costume fitting. Carmen's seemingly offhand comment about finding sand in the dressing rooms, her gentle musing that actors "bring the strangest things back with them."

"The sand," Vivi whispered, her voice barely breathing. Her eyes were wide as she looked from the baggie of impossible sand to Carmen's sorrowful face. "When you were fitting my Viola costume... You mentioned finding sand in the hems."

Carmen met her gaze, and a sad, knowing smile touched her lips, a smile that held thirty years of silent watching. "I did. And you, my dear, had the faintest scent of sea salt in your hair that day. I was checking." Her eyes held Vivi's, full of fierce, quiet compassion. "I was asking, in the only way I could without getting you locked away or losing my job. It was my quiet way of letting you know you weren't alone. That someone saw."

A wave of immense gratitude washed over Vivi, so powerful it almost buckled her knees, mingled with the deeply unsettling feeling of having been seen in her most secret, vulnerable moments. This quiet, unassuming woman had been a guardian angel hiding in plain sight, a secret keeper watching over all of them. Carmen hadn't been making a quirky observation about messy actors. She had been extending a lifeline, a thread of connection that Vivi had been too lost in her own beautiful, hollow world to see.

"I'm so sorry," Kevin said with an emotion he rarely let surface. He was staring at a small, tarnished silver locket in another box, the engraved initials worn smooth, marked *Phantom, '09*. He, too, was connecting the dots of his own terrible journey, realizing with a sick jolt that he had never been as uniquely, beautifully tortured as he had believed. He had just been the next one in line.

"There is nothing for you to be sorry for," Carmen's voice was firm but kind, a mother speaking to a child who has finally come home. "You were all fighting a battle no one would have believed you were in. My job was to collect the evidence, just in case. And sometimes... to nudge."

"Nudge?" Tyler asked, his reporter's notebook now open on his knee, his pen moving across the page in swift, urgent strokes.

"Sometimes an actor would be... lost. Disconnected from us," Carmen explained, her gaze distant for a moment. "They would start to talk in the cadence of their character, or their eyes would have a look in them like they were seeing a different room than the one they were standing in. So, I would take an item, one I had collected before from their character's world. A seashell still crusted with salt from Illyria's shore. A piece of dried, dark heather from the Scottish play." Her hands smoothed over the lid of a box as if soothing it. "I'd leave it in their coat pocket. Tuck it inside their script. Once, I mended a tear in an actor's jacket with a single thread of shimmering gold that came from a fairy-tale costume. A tangible piece of fantasy, right there in the solid, real world. A small, strange thing to help their mind question the barrier between the two. A nudge back toward reality."

The sheer, breathtaking empathy of her strategy, born from decades of helpless observation, silenced them all. She had not been a passive archivist, a librarian of sorrow.

She had been an active, subtle warrior, fighting a secret war with the only weapons she had. A needle, a thread, and a quiet, unshakeable faith in the people she thought of as her children. She had been leaving breadcrumbs not to help them find their way back, but to remind them that there was a 'back' to find at all.

Cate stepped forward, moving with a slow, deliberate grace, and placed a hand on Carmen's shoulder. "Carmen," she said, and her voice was thick with an emotion she rarely showed, a raw astonishment that broke through her carefully constructed walls. "Your quiet courage puts every one of us to shame. Thank you."

The burden Carmen had carried in silence for over thirty years—a weight that had settled into the lines on her face and the stoop of her shoulders—finally lifted. The validation in the room was a palpable force, a collective wave of respect and gratitude that was warm enough to push back the basement's persistent chill. Her years of secret, thankless work weren't just seen. They were honored.

She gave a slight, shaky nod, her eyes glistening with unshed tears. Then her gaze shifted, moving past the faces of her friends, settling on one specific, plain-looking box set slightly apart from the others. It was simple, unadorned cardboard, its edges softened with age, with brown paper peeling at the corners. It had no production label, no year scrawled in faded ink. Only a single name, written in a delicate, looping script that had bled and feathered over time. *Ophelia.*

"I've documented everything I could," Carmen said,

voice softening, dropping into a whisper that held the texture of old grief. The raw pain of losing her friend was still present in her, a ghost that had never left her side, a sorrow so old it had become a part of her posture, of the way she held her hands. As she looked at the box, her own hand trembled slightly—a minor, involuntary betrayal of the calm she had projected. "But that one... that one was Clara's. It holds what she left behind."

She looked up, her gaze meeting each of theirs in turn, a silent, heavy question passing from the theater's first, secret guardian to its new, official ones.

"It's the only one I never opened."

THIRTY-FIVE

DANNY'S GROUNDING INFLUENCE

The Green Room was a place built for feelings that were supposed to pass, but tonight it felt thick with a permanence that settled in the air like dust on a forgotten heirloom. Faded posters from productions long past, their comedies and tragedies all gone to ghosts, looked down like a silent chorus of ancestors. The whole room held the familiar scent of old velvet upholstery breathing out its history, mixed with the sharp perfume of whiteboard markers and the ghost of stale coffee. On that board, a half-erased diagram of their new buddy system looked as fragile as a promise, a hopeful little scribble against a threat too vast to name.

They had gathered here again after the tense, soul-baring session in the basement. Carmen's secret history, a lifetime of impossible evidence kept in floral hat boxes, had been moved with the care of a holy relic to Cate's locked office. The last box, bearing only the name Ophelia, sat in the corner of Cate's desk, a silent, unopened tomb that they had all agreed to leave be for now. The past was a wound best tended to later. The immediate future and the safety of the family that remained were the things that mattered most.

Danny Kim stood just outside the circle, his communication headset hanging loose around his neck like a forgotten garland. The familiar comfort of his stage manager's clipboard was a solid presence in his hands. From where he stood, he could see them all, a fragile and determined ecosystem of artists trying to plant a garden of order in a world of chaos. He just listened.

"The check-in and check-out sheet is on the main call board," Vivi said. Her voice was clear and measured, the sound of a leader who had found her footing in the storm. She pointed a steady finger toward the list on the whiteboard. "Everyone signs in the moment they arrive and signs out with their buddy when they leave. There are no exceptions."

"And we're all clear on the two-person rule for any of the high-risk zones," Kevin added, his own tone solid. He sat on the worn-out couch, Sarah a quiet, steady presence beside him. "The dressing rooms, the archive, all the basement rehearsal spaces. No one goes into those places alone. Not ever again."

Zoe, who still wore her guilt like a heavy costume she couldn't take off, nodded with fierce energy. "We also have the safe zones. Here in the green room, the lobby, and the main stage during a full company call. Places where that... that feeling is weaker."

Tyler leaned against the wall near her, his arm a subtle

but constant anchor. He made a note in that reporter's notebook of his, having shifted from a skeptical observer to a full-fledged participant. His cynicism had burned away, leaving behind a protective, practical core. "So, we've got accountability, restricted areas, and safe zones. It's a start."

Cate and Malcolm watched from the room's center, their faces holding the same weary vigilance they always wore, a map of old sorrows. "It is good," Cate's voice was a low, certain rumble. "It is community as a shield. It is what we should have had thirty years ago."

A moment of hard-won pride settled over the room, warm and quiet. They had faced down a crisis of spirit, rescued two of their own from the edge of oblivion, and built something together to keep it from happening again. They had created a plan from the ashes of shared trauma and mutual care. It felt solid. It felt right.

Danny clicked his pen.

The small, sharp sound cut through the warm consensus like a shard of glass. Every eye in the room turned to him. He had not spoken a word in twenty minutes, just observed, his pen making minor, precise marks on a fresh sheet of paper on his clipboard, the kind with glow tape along the edges for finding his way in the dark.

He looked down at his notes, then up at the earnest, hopeful faces staring back at him. He hated what he was about to do, but his job wasn't to manage feelings. His job was to organize reality.

"It's a great first draft." This was the same voice he

used to announce a fifteen-minute hold during a technical disaster that had everyone else ready to tear their hair out. "But what you've made here isn't a safety protocol. It's a group hug put down on paper."

The warmth in the room vanished as if a door had been thrown open to a winter night. Faces fell. Kevin's shoulders tightened. Zoe looked as though she had been struck. Cate's expression hardened into stone. Danny's blunt, process-driven truth was a hand dismissing their deeply personal, heartfelt work.

"What do you mean by that?" Vivi asked, her voice losing its foundation of certainty, a hint of defensiveness creeping in like a chill.

Danny didn't so much as flinch. He walked to the whiteboard, his steps measured and full of purpose. "Your check-in sheet. Who is responsible for checking it at the end of the night? Is there a designated person who cross-references it with the building lock-up schedule and the fire marshal's headcount log? What's the escalation process if a signature is missing? Who do they call, and in what order? What's the timeline for that call? Ten minutes overdue? Thirty? An hour?"

He gestured to their list of restricted areas. "The two-person rule. What's the procedure if a buddy has to leave the room for an emergency? Does the other person have to evacuate immediately? What if they're in the middle of something delicate? Is there a designated all-clear signal? Is it verbal? Is it a light cue? What's the contingency for a building-wide power failure, a dark-stage protocol?"

He faced them, his expression not unkind, but as

unyielding as concrete. "I'm not questioning the threat. I believe you. I saw what happened. I'm questioning your response to it. You're all coming to this like artists. You're trying to solve a problem with emotion, with trust, with community spirit. And all of that is important. That's the 'why' of it. But it is not the 'how.' This is a workplace safety issue. It's an occupational hazard, same as a faulty fly rig or a cable that isn't grounded. This one happens to be a hazard that can send you to a fairy-tale kingdom."

The deflation in the room was palpable, a weight that pressed down on their shoulders. They had been so sure of themselves, so certain their unity was a fortress. Danny's cool, logistical dismantling of their plan left them feeling like amateurs. Their passionate work had been reduced to a list of gaping, unexamined holes.

He saw the looks on their faces. The disappointment. The hint of resentment. He softened his tone, just a fraction, shifting from a critic to a guide.

"Look," he said, and his gaze swept the room, landing on each of them in turn, a quiet acknowledgment. "I manage the safety of fifty people from falling scenery, frayed electrical wiring, and the occasional burst of pyrotechnics every single night. That is my job. This... this is just another hazard on the list. It has different rules, I'll grant you that, but it needs a process. A real one."

He looked at their hopeful diagram on the whiteboard, the lines and circles that were a testament to how much they cared for each other. "Your buddy system was the right first step. Think of it as Version one-point-oh. It shows you care, and that's the foundation for any real safety culture. Without that, no protocol in the world would ever matter." He paused, letting that piece of validation settle in the air between them. "Now we make it work. Let's build a real process."

He provided them with an analogy they could understand, grounding the unbelievable in the language of their profession. "An open trapdoor on a blacked-out stage isn't something you handle by telling folks to 'be careful.' You have a process. The area is taped off in glow tape that burns a warning into the dark. It's marked in blood red on every schedule. You have a dedicated crew hand whose entire job is to personally check that it's secure before and after every single scene. A mirror that might swallow you whole is that open trapdoor. We need a process, not a prayer."

The shift in the room was immediate, like a key turning in a lock. The language of the stage, of professional rigor and unbending process, was a language they all spoke. They understood. The dejection on their faces gave way to a dawning realization, a sudden respect for an expertise they didn't have. They weren't artists failing at logistics. They were a team that had just found its logistics expert.

Cate Hart stepped forward, her expression clear and decisive. She gave a single, sharp nod that left no room for argument. "Danny is right," she declared, her voice ringing with authority. She turned to face him fully. "As the director of this company, I am formally ceding all authority on operational safety protocols, supernatural or otherwise, to you. You have the final word. Tell us what you need."

Malcolm nodded in solemn agreement beside her. One by one, the others followed, a quiet chorus of assent rippling through the room. Vivi, Kevin, Tyler. They were deferring not from a place of weakness, but from a mature understanding of their own limits and his undeniable strength. This was the moment when a loose collective of guardians became a truly structured and effective team.

A familiar weight settled on Danny's shoulders, comfortable as a well-worn tool belt. The weight of responsibility. This was something he knew how to handle. He unclipped the flimsy, heartfelt sheet from his clipboard and let it drift down to the table. Then he pulled a slim, ruggedized tablet from his tote bag, its screen glowing to life with a clean, empty document. He had taken on this role not because he doubted the magic, but because he believed, with every fiber of his being, in the process.

"Okay," he said, all business now. His fingers flew across the screen, creating headings and sub-bullets in a clean, sharp font. *Risk Assessment. Accountability Matrix. Escalation Procedure. Contingency Planning.* This was his art form.

He looked up at the faces watching him, their expressions now a mix of profound relief and intense curiosity. They were his team. He had their trust. Now, he just needed their data.

He held their gaze, his own expression one of complete

and utter seriousness, the practical anchor in their sea of impossible things.

"Right. First, I need a risk assessment matrix. On a scale of one to ten, what is the probability and impact of... spontaneous trans-dimensional travel... in the props closet versus, say, the main stage?"

A stunned, absolute silence fell over the Green Room. The jarringly corporate question, applied to their wild and terrifying new reality, made every single one of them freeze in place. They had found their practical expert. They were beginning to realize what a strange and surreal partnership this was going to be.

THIRTY-SIX

THE SUPPORT NETWORK

On the sagging floral couch in the Green Room, a piece of furniture that had absorbed decades of actors' opening-night jitters and closing-night tears, Vivi and Marc sat so close their shoulders touched, a silent promise of solidarity. The room smelled of old velvet, warm electronics, and the lingering, sharp scent of ozone that seemed to follow any brush with the theater's more profound truths. Into this fragile peace, Danny Kim's question fell with all the grace of a dropped sandbag.

He asked about a risk assessment matrix.

The words, so sterile and plucked from some corporate manual shepherding a world of spreadsheets and liability waivers, seemed to suck the very warmth from the room. The shared relief that had settled over them like a warm blanket moments before was ripped away.

Tyler was the first one to find air. A short, sharp sound tore from his throat with a laugh born of humor and the kind of jarring disbelief that comes when the world tilts sideways. "A risk assessment matrix," he said, the words tasting like absurdity on his tongue. He shook his head, a slow gesture of wonder. "For what, exactly? Spontaneous, unscheduled trips to Shakespearean England?"

Danny didn't so much as twitch. His focus was a laser point on the screen of his tablet, a heavy-duty device encased in black, reinforced rubber. It looked like something designed to survive a fall from a high loft, and he held it like a shield. "Probability and impact," he stated, his voice an unshakeable monotone. "It's standard operating procedure. We can't build a defense for a threat we haven't measured. So, the props closet. It has low foot traffic and a single point of entry. What is the statistical likelihood of a portal manifesting in there compared to, for instance, one of the seven dressing rooms on the second floor?"

A gallery of stunned faces stared back at him. They had just walked through a fire that burned the soul, guided only by the fragile threads of trust and love. Now, Danny was asking them to analyze the ashes and file a report.

Kevin broke the spell. He rose from the couch, a restless energy coiling in his frame, and the shift in him was immediate and unsettling. The quiet, hard-won calm he had cultivated for weeks seemed to peel away, revealing the man he used to be. His voice, when it came, was a low, resonant thing, the same brooding timber that had once been both his artistic signature and his cage. "This is madness," he said, the words a low rumble that seemed to vibrate through the worn patch of carpet, and he began to pace. "We aren't talking about a faulty lighting grid,

Danny. We are talking about the very thing that makes this place breathe. We're talking about inspiration."

His eyes, a deep and turbulent blue, swept over them, burning with a fire they all recognized. "You can't measure it. You cannot put the human heart on a spreadsheet and slap a warning label on its deepest needs. That's not protection. That's desecration."

He stopped, his hands gesturing, painting a picture of the prison he feared. "The path Vivi and I walked was born of that need, both dangerous and wrong, I know that. But its roots were in something real. The desire to connect, to go deeper into the work than our own skins would allow. If you turn this theater into a fortress of checklists and regulations, if you start treating every moment of profound, personal discovery as a potential 'containment breach,' you will starve the very art you think you're saving. You'll build a beautiful, safe, sterile box with nothing alive inside it."

Cate Hart's head came up. The weary lines around her eyes, etched there by forty years of vigilance, hardened into something brittle and sharp. In her hand, a ceramic mug filled with the gingery, calming tea Malcolm always made for her suddenly seemed fragile. She set it down on a side table with a sharp clink, the sound of a gavel falling. The comforting scent was lost, overpowered by the sudden draft of her memory.

"A prison?" she shot back, her voice stripped of all warmth. "You want to talk about prisons, Kevin? I have seen a real one, a world stitched together with paranoia and painted in shades of drying blood. It had a sky the wrong color, and the very air tasted of ambition, a sickness that infected the man I watched it consume. You think this magic is some gentle muse. It's not. The darkness doesn't send an invitation. It doesn't knock. It finds the cracks you leave open because you were too proud or too foolish to seal them."

A tremor ran through her voice, a fine vibration born not of weakness but of the sheer, unyielding force of a memory that had never stopped being real. "Your 'inspiration' nearly cost us two of our own. It nearly tore this place apart at the seams. Anything less than absolute, unbending protocols is a welcome mat for the next disaster. We use the buddy system; there are no exceptions. We identify the high-risk rooms, and they are locked down. We run drills. No one is ever, ever alone in this building. Not for a moment."

Zoe flinched, the force of Cate's words striking her with the sting of a physical slap. A knot of shame tightened in her stomach. Cate's 'prison' of blood and paranoia was a nightmare, but Zoe's own fairy-tale kingdom, with its glittering balls and prince, had been a prison too. One she'd walked into with a smile, believing its cloying sweetness was a gift. She remembered the blissful ignorance, the certainty that her connection to that world was a sign of her own specialness. She risked a glance at Tyler, and the deep worry carved into his face sent another wave of sickness through her. He knew. He'd seen how close she'd come to choosing the perfect, empty story over their messy, real one.

The room had split down a fault line of fear and

conviction. On one side stood Kevin, the artist who had almost drowned in his own romanticized darkness, now arguing for the very freedom that had nearly been his undoing. On the other hand was Cate, the guardian who had survived the inferno, now demanding walls so high no spark could ever get in or out again. Between them, Vivi and Marc exchanged a look, their shared anxiety a current passing.

"It is not about suffocating anyone. It's about keeping them alive," Cate insisted, her voice rising with a sharp, brittle edge.

"Safety is not the complete removal of risk, Cate. It's the intelligent management of it," Kevin retorted, his hands moving with the dramatic flair of a man born for the stage. "We're actors. Our entire profession is built on taking risks."

The two opposing forces met in the middle of the room and created a perfect, immovable stalemate. They were all passion and all fear, locked in a battle with no possibility of victory. They were stuck.

Then, Sarah moved. She had been a pool of calm in the churning waters of the room, sitting quietly in an armchair, her pen held loosely over a fresh page in her notepad. The soft click of her setting the pen down on the end table beside her was a tiny sound, yet it sliced through the tension, drawing every eye. She looked from Kevin's fiery, impassioned face to the white-knuckled grip Cate had on the edge of the table, and a deep, knowing sadness touched her expression.

From a small, carved wooden bowl on the table, she

picked up a smooth, grey river stone, one of several she kept in her office and here in the Green Room, small, tangible anchors to the present moment. She turned it over and over in her palm, the rhythmic, soothing motion a stark contrast to the jagged energy filling the air.

"You're both right," she said. Her voice wasn't loud, but it carried a gentle authority that made everyone lean in. The room fell silent, waiting.

She met Kevin's gaze first, her eyes full of understanding. "You are absolutely right, Kevin. If we make this place a cage of rigid rules, we are essentially criminalizing the artistic process. We would be telling our actors that the deep, vulnerable, and sometimes dark places they must go to find truth are off-limits. That will only ever create fear and secrets. And we all know secrets are the things that give this magic its teeth."

A fraction of the defiant tension in Kevin's shoulders eased. He gave a slight, almost imperceptible nod. He had been heard.

Then Sarah turned her gaze to Cate, and her expression softened with a wave of profound empathy. "And you're right too, Cate. Our current system, as Danny's perfectly logical and deeply unsettling question just high-lighted, is built on a foundation of hope and good intentions. It is not a process. It is full of holes. And you know better than anyone on this earth that the darkness doesn't wait for an invitation. It waits for a door left unlocked."

Cate's jaw remained a tight, stubborn line, but the unyielding stiffness in her spine relaxed, just a little. Her fear had been given its due.

Sarah let the acknowledgment settle into the space between them, a quiet moment for the two opposing truths to coexist. She continued to smooth the stone in her hand, as if polishing her thoughts before she offered them. "We are looking at this problem from the wrong angle. We aren't trying to build a prison." She looked pointedly at Kevin. "And we aren't leaving the doors unlocked for monsters to wander in." She looked directly at Cate. "We are upgrading a climbing gym."

The metaphor, so unexpected and straightforward, landed in the room like a single, clear bell toll. It hung in the air, clean and pure.

"This theater," Sarah continued, her free hand starting to sketch the concept in the air, "is a place where we ask people to climb. We ask them to reach breathtaking creative heights that they cannot possibly reach on the ground. That's a beautiful goal. It's a worthy goal. But it is, by its very nature, a high-risk activity. You don't stop people from climbing a mountain because it's dangerous. You give them the right equipment. You give them professional-grade harnesses and ropes. You provide certified, experienced spotters. You teach them how to check their knots, how to communicate with their team, and how to recognize when they're too tired to go on."

The idea clicked into place for every single person in the room at the same time. A wave of comprehension washed through them, easing the hard lines of their faces.

"So," Sarah's eyes found Danny, who was watching her with an expression of intense, focused curiosity. "Let's build the best, safest climbing gym in the world. We reinforce the buddy system for all work in high-risk rooms and for all solo rehearsals. That's our mandatory, professional-grade harness. No one climbs without one. No exceptions."

She then turned her attention back to the actors, the artists who would be doing the climbing. "But a harness is only there to save you after you have already fallen. We need a spotter. We need someone whose job it is to help you get down from the wall safely, before your muscles give out, before your grip fails. So, we add a second protocol. Protocol Two will be a mandatory cool-down."

"A cool-down?" Vivi asked, her brow furrowed with intrigue.

"After any intense solo work, or any scene work that takes place in a room we've designated as high-risk, you're required to have a ten-minute conversation with your partner, or a designated mentor," Sarah explained, her voice steady and clear. "The conversation must be about something completely unrelated to the show, such as what you're planning to have for dinner. A stupid movie you watched last night. Your plans for the weekend. The goal is to verbally and consciously pull yourself back into the mundane, grounding details of reality. It's a gentle, guided reentry into the real world. It is your spotter, talking you safely back down the wall before you realize you're exhausted."

Brilliant. The understanding rippled through the group, a shared wave of relief and excitement. This wasn't a rule born of mistrust or restriction, a protocol born of therapeutic care, one that deeply respected both the work and the artist. It honored Kevin's passionate need to explore the depths and Cate's visceral need for a safe return.

Danny, who had been listening with the rapt attention of an engineer studying a new blueprint, gave a single, sharp nod. His fingers were already a blur across the screen of his ruggedized tablet, the stylus clicking with precise, efficient taps. "Got it," he said, the word clipped and final. He looked up, his pragmatic mind already constructing the logistical framework. "Protocol One: Buddy System. That is our harness. Protocol Two: Mandatory Cool-Down. That is our spotter." A ghost of a smile touched his lips. Harnesses and spotters. I can build a process around that."

The suffocating tension in the Green Room had not merely vanished. It had been transformed into something new, a focused, collaborative energy that hummed with purpose. They had found their guiding principle. They had a path forward that didn't force them to choose between Kevin's passionate freedom and Cate's hard-earned fear. They had stopped being survivors reacting to a crisis and had become architects, designing their own future.

A moment of quiet satisfaction settled on them as Danny continued to jot down the framework of their new rules, his face a mask of pure concentration. He was in his element, turning chaos into order, creating a system where there had only been hope. He looked up from his list, his practical gaze sweeping over the faces of the people in the room, his people. The witch, the ghost of a Scottish king, the recovered addicts, the steadfast partners, the quiet archivist, the therapist. This was his company now. This was his process.

He tapped his stylus against the tablet screen, the sound small and decisive. "This is great for us," his tone was matter-of-fact. "This is a solid framework for the people in this room, for the people who already know the risks and have seen what's on the other side of the mirror."

He paused, letting his gaze rest on each of them in turn. "But how in the hell do we explain any of this to the next brand-new actor who walks through that door for an audition, without sounding like we belong in a straitjacket?"

The question, so brutally practical and profoundly unanswerable, hung in the air, a stark and heavy reminder that their work as guardians of this strange, beautiful, and dangerous place had only just begun.

THIRTY-SEVEN

ZOE'S GROWTH

Cate let out a long sigh, rubbing the deep grooves at her temples. The lines of fatigue etched on her face seemed to have settled in for good, a permanent map of the roads they'd all been forced to travel. "We can't exactly hand them a welcome packet that includes a waiver for 'magical mirrors and their soul-stealing, devastatingly handsome inhabitants'."

Malcolm, who always seemed to be the calm eye of her personal storm, suggested a tiered system. A slow, careful acclimation to the theater's unique character. A mentorship program that was about more than just hitting your marks and learning your lines.

"For now," Marc said as his steady gaze swept over the circle of tired but unbreakable faces, "we keep this circle small—the eight of us, plus Carmen and Danny. We'll be the first line of contact. We'll be the spotters, the buddies, the harness. We'll figure out how to write the 'welcome to the madhouse' pamphlet later."

A soft murmur of agreement rippled through the room. A bandage, not a cure, a way to hold the line until they could rebuild the wall. They set aside the bigger, more daunting problem, letting it rest so they could focus on the immediate, tangible future of the spring season.

Months later, the unforgiving glare of a single Fresnel stage light pinned Zoe to a set that was the antithesis of everything she had ever been. The light was a physical weight, hot on her skin, bleaching the color from the minimalist apartment, a world rendered in shades of grey, little more than a table, two chairs, and the stark, skeletal outline of a window frame. This was the world of *The Shattering*, a brutal contemporary tragedy about a woman hollowed out by the sudden, violent loss of her family, a universe away from the glittering fantasy of Cinderella's ballroom. And a truth she had spent her entire life running from.

She stood center stage, the breath caught in her throat like a trapped bird. From the consuming darkness of the house, the director's voice echoed, impatient. "From the top of the monologue, Zoe. And I need it this time. I truly need to see the rage. She just found the letter. Her whole life, everything she believed was a lie. Where is the anger?"

Zoe nodded, her throat a tight knot of compliance. She could feel the old, familiar instinct rising in her, a phantom limb twitching with a muscle memory she'd honed for twenty-six years—the people-pleaser's reflex. *Give him anger. Perform it for him.* A furrowed brow, a clenched fist, a voice made sharp and cutting.

She took a shallow breath, ready to manufacture the rage on command, but then her eyes found them. Marc, a quiet silhouette in the soft glow of the lighting booth, his expression radiating a deep, unhurried patience. And Vivi, sitting in the front row, not as a critic but as a silent, knowing witness. Vivi gave her a slight, almost imperceptible nod. They weren't asking her to perform. They were waiting, quietly and lovingly, for her truth.

The fear that hit her was immediate and suffocating, a wave washing over the hot stage lights. What if she finally touched real anger, and it consumed her? What if it burned through her and she couldn't find her way back? What if the character's shattering grief dredged up her own, the crushing guilt over the chaos she had caused, the hollow, aching void of the love she'd lost for a man who was never real? What if she finally showed them all the ugly, messy, broken pieces of herself and they turned away in disgust? What if she became unlikable? The thought was a shard of ice in her heart.

The director's sigh was a gust of wind from the dark. His patience had worn thin as an old thread. "Alright, that's fine. Let's move on to the next—"

"No, wait," Zoe said. She held up a hand, a gesture that was both a plea for time and a command to stay. "Just give me a minute."

She closed her eyes, shutting out the director's expectant silence, the vast emptiness of the stage, the waiting, loving eyes of her friends. She didn't try to imagine the character's grief. She didn't need to. She just had to stop running from herself. She reached down, deep inside herself, and let the mask of the eternal optimist, the one she had painstakingly crafted and worn for a lifetime, finally, completely, fall away. It shattered on the floor of her heart without a sound.

And then she let herself feel it all.

The profound, soul-deep loneliness of her years spent performing happiness for everyone, including herself. The quiet terror of being seen as not enough, of knowing that the sunshine everyone loved was just a trick of the light. The sharp, bitter sting of Prince Adrian's beautiful, hollow lies, the memory of his words that were as empty as a stage set after the show. The shame, hot and furious, of knowing her desperate escape had endangered the people she loved most in the world. And beneath it all, a white-hot, furious grief for the girl she used to be. The girl who thought an ending was something you could find, like a lost slipper, instead of something you had to build, nail by nail, with your own blistered hands.

She dug her nails into her palms, the sharp crescents of pain a welcome anchor to the real, physical world. She let the fury and the sorrow rise, a hot, acrid tide climbing her throat.

She opened her eyes, burning with unshed tears.

"You son of a bitch," she whispered, and the words weren't for the character's absent, deceitful husband. They were a venomous prayer for the ghost of a prince. The whisper was raw, jagged, filled with a poison she never knew she possessed. Her body trembled with the bone-deep shudder of a soul cracking open to the light.

She stumbled toward the simple grey table, her hand

sweeping a stack of papers, her character's entire life, onto the floor in a cascade of white. "You promised me!" she screamed, the sound tearing from a place deep within her, a raw, ragged cry of ultimate, absolute betrayal.

And then came the sob with a guttural, ugly, wrenching sound of pure, undiluted agony. She collapsed into the chair, her body wracked with a grief so authentic, so horrifically real, that it silenced the entire theater.

She wept. For her character. For Clara, the lost Ophelia. For herself. For the girl who just wanted a fairy tale and the woman who had to learn to live without one.

The silence that followed was absolute and reverent, as if the whole building were holding its breath. Out in the darkness, the director just breathed two words. "Yes. That."

Later that night, the door to the apartment she now shared with Tyler clicked shut behind her, the sound a soft, final note on a long day. The space was a reflection of their two lives braided together. His towering stacks of books and vinyl records, smelling of old paper and history, coexisted with her cheerful, colorful throw pillows. One of his favorite records, a quiet folk album, sat next to a stack of her brightly colored playscripts on the coffee table. The air smelled of his dark-roast coffee and the lavender soap she always used.

She found him in the living room, reading under the warm, golden glow of a single floor lamp. He looked up the moment she entered, his face softening with immediate concern. "Hey. Long rehearsal?"

The old Zoe would have manufactured a bright smile.

It was great! So productive! We made so much progress! The new Zoe, the one who was still vibrating with the emotional aftershocks of the exorcism she'd performed on stage, just nodded. The weight of it all was still settled on her shoulders like a heavy coat. She walked over and sank onto the couch beside him, curling into his side without a single word.

He wrapped an arm around her, his touch solid and grounding. He didn't push or pry. He just waited, offering the silent, sturdy support that had become her anchor in the unsteady waters of her new life.

"I did it today," she whispered, her voice muffled against the soft, worn fabric of his flannel shirt. "I let myself be angry. On stage. For real."

"I bet you were terrifying," he whispered against her ear, a sound that felt like home.

She pulled back just enough to look at him, her eyes searching his for any shadow of disappointment, any sign that he preferred the sunny, uncomplicated girl he had first met. She found nothing but a deep, steady love. A love that wasn't afraid of her darkness, that didn't ask her to hide her storms.

"Ugly," she admitted, her voice small and laced with the last remnants of her fear. "And I was so scared that if I touched it, I'd get stuck there. Or that you... that it would be too much for you."

Tyler's hand came up to cup her cheek, his thumb stroking her skin with a tenderness that unraveled the last knot of tension in her chest. "Zoe," his voice serious, his gaze unwavering and true. "I fell for the sunshine, it's true.

I did. But I'm in love with the whole damn sky. The clouds, the storms, the works. You don't ever have to perform for me."

The raw, unconditional acceptance in his words was more potent than any fairy-tale declaration she had ever dreamed of. This was the happily ever after she had finally, painfully, redefined for herself. Not a perfect, unchanging story, but a shared, messy, beautiful reality.

Her artistic breakthrough on stage had been a necessary release. But this moment, here in the warm safety of their home, was the valid reward. The vulnerability she had unlocked for her character was now hers to keep, a key to a deeper intimacy she had never known was possible.

She leaned in, and the kiss was different from any they had shared before. There was no performance in it, no hesitation, no part of her held back in reserve for fear of being too much. This kiss deepened, becoming a silent conversation of shared trust and accepted flaws, a language of scars and healing.

Later, tangled in the soft, worn sheets of their bed, lying in the peaceful dark, Zoe felt a sense of rightness settle deep in her bones. For the first time in her life, intimacy wasn't a role to be played or an escape to be chased.

She traced the strong, specific line of his jaw in the dim light, a map of the man who had seen all of her, the dark and the light, and had not run.

"This is real," she whispered, the words a quiet, definitive declaration against the darkness.

THIRTY-EIGHT

THE MAGIC STABILIZES

The Meridian Theatre breathed around them with sounds the company had learned to place, a low architectural sigh of old wood settling and velvet curtains drinking in the silence. Months had passed since the crisis that had nearly pulled their world down around them, and a peace as fragile as a held note had settled in its place. The hurried, desperate energy of emergency meetings had faded, replaced by the quiet, focused hum of a new production, a new season, a new way of living with the ghosts they knew by name.

The pre-show rituals, once a desperate invention born of fear, were now as familiar as a worn-in pair of shoes. Before every rehearsal, Malcolm would gather the cast and crew on the main stage. He never spoke of magic, never mentioned the worlds that waited behind the glass. He led them through a grounding exercise, a shared moment of reconnecting with themselves. The group would arrange itself in a circle, standing on floorboards that had been polished over the decades by previous storytellers, and pause to gather its thoughts. Inhale the scent of set paint and the history settled in the thick fabric of the seats. Exhale the day's worries. Feel the solid, undeniable truth of the room.

Tonight, the theater was mostly empty, the seats a vast, dark ocean of plush velvet. A single, powerful Fresnel lamp cut a bright circle of light on the stage, pinning a young actor named Leo in its beam like a butterfly to a board. He stood beside a simple table, his face a mask of frustration. In the wings, his designated buddy, a girl named Maya, watched with the patient, unobtrusive gaze required by Danny Kim's new protocols.

"I'm just not getting there," Leo's voice was a lonely echo in the cavernous dark. He raked a hand through his hair, the gesture sharp with irritation. His script for the theater's new play, *Inheritance*, was a tight fist in his other hand. "He's just found out his father isn't his father. The man who raised him is gone, and was a stranger the whole time. It should be... shattering. But I feel nothing. It's just empty."

From the darkness of the house, the director's voice was a calm, steady anchor. "It's a hard scene, Leo. This kind of grief isn't a storm. It's the slow cracking of the world beneath your feet. Don't push for the emotion. Just find the truth of the moment. Let's take five."

Leo nodded, the gratitude a visible release of tension in his shoulders. He walked off stage, the sharp edge of light falling away as he stepped into the dimness backstage. He leaned his back against the cool brick of the wall, the faint, distorted shape of his face looking back at him from a large, simple pane of glass propped nearby. It was a set piece, a stand-in for a picture window in a later scene. It wasn't an antique mirror, gilded or ornate. Just glass, but in the Meridian, nothing was ever only what it seemed.

He stared at the ghost of his own reflection, his frustration a sour taste on his tongue. He'd heard the stories, the hushed whispers about the Meridian's 'atmosphere,' the strange intensity that seemed to settle over specific productions like a low-country fog. He'd seen the quiet, knowing looks exchanged between the veterans, between Asbury, Brooks, and Reeves. He had seen the way Cate Hart watched over them all, a fierce, protective shepherd guarding her flock from a predator no one else could see. He wanted to be a part of it, to tap into that legendary power, but all he felt was the hollow echo of his own limits.

He closed his eyes, the words of the monologue a prayer on his breath. "All that time... all those years... who were you?"

As he spoke, a strange sensation prickled the air. The familiar scent of wood and old fabric was suddenly overlaid with something else, a clean, sharp smell like the air after a lightning strike, a whisper of ozone that made the hairs on his arms stand up. He opened his eyes. The glass was just glass. But as he looked at his own reflection, it felt as if something was looking back from a place deeper than his own eyes.

He didn't see a sun-drenched coast or a gothic lair.

There was no intoxicating pull, no dizzying promise of escape. Instead, a feeling washed over him, a wave of pure, crystalline emotion that wasn't his own. But threaded through the sorrow was something else, a tough, resilient fiber of strength. The lie didn't erase the love; it made it more complicated. The pain wasn't an end; it was a becoming. The pure, unvarnished feeling of grief was the heart of the scene, delivered as a gift of feeling, not of forgetting. The stabilized theater amplifies feelings; it didn't generate new content.

The feeling crested and then receded, leaving him breathless. He felt... empty, but not in a hollow way. He felt clear, like a glass held up to the light.

From the back of the house, hidden in the deepest shadows of the last row, Cate and Malcolm watched. They had felt the subtle shift in the air, the familiar thrum of the theater's power focusing on the young actor like a held breath. Cate's hand instinctively found Malcolm's, her grip tight, a reflexive brace against a blow she'd felt too many times before. She watched Leo, her body tense, every fiber of her being ready to run, to intervene, to scream a warning that might already be too late.

Leo pushed himself off the wall and walked back into the circle of light. He carried himself differently. The frustration was gone, replaced by a deep, weary stillness that seemed to add years to his face.

"From the top."

He began the monologue. The words were the same, but they were no longer just words. They were vessels filled with the devastating weight of his discovery. His voice didn't break. He didn't scream or rage. His performance was a study in profound, controlled sorrow. A single tear traced a path down his cheek, catching the light like a falling star, a perfect, honest expression of a heart breaking not with a bang, but with a slow, grinding fracture—a breathtaking, beautiful, and utterly actual performance.

In the wings, Maya forgot she was a spotter. She was just an audience member, transfixed, her own eyes filling with sympathetic tears.

In the back row, Cate's breath left her in a long, shuddering exhalation. She felt Malcolm's hand tighten over hers, a shared, silent acknowledgment of what they had just witnessed. The magic had offered the feeling, but it had not provided an escape. It had deepened the art, not consumed the artist. It had provided the spark, but it demanded that the actor do the hard work of turning that spark into a flame.

Cate looked at Malcolm, her dark, intense eyes shining in the dim light. A slow, quiet smile spread across her face, a smile of such profound, hard-won relief that it seemed to erase years of fear from around her eyes. He returned it, his own expression one of quiet, parental pride. The protocols were working. The rituals were holding. They had done it. They had taken a wild and hungry thing and taught it how to sing.

When Leo finished, the silence in the theater was heavy and sacred, like the air in an old church.

Then, Maya stepped out from the wings, her movement breaking the spell. She followed her training. She didn't mention the performance. She didn't ask him how he'd found that emotion. She just gave him a small, supportive smile that was all her own.

"Hey, that was… something. Rehearsal's almost over. You wanna grab a slice at Vinnie's after this? My treat. I heard they brought back the garlic knots."

Leo looked at her, his eyes still distant. He blinked, the character receding from him like a tide going out. He was just a young actor again, tired and emotionally spent, but clean. There was no addictive high, no desperate craving for more. There was only the satisfying exhaustion of a job well done.

"Yeah," he smiled. "Pizza sounds great."

As they walked off stage together, their voices a low murmur about toppings and whether Vinnie's old jukebox was still broken, the theater settled back into its quiet, watchful silence. The moment had passed. The magic had been respectfully used and then respectfully set aside.

An hour later, the stage was empty save for the single, stark beam of the ghost light. Its base was heavy, cast iron from some long-gone opera house, a relic meant to keep the real ghosts company. The silence was absolute now, a living presence. Malcolm walked out from the wings, his footsteps soft on the boards. He stopped at the center of the stage, the ghost light casting his long shadow across the empty seats like a silent watchman.

He pulled a small, handsome logbook from the inner pocket of his jacket, bound in dark, unadorned leather that smelled of tannin and new promises, a sacred and necessary object. He opened it to the first, clean page and took a pen from his pocket. The click of the pen was the only sound in the vast, quiet space.

He wrote the date at the top of the page. Underneath, in his neat, steady hand, he wrote a single, momentous sentence.

Equilibrium holding.

He closed the book. The soft thud of the cover echoed slightly. The war was over, but peace was a fragile, living thing. The long watch had only just begun.

THIRTY-NINE

A FOUNDATION OF TRUST

The future, Vivi Asbury had decided, smelled like fresh paint and the sweet, heavy promise of rain on hot pavement. The scent clung to the air in the loft apartment she and Marc had chosen, a sprawling space carved from the bones of an old Westgate textile mill. Its ceilings soared toward exposed heart-pine beams, and enormous, mullioned windows flooded the main room with the silver-grey light of a Southern afternoon. Cardboard boxes stood in haphazard mountains, a testament to two lives waiting to be unpacked and pieced together.

Marc was in the kitchen area with his back to her, patiently wrestling with the hieroglyphics of assembly instructions for a new bookshelf. The quiet sounds of his work were a comforting anchor in the cavernous space. The scrape of metal on wood and a low, frustrated mutter created a rhythm that grounded her, a simple melody of a life being built. A distant train whistle blew, a long and lonely sound that somehow became hope. Vivi stood by the long concrete countertop that divided the kitchen from the living area, a thick stack of papers in her hand—the lease agreement.

She traced the final signature line with a hesitant finger. Vivianne Asbury. Marc Middleton. Two names, bound together by black ink and the unforgiving certainty of legalese. Twelve months. A full circle of seasons in this new home. A year of waking up together, of shared coffees and quiet evenings that stretched into the humid dark. A year of being known.

A knot tightened deep in her stomach.

She drew a sharp, panicked breath, and the smell of paint turned thick and suffocating. The light from the windows suddenly felt harsh; the generous space of the loft was no longer a canvas, but a cage, a beautiful cage, of course. Gilded. Just like the marble terraces and sun-drenched gardens of Illyria had been. The lease in her hand felt impossibly heavy, each clause another bar, each signature a lock turning. She was signing herself away. She was choosing to be trapped.

The old instinct rose, swift and familiar as a reflex. Retreat. Build the wall. Find a quiet corner and analyze the feeling until it is a dead thing, an academic specimen pinned to a board for study. She could feel the mask of cool, professional competence settling over her features like a second skin. She would put the papers down, make a witty, detached comment about the absurdity of rental contracts, and walk away. She would handle it. Alone.

But she didn't.

She looked at Marc's back, at the solid, reassuring set

of his shoulders beneath his worn flannel shirt. She thought of the promise she had made to herself while standing in the ruins of a shattered mirror, her knuckles raw and bleeding. *No more performance. No more hiding.* Vulnerability wasn't a weakness to be conquered but a muscle to be trained, and it ached with disuse.

"Marc," she said. Her voice was thin, a pale version of its usual clarity, barely a whisper in the echoing room.

He turned, a screwdriver in his hand, a warm, easy smile on his face. The smile faded the moment he saw her expression. He set the tool down on a box and crossed the room in three long strides, his brow knitting with concern. "Vivi? What is it? You look like you've seen a ghost."

"Worse," she whispered, holding up the lease like an indictment. "I've seen a contract."

He looked from the papers to her pale face, and his expression softened with an understanding that was so complete it almost undid her. He didn't laugh. He didn't dismiss her fear. He just waited, giving her the space to find her words.

"This is stupid," she said, the words tumbling out in a rush of self-recrimination. "It's just paper. It's what we wanted. But holding it, seeing our names... it feels so permanent. It feels like a beautiful prison. Like I'm locking myself in, and what if... what if it's a mistake? What if I'm not... what if I can't..."

She could not finish. She could not give voice to the old, familiar litany of fear. *What if I'm not enough? What if you see the real, messy me, and you leave?*

Marc's hands came up to gently take the lease from

her. He set it on the counter with a quiet finality. Then he took her hands in his. They were warm and steady, callused from real work, a grounding touch of reality against her own trembling skin. "Hey," he said softly, his eyes searching for hers. "Look at me. This isn't a prison. It's a stage. Our stage. And unlike Illyria, the script isn't written. We write it. Every day."

He squeezed her hands, a simple, solid pressure. "And you're right. It is a cage, in a way. I am caging you for at least twelve months. I'm trapping you here with my terrible taste in music and my inability to assemble furniture. It's going to be absolute hell." A slow grin spread across his face, crinkling the corners of his warm, brown eyes. "But the bars are made of pizza boxes and movie nights. The lock can be picked with a simple conversation."

He lifted one of her hands and kissed her knuckles, right where the scars from the mirror had long since faded into a pale memory. "If you ever feel trapped, you tell me. And we'll smash a wall down. Or we'll paint it a ridiculous color. Or we'll pack a bag and leave for a week. A lease doesn't own us, Vivi. We are architects here. We decide what this place is."

The panic receded, washed away not by some grand, poetic declaration, but by the simple, sturdy promise of partnership. He wasn't afraid of her fear. He was offering to help her renovate it. The suffocating feeling in her chest eased, replaced by a profound, breathtaking wave of love that left her dizzy. This was real. This was what it felt like to be truly seen, flaws and all, and not just accepted, but cherished. She leaned in and kissed him, a kiss of profound gratitude, a promise sealed not with ink, but with a shared, messy, and beautifully imperfect truth.

The restaurant was an island of quiet intimacy in the bustling heart of the city, a place of dark cypress wood and slow-turning ceiling fans that stirred the air. Low lights glowed, the soft clinking of wine glasses, and the murmur of conversation creating a romantic score for the evening. Kevin Brooks sat opposite Sarah, her hand in his, providing comfort. One year, a lifetime ago, he had been a ghost haunting the basement of the Meridian, a man who had mistaken his own shadow for depth.

"Happy anniversary," Sarah's smile was as warm and steady as the candlelight between them. It had been two years since they met, and one year since this first real date.

"Happy anniversary," he replied, his voice thick with an emotion he no longer tried to hide. "Thank you for... well, for everything. For not giving up on the difficult, brooding actor in the corner."

"He was worth the effort," she said softly, and the simple sincerity of it filled a space in him he hadn't known was empty.

His phone, set face down on the white linen tablecloth, buzzed. A single, sharp vibration. He ignored it, probably just an email, a press release from the theater. Nothing important.

It buzzed again. Then a third time. A series of rapid-fire notifications, insistent and sharp.

Sarah's brow furrowed slightly. "Everything okay?"

"I'm sure it's nothing," he said, but a familiar knot of

anxiety was tightening in his gut, a practiced fear. With a sigh, he picked up the phone, a series of texts from Vivi, then Zoe, then Marc—all of them variations of the same concerned chorus.

> Please don't read it. It's garbage.

> He's a hack, Kevin. Everyone knows it.

> We love you. Call us if you need to.

His blood ran cold. He knew exactly what "it" was. The first review from *Inheritance*, the play he had poured his healed, authentic self into, had just been published. His fingers felt clumsy as he swiped through the notifications and opened the link on his phone.

The headline was brutal. *Brooks' Brooding Performance Lacks Authentic Fire.* The article itself was worse. The critic, a man notorious for his acidic prose, tore him apart piece by piece. "A performance so mired in self-conscious melancholy it forgets to have a pulse... a tedious exercise in navel-gazing... a fraud pretending at depth."

Fraud.

The word struck him with the force of an old wound reopening. Christine's voice, whispering from the grave of his memory. The seductive, poisonous lie she had continuously fed him, that without the grand performance of his pain, he was nothing. A hollow man. A fraud. The old, familiar spiral began, the dread coiling in his stomach. The voice in his head was a venomous hiss. *They see you. They see you're worthless without the darkness. Sarah will see it too.*

She'll see she fell in love with a character, and the real you is... this—an empty suit.

He could feel the pull, the instinct to retreat into the comfortable gloom, to push Sarah away with sarcasm and brooding silence before she could leave on her own. The escape route was so familiar, so well-trod, practically a part of him.

He looked up and met Sarah's watchful, worried gaze. He saw the question in her eyes, the fear that he would slide back down the hole he had worked so hard to climb out of. He had a choice. He could retreat into the ruins, or he could stand in the light with her.

He took a deep breath that shuddered on the way out. He put the phone face down on the table, its black screen a small, dark mirror reflecting nothing.

"Okay, it's a bad one. And the voice... Christine's voice... is very loud right now."

Sarah didn't offer platitudes. She didn't say the review didn't matter. She nodded, her presence a solid, unwavering anchor in his storm. "Okay," she said back. "What's the plan?"

The plan. The one they had built together with his therapist. A step-by-step protocol for when the ghosts came knocking, a tool not of suppression, but of navigation.

"Step one," Kevin recited, the words a lifeline he clung to. "Acknowledge the feeling. I feel like a complete fraud, and I'm terrified that you're about to realize it."

"Acknowledged," Sarah's hand tightened on his. "And for the record, not a chance. What's step two?"

"Step two is to ground myself in reality." He scanned the restaurant, making himself identify and list objects in the present moment. "The tablecloth is white. The candle smells like vanilla. Your eyes are the warmest brown I have ever seen. And you're here with me."

"I'm here," she confirmed, her gaze unwavering. "Step three?"

"Step three…" He hesitated. This was the most challenging part, the one that went against every instinct he had. "Step three is to reach out. To not isolate." He swallowed, the old pride warring with the new, hard-won wisdom. He picked up his phone, his thumb hovering over his therapist's number, like lifting a mountain. He pressed the button.

As the phone rang, he looked at Sarah, and the love and gratitude he felt for her were so immense that they threatened to break him wide open. He did not run. He had not hidden. He had been hit with a direct shot to his oldest wound, and instead of bleeding out alone in the dark, he had reached for the light, the hardest thing he had ever done. And also, the easiest choice he had ever made.

The first sign of trouble was the smell. A sharp, acrid scent of something deeply, irrevocably burnt. The second was the thin plume of grey smoke pouring from the oven door like a distress signal. The third was the high-pitched, frantic shriek of the smoke alarm.

Zoe Reeves stared at the oven; a spatula held limply in her hand like a forgotten prop. Inside, the beautiful, herb-crusted roast chicken, meant to be the centerpiece of her and Tyler's first-ever dinner party, was a blackened, carbonized husk, a culinary failure.

The old Zoe would have panicked. She would have become a frantic, high-energy whirlwind of apologies and desperate attempts to fix the unfixable. She would have been mortified, her cheeks burning with a shame that felt hotter than the oven. The evening would be ruined. Her performance as the perfect, capable hostess would be a complete flop. She would have felt the familiar, crushing weight of not being good enough. Prince Adrian would never have burnt the chicken.

Their guests, Vivi, Marc, Kevin, and Sarah, were frozen in the living room, a polite, awkward tableau of concern. Tyler came rushing in from the small balcony, where he'd been trying to fan the smoke away from a tangled jasmine vine climbing the brick wall. His face was a mask of crest-fallen defeat.

"I'm so sorry," he said, looking at the charred remains of their dinner. "I...I lost track of time. I ruined it."

Zoe looked from the smoking oven to Tyler's guilty face, to the worried expressions of her friends. She felt a brief, familiar pulse of her old panic, the urge to plaster on a bright smile and insist that everything was fine, that she could whip up something else in five minutes, that the disaster wasn't a disaster.

And then, a strange, new feeling bubbled up in her chest, a sense of pure, unadulterated absurdity. She looked at the blackened chicken, a funeral pyre for her domestic ambitions. She looked at her wonderful, loving, imperfect friends, standing awkwardly in her beautiful, imperfect home. She looked at the man she loved, who was more worried about her disappointment than the ruined meal.

She laughed.

It wasn't a nervous titter or a performed chuckle, but a deep, genuine, rolling laugh that started in her belly and filled the smoky kitchen, a laugh of pure, unburdened relief.

Tyler stared at her, utterly bewildered. "You're... laughing?"

"It's a charcoal briquette!" she gasped, tears of mirth streaming down her face. "It's a fossil! We could donate it to a museum!"

The tension in the room shattered like glass. Kevin let out a short bark of a laugh, and Vivi's lips quirked into a rare, genuine smile that reached her eyes. Marc was grinning from ear to ear.

Zoe walked over to Tyler and wrapped her arms around his waist, burying her face in the comforting fabric of his chest. "Oh, it's so perfectly ruined," her voice muffled by his shirt. She looked up at him, her eyes shining with a light he had never seen before. "I'm not a perfect hostess. You're not a perfect cook. And we are never, ever going to have a perfect dinner party."

She stood on her toes and kissed him, a quick, happy, smoke-scented kiss. Then she turned to their guests, her smile wide and real, utterly devoid of performance.

"Well," she announced, gesturing grandly at the kitchen disaster. "I guess we're officially a pizza-for-dinner-parties household. Who wants pepperoni?"

An hour later, they were all squeezed around the

dining room table, greasy cardboard pizza boxes spread between them. They were drinking cheap red wine from a bottle they'd bought at the corner market, sloshing it into their glasses with abandon. The conversation was loud, the laughter was easy, and the connection was as real and tangible as the warm, humid night air drifting in through the open windows.

Zoe looked around the table at the faces of her found family. Vivi, leaning against Marc's solid shoulder, her expression relaxed and open in a way it never used to be. Kevin engaged in a passionate, friendly debate with Tyler, with Sarah watching him, her pride a quiet, steady glow. This was it. This was the happily ever after. Not a castle, not a prince, not a perfect, static fantasy. This messy, loud, imperfect, and breathtakingly beautiful reality. A reality they had all fought for, a reality they were now building together, one burnt chicken, one vulnerable confession, and one shared pizza at a time. And more satisfying than any fairy tale.

CHAPTER

FORTY

STAR-CROSSED LOVERS

The Meridian Theatre was a lung holding its breath, having held it for a century. On the main stage, where painted kings had fallen and star-crossed lovers had found their forever, a single ghost light burned. It cast a stark, lonely circle of light on the worn floorboards, a tradition as old as the boards themselves. A beacon that meant to ward off restless spirits, or maybe, to welcome the right ones home. On this night, steeped in the thick, humid air of a Southern summer, was doing both.

Within that solitary circle of light, ten people sat on a makeshift gathering of stage blocks and overturned prop crates. A few thick, beeswax candles stood between them, their small flames wavering in the cavernous dark, casting their faces in soft, shifting gold. This was the heart of the Meridian, the ten who had looked straight into the beautiful, hungry abyss of this place and made the choice to stay. Vivi and Marc sat near one another, his arm a solid, grounding weight around her shoulders. Kevin's hand was

327

laced with Sarah's, a quiet, specific anchor. Zoe had tucked herself against Tyler, her head resting on his shoulder in a posture of hard-won peace. And at the head of their circle, like the sovereigns of some strange and fragile kingdom, sat Cate and Malcolm, flanked by Carmen and Danny, the silent witness and the steady hand.

They were calling it the Legacy Reading—a new tradition for a new time.

"A story is a promise." Cate's voice was a low, clear tone that carried through the vast silence without effort. "It's a promise that the things we walk through have meaning. Tonight, we will make a new one. We tell our own stories, not the way they were, but the way they are now. We give them their truth."

She gave a slight nod to Zoe, whose face was warmed by the gentle candlelight. Zoe took a soft breath, her eyes finding Tyler's in the shadows.

"There was once a princess," she started, her voice stripped of all its usual bright performance, leaving something softer and truer. "She lived in a beautiful castle made of spun glass, where the sun was always shining and every single day was a ball. She had a handsome prince who adored her, who promised her a whole life of flawless happiness. But the princess started to notice the glass was cold to the touch. The sun never moved in the sky. And the prince's love, while perfect, was always the same. So, one day, she broke a window. And she ran. She ran until she came to a messy, muddy, wonderful village where the weather changed, where things got broken, where people laughed and cried and got into fights. And there, she met a man who wasn't a prince at all, but a builder. He didn't promise her a castle. He promised he'd help her build a home, one crooked, imperfect, and very real brick at a time."

A quiet knowing settled over the group, as soft as the settling dust motes in the air. Zoe's story, made new. Next, Kevin looked down at his own hands, then over at Sarah, who gave him a gentle squeeze that spoke volumes.

"There was a soldier," his low baritone seemed to vibrate through the floorboards. "He fought a thousand wars, and every one of them was in the shadows of his own mind. He believed his armor was his strength, and he wore his wounds like medals of honor. He saw peace as a kind of surrender, a boring, empty field after the glory of battle. He met a healer who offered him a place to rest, but he mistook her kindness for a new kind of weapon, something meant to strip him of the only identity he had. But the wars left him bone-weary, and one day, he was too tired to lift his sword. The healer came to him then, not with medicine, but with bread and water. And he learned that real strength wasn't in the fighting but in having the courage to finally lay your arms down and build a home in the quiet field you once thought was empty."

Vivi was the last one. She looked at Marc, at the patience and strength she saw in his eyes, the man who had waited for her, not to return from some faraway place, but to come home to herself.

"A shade haunted a beautiful house," she said. Her diction was as precise as ever, but warmed now by an emotion that was finally her own. "She was bound to it, a guardian who had forgotten she was also its prisoner. She polished all its surfaces until they gleamed like mirrors, each one reflecting a perfect, empty order. She believed her duty was to keep the world out, to protect the house's perfect, silent story. But a visitor came, a man who wasn't afraid of a little dust. He was a gardener. He didn't try to cast her out. He opened a window to let in the sun and the smell of rain on thirsty soil. He showed her that the garden outside was dying from neglect. And the shade learned that true guardianship wasn't about protecting a flawless, dead thing, about joining the living, getting your hands dirty, and helping a messy, beautiful garden grow."

The three stories hung in the air, a braid of survival and rebirth. They had taken the shape of their private pain and woven it into a shared mythology, a founding legend for the Meridian itself. The hopeful silence that followed was its own kind of victory, a quiet space filled with everything they had won back.

Malcolm broke that silence. His expression was solemn as he stood and picked up a thin, worn folder from a nearby crate. The paper inside was yellowed, so brittle with age that it looked like it might crumble into dust in his hands. This was the list Tyler had first put together in the library, the one Carmen had added to from her own secret archives—the list of the lost.

"We have told the stories of the saved," Malcolm said with a purpose that gently displaced the joy in the air. "Now, we have to honor the stories that were never finished."

Cate stood beside him, her face a mask of iron

certainty. This was the other half of their new charter. Not to celebrate that they had survived, but to bear witness to the failures that came before them. This was the moment they chose to shoulder the full weight of their history, rather than burying it. Their trauma would not define them, but they would never forget what it had cost.

The theater seemed to agree. The ambient magic in the air, which had felt warm and alive during the storytelling, now settled. It grew quiet and still, profoundly respectful, like a breath being held in reverence.

Cate took the first page. "James Armitage," she read, her voice clear and unwavering. "Cast as Macbeth, 1988. Vanished during dress rehearsal."

Malcolm took the next name. "Eleanor Vance. Cast as Lady Macbeth, 1988. Lost to madness."

Carmen, her hands trembling slightly, read a name from her own hidden records. Her fingers brushed unconsciously against a pocket of her work apron, a nervous habit that came from years of tucking away impossible things. "Daniel Cruz. Chorus, *Sweeney Todd*, 1995. Walked out of the theater and was never seen again. I found a silver locket in his costume, filled with sea salt."

One by one, they passed the pages around the circle. They read the names of the vanished, the broken, the lost. Each name was a ghost in the room, a story cut short. With every name spoken aloud, the air grew thicker, the circle of ten bound tighter by the solemnity of their promise.

Tyler, the cynic who had become a true believer, read a name with a raw, cracked voice.

Then Sarah, her clinical expertise melting away to reveal a simple, human sorrow.

Marc, his voice low with respect for the artists and dreamers who had walked these boards before him.

Danny, his usual pragmatism giving way to the sheer, tragic weight of the list.

They read the last name, the one that had become their own grim North Star. "Clara Mayhew. Cast as Ophelia, 2003. Declared a missing person."

The final name fell into a deep, shared silence. The candles wavered, their small lights seeming fragile against the vast, listening darkness of the house. The weight of all those names settled on their shoulders, no longer a history, but a responsibility—a sacred trust.

"We remember them," Vivi whispered into the quiet.

"We will not let it happen again," Kevin stated, the words a formal oath.

"We are the guardians now," Zoe added, her voice filled with a new kind of strength, hard as steel.

They had done it. They had taken the sharp edges of their grief and given them a purpose, building a shelter from the pain instead of a monument to it. They had forged a new charter, written in the ink of sorrow and the light of a hard-won hope. The Meridian was a sanctuary, and they were its keepers.

After a long, shared silence, they carefully folded the list. They placed it inside a simple wooden box Carmen had brought, made of old heart pine, salvaged from a wall torn down during a long-ago renovation, its wood saturated with the essence of the theater. This would be their memorial, a permanent fixture backstage, a quiet, constant reminder of their vow.

The ceremony was over. The group stirred, the heavy stillness of the moment giving way to the quiet exhaustion that follows a night dense with meaning.

Marc stood up, stretching his back. He walked away from the candlelight circle toward the backstage area, his footsteps the only sound on the wide planks of the stage. He moved toward the call board, a place that had held so much hope and heartbreak over the years. With gentle hands, he took down the faded, curled posters from the last season. *Twelfth Night. The Phantom of the Opera. Cinderella.* Relics of battles won. On the *Twelfth Night* poster, Vivi's face stared out, impossibly young, her eyes guarded and lost, a ghost of the woman she was before she found her way home.

He tacked up a single, clean sheet of white paper in their place.

Drawn by the quiet purpose in his movements, the others drifted over from the stage, gathering around the board. A gentle current of air, smelling of old wood and new beginnings, seemed to brush past them, as if the building itself had let out a long, slow breath. In the dim spill of the ghost light, they read the simple, typed words, stark and black against the white page.

AUDITIONS: THE PHOENIX SEASON.

All are welcome.

The story was over. The legacy was beginning.

EPILOGUE

EVER AFTER

A year later, the Meridian Theatre was back in business.

The grand old building, a place that had held its sorrows like a breath held too long in its lungs, now seemed to exhale a contented, golden sigh. The deep velvet of the seats absorbed the joyful noise, a sound that settled deeply into the fabric of the place. The familiar, nostalgic scent of old wood and history—a perfume of stage dust and time—was sweetened tonight by the crisp spirit of champagne and the faint, happy fragrance of a family brought back together under one roof. Strings of tiny lights were woven like constellations through the rigging high above, their gentle sparks mingling with the warm, professional glow of Marc's carefully set stage lighting. This wasn't a performance but a homecoming.

The stage itself had become an impromptu ballroom floor. A soft jazz trio played from the corner where a throne for a doomed Scottish king once held court, the saxophone's notes curling through the air like lazy smoke on a summer evening. On a long table heavy with food and the chime of champagne flutes, a small, framed photograph held a place of honor. It showed a kitchen filled with smoke and six people dissolving into helpless, gut-deep laughter around a tragically blackened chicken.

This was their happily ever after. Not an ending. But the beginning of the work.

Kevin Brooks stood near the edge of the stage, his arm looped with a loose and easy ownership around Sarah's waist. He watched Zoe and Tyler slow dance. Tyler's mouth, usually drawn in a cynical line, had softened into something achingly tender. Zoe's smile was a radiant thing, a light that was finally, entirely her own. Two years. Two years since Sarah had offered him coffee and a quiet corner of the world to put himself back together in. After two years of effort, challenges, and consistent support whenever needed.

Danny Kim, forever the stage manager even at a party, tapped a microphone. "Alright, alright, settle down, you beautiful disasters. A few words." A chorus of fond, laughing jeers answered him. He grinned, an honest and unguarded thing. "We're here to celebrate one year of the Phoenix Season, the most successful and least supernaturally infested run in this theater's recent memory."

The room erupted in a wave of laughter, a sound built of shared relief and the kind of joy that only comes after the sorrow.

"But more than that," Danny went on, his voice gentling, "we're here to celebrate the people who make this building a home. So, to get us started, I believe Mr. Brooks has something he wants to say."

A warm river of applause followed Kevin as he stepped to the microphone. He kept Sarah's hand held tight in his, her palm a solid, warm anchor in a world that had once been a storm-tossed sea. He looked out at the small crowd, at the faces of the people who had built a wall of light around him and refused to let the darkness win. His heart felt too big for his chest, a whole and heavy thing.

"I'm not a man who's good with speeches," he began, his voice a low, steady baritone that carried through the room without any need for the microphone. He felt the familiar grain of the stage floor beneath the soles of his shoes, the same boards he had collapsed upon. "But I have to say something. Two years ago, Sarah and I had our first real date. And a little over a year ago, I was standing right here, on this stage, and I broke down. I thought that was it. The final curtain call."

He paused, the memory of a ghost that no longer had the power to haunt him. He had to swallow past the thickness in his throat. "I was wrong, this was an overture. Because when I fell, I didn't hit the ground. I fell into a safety net. A net woven by every single person in this room."

His eyes found Cate and Malcolm. They stood near the wings, the same way they always had, like watchful guardians who had finally earned a moment of peace. "Cate, Malcolm. You taught me that strength isn't about how much pain you can endure by yourself. It's about having the courage to let someone else help you carry it. Thank you."

He looked at Carmen, who was a vision in a dress of her own brilliant design, a physical manifestation of the creative soul she now let shine so freely. "Carmen, you saw we were all wearing costumes long before the play started. You patiently waited for us to be ready for one last fitting, the one where we finally got to wear our own skin. Thank you."

He turned to Danny. "Danny, you kept the real world turning when ours was flying apart. You kept the lights on, in every way that matters. Thank you."

His gaze fell on Vivi and Marc, then on Zoe and Tyler. "You guys. You showed me what it looked like to fight for your own light, even when you were terrified of the dark. My chosen family."

Finally, he looked down at Sarah. The love he felt for her was a bright, steady flame inside him, a warmth that had chased out all the cold. His eyes shone with tears he had no shame in showing. "And Sarah. You are the architect of my entire second act. My recovery, my happiness. I didn't win any of it by myself. All of you built it. You are my home." He raised his glass, his hand steady. "To the safety net. To my home."

"To home," the room echoed back, a chorus of voices and clinking glass that rang with a profound, tear-soaked gratitude.

As the music swelled up again, Cate and Malcolm shared a quiet look in the shadows of the wings. He took her hand, the familiar weight of it a comfort that had seen them through decades and worlds. She leaned her head against his shoulder, a rare and public gesture of softness that spoke volumes. The air backstage smelled of old rope, sawdust, and a faint, clean scent like the air after a storm —a smell of creation, not destruction.

"We did it," he whispered, his voice meant only for her. The vibrant, messy, life-filled joy playing out on the stage before them. "All that pain. It became the foundation they built their lives on."

Cate's grip tightened on his hand. Her gaze, once haunted by the bloody ghosts of Dunsinane, was now clear and deeply peaceful. "And that symbol, Mal? The one on the back of the old mirror?"

A slow, easy smile touched his lips, a smile that finally reached his weary eyes. "I heard back from the university library. Carmen's research was right. It was the mark of a defunct mirror-makers' guild from the seventeenth century. Their maker's mark. A historical footnote, after all. A story with a perfectly rational, wonderfully boring ending."

They stood there in a comfortable silence, watching their found family. Malcolm reached for a passing tray and selected a small pastry; something filled with sweet cream and dusted with cinnamon. He took a bite, closing his eyes for a second, quiet reverence for a simple, authentic flavor he'd learned to cherish after years of watching Cate struggle without them. Their own long, painful journey, the trauma, the flight, the decades of fearful watching, was all reflected and redeemed in the honest laughter on that stage. They had not only healed. They had turned a curse into a legacy.

Later, as the party reached a joyful, humming crescendo, Marc stepped to the microphone. He was a man more comfortable with steel pipes and electrical cables than with public declarations, and the nervous way he held himself was deeply endearing.

"I'll keep this short," his warm eyes finding Vivi in the crowd. "This theater, for all its... personality... is a place where stories get told. And for the last year, I've been lucky enough to be part of the best story I've ever known." He held out a hand to Vivi. She walked toward him, a questioning smile playing on her lips, her every step as graceful as a line of poetry.

He took her hand, his thumb tracing the spot where her knuckles had once been raw from a desperate act of self-preservation. "Vivianne Asbury," his voice becoming suddenly intimate even with everyone watching. "You are the most stubbornly, infuriatingly, brilliantly real person I have ever met. You didn't teach me that love is about finding someone perfect. You showed me it's about finding the person whose broken pieces fit with yours and then having the courage to build something new and strong in the spaces between."

He knelt, the motion both beautifully awkward and deeply graceful on the stage that was his second home. From his pocket, he produced a small, simple wooden box. A collective, happy gasp rippled through the room.

"I don't want a flawless fantasy, Vivi. I want our

messy, chaotic, wonderful reality. I want it forever. Will you marry me?"

Vivi stared down at him, her classically trained poise shattering into a million pieces of pure, unscripted shock. Tears filled her clear, gray-blue eyes. She thought of the woman she had been, the one who had analyzed her own feelings in a journal and believed herself to be an emotional fraud. The woman who would have run from a moment this vulnerable, this terrifyingly real.

She looked at the man kneeling before her. He wasn't offering a perfect, scripted romance. He was offering a lifetime of co-writing their own story, with all its rewrites, crossed-out lines, and beautiful, unexpected turns. She threw her arms around his neck, her answer a sound that was part sob and part laugh and one single, fervent word. "Yes. Always, yes."

The room exploded into cheers. As Marc slipped the ring onto her finger, Zoe caught Tyler's eye across the room. The ring itself was a simple, elegant band of unadorned platinum, solid and trustworthy, holding a single, clear diamond that shone with the honest fire of a perfectly aimed stage light.

"Can you believe it?" Zoe mouthed, her own eyes wet with happy tears for her friend.

He grinned and made his way to her side, navigating the celebrating crowd with a quiet purpose. "I can. They're a good team." He nudged her gently, his touch a familiar comfort. "Speaking of teams. I found a place. Two bedrooms, a balcony big enough for a couple of chairs, and a kitchen that comes with a fire extinguisher already installed."

Zoe's breath caught in her throat. Her heart gave a great, hopeful leap. "Are you serious?"

"I put a deposit down this afternoon." His gaze was steady and sure, all the cynicism washed away, leaving only a profound, quiet certainty. "If you'll have me, Reeves. I would very much like to start burning dinners with you permanently."

She didn't need to answer with words. She launched herself into his arms, her heart so full of a bright, bubbling joy that it might spill over and fill the entire theater.

The toasts continued, each one filled with more laughter and joyful tears. Vivi gave the last one. Her hand rested on Marc's chest, the ring a small, bright star on her finger, a promise made real.

"Tonight is about celebrating happily ever after," her voice clear and strong, the voice of a leading lady who had finally found her truth. It carried all the way to the very back of the house. "But I think we have all learned that ever after is not a destination. It is not a final scene where the lights fade to black on a perfect, unchanging picture. It is a choice. It is the choice you make every single morning to keep building, to keep talking, to keep showing up for the messy, difficult, beautiful work of a life you share with someone."

She looked around at their family, at the faces of people who had fought their way back from the edge of their own private darknesses. "Happily ever after is the process. It is the journey. And I, for one, cannot wait to see what happens in Act Three."

As the last guests finally trickled out into the cool night air, leaving behind a happy chaos of empty glasses and plates, the three couples stood together on the softly lit stage. Vivi and Marc, their hands linked, the newness of their engagement, a quiet, shimmering thing between them. Kevin and Sarah are a living testament to the complex and beautiful work of healing—Zoe and Tyler, standing on the precipice of a new and wonderful beginning. The soft jazz had long since faded, and the theater settled into its own quiet rhythm. A gentle, warm energy, the theater's new and benign magic, seemed to sigh contentedly around them, a soft hum of approval that became a blessing.

They looked out into the empty, velvet seats, not with fear or with the ghosts of the past, but with a profound sense of ownership and of peace. The story wasn't over. It had simply become their life, a quiet promise whispered into the heart of the old building to continue choosing the messy, beautiful, and authentic reality they had built together, day after day, for all the ever afters to come.

OTHER FLORID ROMANCE BOOKS

To be notified of new releases and special promotions from Florid Romance, please join our email list:

https://floridromance.lmbpn.com/about/sign-up-for-our-newsletter/

For a complete list of books published by Florid Romance please visit our website:

https://floridromance.lmbpn.com/

BOOKS BY KELLI ROBYNS

The Enchanted Orchard

The Orchard (Book 1)

Family Curse (Book 2)

Crystal Heart (Book 3)

The Charmed City

Spellbound (Book 1)

Prophecy (Book 2)

Ultimatum (Book 3)

Crescent City Curse

Beignets and Bad Omens (Book 1)

Moonlight and Muddy Waters (Book 2)

Queen of the Quarter (Book 3)

In My Mind's Eye

Oracle Project (Book 1)

Dark Dreams (Book 2)

Seer's Visions (Book 3)

Crimson Star

Healing (Book 1)

Exposure (Book 2)

Blackout (Book 3)

Spellbound Games

Magical Court (Book 1)

Foul Play (Book 2)

Sudden Death (Book 3)

The Backstage Mirror

Twelfth Night Magic (Book 1)

Phantom's Promise (Book 2)

Fairy Tale Finale (Book 3)

BOOKS BY MICHAEL ANDERLE

Sign up for the LMBPN email list to be notified of new releases and special deals!

https://lmbpn.com/email/

For a complete list of books by Michael Anderle, please visit:

www.lmbpn.com/ma-books/

Connect with Michael Anderle

Website: http://lmbpn.com

Email List: https://michael.beehiiv.com/

https://www.facebook.com/LMBPNPublishing

https://twitter.com/MichaelAnderle

https://www.instagram.com/lmbpn_publishing/

https://www.bookbub.com/authors/michael-anderle

9 7 9 8 8 9 7 9 0 0 6 9 5